RWBY

AFTER the FALL

RWBY
AFTER the FALL

By E. C. MYERS
Story by KERRY SHAWCROSS and MILES LUNA
Based on the series created by MONTY OUM

Scholastic Inc.

ROOSTER TEETH®

© 2019 Rooster Teeth Productions, LLC

All rights reserved. Published by Scholastic Inc., *Publishers since 1920*. SCHOLASTIC and associated logos are trademarks and/or registered trademarks of Scholastic Inc.

The publisher does not have any control over and does not assume any responsibility for author or third-party websites or their content.

No part of this publication may be reproduced, stored in a retrieval system, or transmitted in any form or by any means, electronic, mechanical, photocopying, recording, or otherwise, without written permission of the publisher. For information regarding permission, write to Scholastic Inc., Attention: Permissions Department, 557 Broadway, New York, NY 10012.

Library of Congress Cataloging-in-Publication Data available

ISBN 978-1-338-30574-6

10 9 8 7 6 5 4 3 2 1   19 20 21 22 23

Printed in the U.S.A.   23

First printing 2019

Book design by Betsy Peterschmidt

Cover illustration by Patrick Rodriguez

PROLOGUE

Velvet Scarlatina's least favorite thing about Vacuo was how it tasted. Of course, Vacuo didn't have much going for it, unless you enjoy blistering heat, scarce food, and scarcer water. Do you like getting lost? Then come to Vacuo, where the desert landscape completely changes overnight—or even from one hour to the next. The most popular items in the tourist gift shops were T-shirts that read, VACUO: THE WRONG PLACE AT THE WRONG TIME and A TERRIBLE PLACE TO VISIT, BUT YOU WOULDN'T WANT TO LIVE THERE.

Of all the things included in Velvet's mental list of "cons" about Vacuo, number one was the lack of *anything* to include under "pros." Number two: the way sand kept getting in her mouth, even when it was covered with a pithy T-shirt.

Chewing fresh cactus leaf helped neutralize the sand's bitter flavor, but all such luxuries were hard to come by in Vacuo. Used to living with hardship, Vacuans simply factored the sand into their food preparation. And hey, if you couldn't deal with the "local spice," you probably didn't belong there.

Velvet definitely didn't belong in Vacuo. She was supposed to be in Vale—beautiful, cool, green Vale. She was supposed to be training at Beacon Academy to become a Huntress to protect people. But Beacon was even less hospitable than the desert these days, as hard as that was to believe. Instead, she and her team— Coco Adel, Fox Alistair, and Yatsuhashi Daichi, known collectively to their schoolmates as Team CFVY (Coffee)—had made their way to Vacuo more than a year ago to finish out their training at Shade Academy. And they had more important things to worry about than the taste of sand.

"What are these things?" Velvet shouted. She ducked as a massive crablike creature thrust a claw at her head. The pincer snapped shut loudly right between her long rabbit ears.

That was too close, she thought. *I'd hate to end up as a "split hare" pun.* Especially after everything else she had survived. The natural wildlife roaming Vacuo was tough for sure, but as a Huntress in training, Velvet had seen the real monsters lurking in the darkness.

Using his Semblance—a special ability unique to every warrior in the world of Remnant—Fox answered her question telepathically, via their special teamspeak. *"Mole crabs,"* he sent. *"Kinda small for the species."*

"Small, huh? Maybe they're babies," Coco said. "They sure fight like babies."

To her left, Velvet heard rapid shots from Coco's Gatling gun, the explosive impact of her Aura-enhanced bullets on a crab's carapace, and soon the sound of the shell cracking and crumbling. The creature screeched horribly as it died.

But Velvet's crab was still very much alive and frisky. It lunged for her again. She dove and rolled out of the way. She just needed her camera—

Suddenly Yatsuhashi was by her side, as always.

The large crab didn't look quite as intimidating next to Yatsu, who was a foot and a half taller than Velvet and much broader.

The creature chittered nervously. Yatsu grabbed its claw with both hands, holding it closed. Then he twisted his torso and tossed the creature up and away with a roar. It spun through the air like an oversized discus with spindly legs, until it crashed into a dune fifty feet away. There it lay, stunned, half-buried in sand.

"Hey, that one was mine!" Velvet said.

"You're welcome. Give me a hand?" He nodded to another nearby crab, which he had also flipped onto its back. Its legs twitched frantically in the air as it struggled to right itself.

Velvet approached the overturned crab, getting close enough to see her face reflected in its beady black eyes, each the size of her head. She looked away, almost feeling sorry for it. She turned to face Yatsu, knelt on one knee, and interlaced her fingers.

Yatsu sprinted toward her, drawing his greatsword from behind his back. As he stepped onto her linked hands, she heaved upward and stood, boosting his jump so he catapulted high over her head. She spun around and watched him fall toward the crab, sword pointed downward purposefully. The blade pierced the mole crab's soft underbelly.

The crab keened and thrashed, but Yatsu held on to his

sword and stayed on top of it. He plunged the blade in deeper. Clear liquid gushed from the wound and drenched him.

Ew, Velvet thought.

The crab's death throes sent sand flying everywhere, including right into Velvet's eyes and—of course—her open mouth. She coughed and rubbed at her stinging eyes until she could see again.

The crab's body still twitched, but it was clearly no longer a threat. Yatsu jumped down and walked toward Velvet. His green robe was soaked dark, almost black. She backed away from him, covering her nose.

"I think it's just . . . water?" Yatsu swept his fingers through his short, damp hair and then examined his hand.

"Stinky water. You smell like a swamp," she said.

"I know," he said sadly.

The liquid was already evaporating in the hot afternoon sun, but the stench remained.

Yatsu wiped his eyes and looked around. "How are we doing?"

Velvet assessed the battlefield with him. Fox was dancing just within reach of his crab, the smallest of the group. It had only one claw; the other jutted out of the sand beside them, neatly severed. Whenever the crab snapped its remaining claw at the lithe, red-haired teen, Fox dodged and slashed at the limb with his bladed tonfas.

"At least Fox is having fun," Velvet said.

Coco walked calmly toward Velvet and Yatsu, the shredded

remains of a crab behind her. She'd managed to avoid getting any of its guts and gore on her brown-and-black ensemble. Lucky thing, because Vacuo wasn't big on designer clothing, although Coco's beret and aviator sunglasses were gaining popularity among Shade Academy's students as fashionable and surprisingly functional desert-wear.

Coco folded her gun up into a handbag and slung its bandolier strap over her shoulder. She flashed a thumbs-up: mission accomplished.

As Velvet returned the gesture, she abruptly remembered the crab Yatsu had tossed into a dune. She looked for it, but the mound of sand it had landed in was gone . . . and so was the crab.

Good, she thought, followed almost immediately by, *Oh no*. She watched as the sand in front of Coco geysered, and Velvet lost sight of their leader.

"Coco!" Velvet bolted toward her, Yatsu right on her heels.

"Fox! Stop playing around!" Yatsu called.

"Coming," Fox sent.

Velvet glanced over as Fox lopped off the crab's head with its own dismembered claw. He dropped the limb and darted toward Coco, who was struggling in the claw grip of the last mole crab. She strained to keep the pincers from closing around her.

Velvet stopped and reached behind her for the rectangular brown box she always carried on her belt. She pressed the stitched heart emblem to open it and then removed Anesidora, her high-tech camera that used special Dust, an energy propellant substance, to print photographed weapons in hard light.

Combined with her Semblance—photographic memory—Velvet could wield these 3-D replicas with skills and moves that otherwise would have taken years of training to master.

Yatsu sped past Velvet, and soon he was engaging the crab. But he couldn't get close enough to hack away its claws like Fox had; this one was too fast. It was all Yatsu could do to parry attacks from its other claw with his sword.

Velvet thumbed through the images stored in the camera, looking for just the right one to help her friends. Professor Port, blunderbuss raised and aimed at a flock of Griffons in Amity Arena. Weiss Schnee, in a rare unguarded moment, with a giant glowing arm and sword hanging from a glyph floating behind her. Green-haired Reese Chloris leaning on her hoverboard after she and the rest of Team ABRN (Auburn) had defeated a Death Stalker.

Velvet came across the last snapshot she'd taken of her friend Ruby Rose and her high-caliber sniper scythe, Crescent Rose—the perfect weapon for cracking open a crab. Still, Velvet hesitated, hand trembling as the memories flooded back.

Beacon was burning. Beacon was falling. All around them.

And they couldn't save it.

The sky was full of the wings and cries of Griffons, terrible flying Grimm monsters that had carried off several classmates and tourists, shattering the peace of the festival. Other Creatures of Grimm—Beowolves, Creeps, Boarbatusks—rampaged through the rubble-littered streets as people ran screaming. The clang and clatter of battle echoed throughout the city, struggling to be heard over the softer sounds that now haunted Velvet's dreams. At least the military's hacked defense robots had been deactivated; now all CFVY had to deal with was the Grimm.

But the Grimm were relentless and vicious, and there were so many of them. More of the dark, deadly creatures poured into Beacon with every passing hour, faster than they could be destroyed. The monsters were the stuff of nightmares, all shadow and bone, fire and fury. They only hunted humans and Faunus, such as Velvet, and they were drawn to negative emotions. They fed off fear and anger and hatred. No one knew where Grimm came from, or why they existed, but they were killing machines. The only way to survive an attack by a Grimm was to kill it first.

Velvet limped along, leaning against Yatsu, who wasn't in much better shape than she was. Still, his strong arm around her shoulders did more than keep her moving—it held up her spirit. Yatsu and the rest of her team made Velvet feel safe, even while they were facing the greatest danger of their lives.

But she also felt guilty; if Yatsu had to take care of her, it kept him from saving other people who needed him more. So far they had rescued seven frightened, hurt tourists and citizens, who were now following them to the docks. But there were plenty more out there waiting for someone to help them.

"I'm fine," Velvet lied. She felt as if she'd been hit by a truck, which was close to the truth. "We have to make sure everyone evacuates."

"An Atlesian Paladin punched you," Yatsu said. "We must get you to the docks. You need medical attention."

"Yatsuhashi's right," Coco said. She paused to fire her gun at a Beowolf. The bullets did little more than annoy it, but still created enough of a distraction for Fox to sneak behind and neatly slice off the Grimm's head. Fox walked through the black mist to rejoin his team as the Grimm disappeared.

"Your Aura's critical, Velvet," Coco continued. With her Aura—the powerful, protective life force tied to everyone's soul—at that low level, one more hit would finish her off. "If it hadn't been for Weiss's Semblance . . ."

"Who knew she could do that?" Yatsu asked.

By "that" he meant summon a massive sword and a giant, ghostly hand to hold it, from out of nowhere.

"It's a Schnee family thing," Fox sent telepathically, somehow managing to sound smug about it. "They can summon avatars of ene-mies they've beaten to fight for them. Handy, huh?"

Coco groaned.

The avatar Weiss had summoned had sliced up the war machine just before it would have finished off Velvet. What was even more impressive than the lifesaving stunt was the fact that Weiss had stepped between Velvet and the Paladin's killing blow, without seeming to know she could stop it.

"I think Weiss was just as surprised at what Velvet's capable of." Coco smiled wearily. "You were terrific."

"Thanks," Velvet said. In taking down the attacking military robots, she'd finally had a chance to prove what she and her camera could do. Unfortunately, she had to burn through some of her best pictures, using weapons she had been saving all semester and losing photos of dear friends— friends she suddenly wasn't sure she would ever see alive or whole again—in the process.

Velvet knew that many Beacon students considered her dead weight on Team CFVY. Some others didn't like her because they discriminated against Faunus-kind—people who possessed animal traits—and Velvet's rabbit ears weren't so easily hidden by a simple disguise. She'd been hoping she would be chosen to fight in the Vytal Tournament, show off a little for a change, but Coco had ended that idea pretty quickly. Velvet wondered if she and Yatsu would have done any better in the battle against Emerald and Mercury.

Coco had wondered that, too. She still smarted from that defeat, the bruises to her ego lasting longer than the bruises on her body. And now she had new bruises on top of those, from fighting a seemingly endless onslaught of Grimm.

The team was utterly spent. In the last hour, they had seen their friend Penny Polendina torn apart by her own weapons. They had helped take down a Nevermore at Amity Arena, fought Griffons and Ursai, faced off against Atlas's finest military machines. And there still was no end in sight. The Grimm just kept coming, and now there was a giant winged Grimm circling Beacon Tower. The smart thing to do was retreat so they could fight another day.

"Heads up," Fox sent.

Coco lowered her sunglasses. Two people were heading toward the school—away from the docks and away from safety. A girl in a white dress and a girl in a black dress with a red cloak. Weiss Schnee and Ruby Rose. Every time Coco turned around, one or more of the girls from Team RWBY (Ruby) was there, right in the middle of the action.

The first-year students skidded to a stop in front of Team CFVY.

"Aren't you going the wrong way?" Coco asked.

Ruby pushed past the question. "Has anyone seen Jaune and Pyrrha?" Coco shook her head.

"The school's overrun with Grimm," Velvet said. "If they're still back there . . ."

Weiss set her jaw. "We're going to find them."

Weiss should have stayed at the docks. It was obvious that she was running on empty . . . but she was still running.

"What about Blake? Yang? Did they make it?" Velvet asked.

Ruby closed her eyes briefly, swallowed whatever she was going to say. She opened her eyes again, and they flashed in the moonlight. "They're all at the docks. We'll see you there soon. With Jaune and Pyrrha."

"We'll help you look," Fox said.

"Are you crazy?" Weiss cocked her hip. "You need to get Velvet out of here."

"I'll take Velvet," Coco tried. "Yatsuhashi and Fox will guard your flank."

"Then who'll guard yours?" Weiss gestured to the civilians who had been following CFVY. They looked uneasy about standing out in the open like this.

Ruby unfolded her weapon and used the sniper rifle to pick off a Beowolf approaching from their right. "Don't split up your team, Coco."

Coco struggled to not smart against what sounded like an order coming from her friend; she'd never seen such a somber look in Ruby's eyes before. Chaos ruled in the ruined city, but for a moment, the two team leaders calmly regarded each other.

"We have to stick together, now more than ever," Ruby said.

Coco nodded.

Then Weiss and Ruby took off again.

"Ruby!" Velvet called. Ruby turned back one last time, her cloak billowing in the bitter wind, the shaft of her scythe draped over her right shoulder. Velvet's camera flashed as she snapped a photo. "Be safe."

"You too." Ruby collapsed Crescent Rose and disappeared into the smoke.

"We should have gone with them," *Fox sent.*

Coco considered. "They're the best two for the job. And we've got our own job: Getting these people out of Beacon. Making sure Velvet is all right."

Velvet flicked past the photo of Ruby, pushing away the thought that it could be the last photo she'd ever have of her friend. While Velvet's injuries were being treated at the docks, Ruby's uncle, Qrow, had arrived with an unconscious Ruby and whisked her onto the next airbus. Velvet never even saw them.

Team RWBY hadn't returned after the fall of Beacon, and no one knew exactly where Ruby, Weiss, Blake, and Yang were now.

Velvet settled on one of her favorite weapons, Sharp Retribution, Fox's bladed tonfas. She was about to activate them and leap into the fray, when she heard a dry, whispery voice nearby. So soft she might have imagined it.

"Help."

Velvet whipped around and scanned the area until she noticed sand sliding slowly down a small hill. She shielded her eyes from the sun and squinted. Something was peeking out of the sand. It looked like the corner of a wagon . . .

And then fingers broke through, frantically pushing more of the sand away.

"Over here!" rasped the voice.

So that's why the mole crabs were hanging out in the area, Velvet thought.

The ground rumbled and more sand fell away. Velvet turned and saw the source: A huge mound of sand was moving toward them, like Pumpkin Pete tunneling under the ground in the old cartoons. Something told her it wasn't going to be an animated bunny.

She glanced back at her teammates. Coco was still in one piece, still trapped in the crab's claw. Fox was on the monster's back, chipping away at the shell with his blades as the crab tried to burrow into the sand. Yatsu had changed tactics and was holding one of the crab's legs, to keep it from submerging in the sand with Coco.

They'll be fine for now, and besides, we don't leave people behind. Not anymore.

Velvet summoned hard-light replicas of Fox's weapons and recalled Fox's fighting style as she ran past her friends, toward the buried wagon.

"Uh, Velvet? Where you going?" Fox sent. *"Could use a little help here."*

It was hard to pretend you didn't hear someone when they spoke in your head.

"Be right there," Velvet said. *I hope.*

She ran alongside the tunneling mole crab, struggling to keep up with it. It was hard enough to run on sand without its surface swelling and swirling in the creature's wake. Then the front half of the monster burst from the desert.

So they do get bigger, she thought. If those other crabs were babies, this could be their parent, easily three times their size, and three times as angry.

Velvet pushed herself to go faster, cutting ahead of the crab as its forward end dropped to the ground, practically on top of her. She looked up and saw the claws preparing to grab her.

Velvet quickly dove forward onto her hands, then pushed off and back. Her feet slammed against the bottom of the crab and she fired bullets from the tonfa blades on her forearms away from it. Her momentum and the recoil from the gunshot blasts carried her and the crab back up off the ground.

When she kicked off of the creature's underside, it tipped up onto its rear legs, while Velvet landed clumsily on her hands and knees.

The giant mole crab balanced precariously above her, waving its claws almost comically. Velvet gave herself a running start and launched herself at it again, this time face-first. As she flew through the air, she twisted her body into a corkscrew and locked the arm blades forward, all while shooting at the crab's soft belly.

The bullets started the job, and the spinning blades finished it, spewing briny fluid and guts everywhere.

Everywhere.

The crab's shrieks set Velvet's teeth on edge. It fell backward, already dead by the time it hit the ground. Velvet felt the body's tremors still as she climbed out of the hot, gory mess she had made of its belly, trying not to gag on the awful stench. The hard-light arm blades faded away.

She jumped off the carcass and surfed down a crest of sand, skidding to a halt in front of the now half-exposed wagon.

Velvet knelt in the sand, coughing and trying to catch her breath. Yatsuhashi was the first to reach her.

"Ugh. You okay?" He covered his nose and mouth. "Why didn't you wait for us?"

"Couldn't." Velvet coughed. She gestured urgently toward the wagon.

"Oh." Yatsu strode forward, grabbed the front of the wagon, and heaved. He grunted and grimaced, straining and sinking to his ankles in the sand. Then up to his knees. But the wagon slowly slid free of the ground. When he held it aloft, sand streamed out of it from the open cabin and wheels. He carefully righted the wagon and eased it down.

Coco and Fox arrived. Velvet glanced back and saw her teammates had cracked the other crab open like a nut.

Fox put a hand on Velvet's shoulder. She nodded. "I'm fine, but I could use a bath."

He wrinkled his nose.

"Hello? Anyone in there?" Coco called.

"Here." An older woman with spiky gray hair and a leathery face poked her head out of the wagon. "Thanks for the rescue."

Yatsu helped her down gently. She was stocky and short, half a foot shorter than Coco, but she looked rugged, like most Vacuo nomads. The woman cradled her left arm, which looked to be dislocated at the shoulder. "And who might you be?" she asked.

"We're Shade Academy's newest star pupils. Team CFVY. I'm Coco, and that's Fox, Velvet, and Yatsuhashi." Coco pointed out her teammates.

"Slate. Nice to meet you all." The woman ran her fingers through her hair, sending sand drifting to her shoulders. Velvet realized that her hair was light brown, not gray.

"How long have you been out here?" Coco asked.

"A day, maybe two?"

Velvet handed the woman a canteen and she sipped the water slowly. "We were fleeing the Gossan settlement after a Grimm invasion. Just when we thought we were in the clear, we found this oasis had dried up and those crabs had moved in."

"Your family just abandoned you here?" Velvet asked.

Slate shook her head. "No family. Not for a long time."

"What about the other survivors, then?" Yatsuhashi asked.

"They *survived*, I hope. I can tell you're new here." Slate looked them over, taking in their outfits. Most Vacuans wore simple, light-colored tunics and linen cloaks and head coverings for crossing the desert. But Team CFVY had to strike a balance between staying cool and being combat-ready, and their clothes were a reminder of where they had come from, who they were. Something normal in their lives when everything was very much *not* normal.

Besides, Coco would always choose fashion over sensibility at the drop of a beret.

"Surviving is what we do here, or don't," Slate went on. "We look out for one another, but if it's down to your life or someone else's, you choose your own. No hard feelings."

"You really believe that?" Velvet asked.

Slate shrugged, then winced and grabbed her shoulder. "What I believe is my own business, but if you're smart, you'll heed that advice. At any rate, the survivors fled, and I couldn't leave the wagon—when I took even a step, the crabs woke up. They use vibrations to find prey, but they lose interest the moment you stop moving."

"You couldn't have mentioned that?" Yatsu glared at Fox.

"Where's the challenge in tiptoeing around our enemies?" Fox said.

"Fortunately, I had this broken wagon," Slate went on. "I stayed with it and hoped for the best."

"That's us," Coco said. "The best have arrived."

"And I'm glad for that. I didn't want anyone else dying on my account, but if someone was gonna show up and distract those crabs, I'm glad it was Huntsmen like you."

"We did more than *distract* them," Fox said.

Velvet still couldn't believe that Slate's friends had left her to die in the desert. If that was the way of life out here, that was one more thing to dislike about Vacuo.

I wish we hadn't come here, Velvet thought, not for the first time. Probably not for the last.

Professor Port had ordered a mandatory evacuation to a safe zone northwest of the city, and General Ironwood had made it clear that there was no shame in leaving.

"You have two choices," he had told the students at Amity Arena. "Defend your kingdom and your school. Or save yourselves."

For Team CFVY, there was no question: They were going to stay in Beacon as long as they could. There were still defenseless people trapped and hiding throughout the city, and a steady flow of Grimm to dispatch.

The only question was whether Velvet would stay with them, or go to safety on her own. They stood in front of the last transport ship while they debated.

"I'm already way better," Velvet said. The on-site medics had patched her up. Her muscles were on fire, her body felt like a giant bruise, and her head was throbbing . . . but she was tougher than she looked. Tougher than anyone gave her credit for, even her own team, apparently.

"I'll be back to normal after a good night's sleep," Velvet said.

"Which you aren't likely to get here, fighting Grimm," Coco said. "Go, Velvet. You can rejoin us after you've rested up. We'll still be here."

Velvet crossed her arms, recalling Ruby's parting words to them. "Don't split up your team, Coco."

Yatsu nodded. He wanted Velvet to be safe as much as anyone, but he figured the safest place for her was close to him. And he certainly didn't want to miss out on the Grimm-bashing action at Beacon.

"We won't be a team if you're dead," Coco said.

Velvet looked hurt. "You don't think I can hold my own."

"You're injured." Coco held up a hand before Velvet could protest again. "And you used all your best photos."

Velvet whipped out her camera and snapped a photo of Coco.

Coco lowered her sunglasses. "Cute."

Velvet stuck her tongue out.

"But you know what I mean," Coco said.

"Hey, we have to get going. They're gonna close the air space soon," the air-bus pilot called.

"Give us a minute, flyboy," Coco snapped.

"Coco," Fox said. Coco looked at him—they each did. Fox spoke aloud only when they were in mixed company, or when he really wanted people to listen. But that was all, a gentle admonishment to their leader.

Coco sighed. "I'm tired. Not thinking clearly."

"That's the first sensible thing you've said today." Professor Glynda Goodwitch strode toward them. "Port told me you were insisting on staying. I'm here to convince you otherwise."

Coco straightened. "With all due respect, Professor, if you're staying, so are we."

Glynda hid a smile. "Is that so?"

"We're students, but we're still Huntsmen," Yatsu said.

"Huntsmen in training," *Glynda said. She looked back at the fallen school wistfully.*

"Huntsmen don't run," Coco said. "Even in training."

"We're sworn to defend those who can't protect themselves. And this is our home," Velvet said.

"I assume there'll be some sort of extra credit for staying," *Fox sent.*

Glynda studied each of them, no longer trying to hide her smile or her pride in them. Team CFVY, all of the students who had defended Beacon this day, were a testament to what Beacon stood for. They were every bit the shining inspirations, the sources of light in a world filled with darkness, that Professor Ozpin had hoped they would be. He had staked his reputation on his ideals, put his life on the line countless times to uphold them.

And if he had given his life in the end, as it seemed he had, it was even more important for his trusted followers to pick up where he left off.

Glynda could certainly use all the help she could get to keep the peace while she rebuilt the school, brick by brick if she had to.

"Velvet, go to the medics. See if they can find you a bed to rest in," Coco *said, taking her cue from the professor. "We'll come back and get you at dawn for another sweep of the city."*

"What are you kids doing out here, anyway?" Slate asked. When she noticed Coco frown, she held up a hand. *"Everyone's* a kid to me. Didn't mean nothing by it."

"Shade Academy received a distress call from Gossan. Professor Rumpole sent us to help," Coco said.

"From Gossan?" Slate said. "We haven't been able to talk to Shade since the CCT went down."

The Cross Continental Transmit System had been offline since the attack on Beacon Tower, which also housed Vale's CCT Tower, cutting off communication among the kingdoms of Remnant. Wireless communication still worked within Vacuo thanks to support towers relaying signals across the continent, but it was spotty farther away from the CCT Tower at the Academy. Sandstorms also tended to cause interruptions, and the smaller towers were often lost to Grimm, further breaking down the network.

"We think someone must have hardwired directly into the Gossan support tower, which boosted the signal strength enough to reach us," Velvet said.

"Must have been someone clever, then. Did you get a name?" Slate asked.

Coco shook her head. "The transmission was faint, but we heard Gossan was under attack, and survivors were going for Feldspar. We were on our way there before all this." Coco swept her hand out.

"That was the plan," Slate said. "Feldspar is the closest big settlement; it has a small oasis, and another CCT support tower."

"Good, then we should be able to report back to Professor Rumpole and update her on our status," Coco said.

"My status is hot, tired, and hungry," Yatsu said.

"You forgot smelly," Fox said.

"I'm trying to ignore that," Yatsu said, "and failing."

"When we get to Feldspar, we can probably take care of most of those problems, at least temporarily," Slate said.

"Then let's get you to your new home," Velvet said.

Slate smiled tightly. "The only home you have in Vacuo is the people you keep close. Don't forget that."

"We'll get you back to your people, then," Coco said.

The ones who abandoned you, Velvet thought. *Some home.*

"One moment." Slate climbed back into her wagon. A

moment later, she emerged with a large canvas pack on her back, a sturdy walking stick, and a scary-big knife.

"What's that for?" Yatsu asked, eyeing the knife.

Slate gestured at the giant crabs baking in the desert around them, already being covered by the drifting sand. Unlike the Grimm, when you killed an ordinary animal, even one of an unusual size, it left behind a body.

"We can't let this food go to waste," Slate said.

"Food?" Velvet covered her mouth and tried not to gag.

"You're kidding," Coco said.

"Mole crab is a rare delicacy," Fox sent.

"Rare because those who hunt the mole crab usually end up feeding the mole crab. But five of them were no match for you!" Slate laughed. "We'll just scoop the meat out of the shell, pack it in sand, and we'll be heroes in Feldspar. There are a lot of mouths to feed. At least I hope there are."

Velvet felt sick. "I'd rather fight another crab than eat one."

"If we take much longer here, you might get your chance," Coco said. "Come on, team. Let's help, but make it quick. The sooner we finish, the sooner we'll be safe at Feldspar."

"I don't know how safe we'll be," Slate said. "Something odd's been going on."

"What do you mean?" Coco asked.

"Let's just say we aren't one big happy family lately. Not anymore. But there's time for that later. I'm taking the big one. Looks like she might be carrying egg sacs." Slate scampered off toward the dead mother crab and then carved out a hefty chunk of meat.

"Gross," Velvet said.

"Dibs on the legs," Fox shouted. He ran off after Slate, arm blades out.

"Even after all the time we've known each other, sometimes Fox is a complete mystery to me," Coco said as she watched him hack off a gigantic crab leg. "I didn't figure him for a leg guy."

"He's different since we got here," Yatsu said. "Vacuo is his home."

"If it's his home, then why did he leave?" Velvet asked. But there was another unanswered question she'd much rather be asking: *Why did we have to leave Beacon?*

CHAPTER ONE

Coco stayed back until her team and Slate entered the makeshift walls of the Feldspar settlement. She lowered her sunglasses and took one last survey of the sweeping desert landscape behind them.

It was just past twilight, and the full moon hung low over the horizon, giving the sand a silvery glow. It was actually kind of pretty, but dangerous things often were. Coco wasn't sure if the moving shadows in the distance were wildlife, lurking Grimm, or the desert sands shifting in the starlight.

Coco had learned that the sand was in constant motion, but even Fox didn't know exactly why or how; for instance, their trail, only a few minutes old, was already disappearing. Vacuo seemed like a good place to go if you didn't want to be followed, if you wanted to disappear yourself. It was also a good place to go to die, unless you were strong enough to survive the extreme temperatures and the even more extreme dangers.

Coco pushed up her glasses and rejoined the others, shaking off her apprehension about what might be out there. There was always something out there. She relaxed slightly—not that she would let anyone notice—now that Velvet, Fox, and Yatsuhashi were safe inside the nomadic settlement. Of course, "safe" and "inside" were relative terms, she realized as she took in the make-shift village.

Coco's dark glasses made her seem casual and aloof, but that couldn't have been further from the truth. Her whole appearance was carefully cultivated to give her an edge over opponents and classmates alike while, of course, looking fashionable. She liked that the glasses hid where her attention was and what she was thinking until she wanted someone to know. Plus, they looked damn good on her, though didn't everything?

But underneath all that fashion, Coco was studying everything around her; silently sizing up everyone, sometimes not so silently. And Feldspar was a dump.

The so-called settlement consisted of scattered tents, trucks, vans, and squat adobe homes haphazardly arranged without any visible defenses. There was no way it could ever compare to Beacon, let alone any village in Vale; there wasn't even a lookout tower, or any sign of guards patrolling. Well, that was what Huntsmen were for, right? That was why Team CFVY was there.

Coco nodded. She always felt better when there was a job to do.

Then it hit her, what was so odd about Feldspar. A moment later, Fox's thoughts echoed her own.

Where is everybody? Fox asked.

The sand was smooth, packed down from the collective weight of people walking over it all day, every day, for months.

But fresh footsteps were visible, suggesting people had been here recently and cleared out in a hurry.

Coco held up a hand and looked around. Fox, Yatsuhashi, and Velvet nodded at the familiar signal to stop and listen. They froze. Then, in the still night, they heard a slight rustle of clothing. Gentle breathing.

"They're all around us," Fox sent to the team. Coco caught Slate's eye and moved her hand in a circle.

Here we go, Coco thought.

"Come on out, folks," Slate called out. "These are my friends. I vouch for them. And they're Huntsmen to boot. Good ones."

They waited. Slate raised her walking stick.

"Slate!" an excited male voice called out. And in a blink, the courtyard was bustling with people, swarming toward Slate.

"You're alive, you old so-and-so." A tall man with dusty hair, dusty skin, and dusty clothes grabbed Slate in a bear hug.

"She seems popular," Fox sent.

"So why'd they leave her?" Velvet asked.

"Bast, put me down or that situation might change," Slate said in a strained voice.

"I'll put you down on the condition that you never pull a stunt like that again," Bast said with a laugh.

"You know I don't like conditions," Slate said. "And I break promises like I break wind. Sometimes you just can't help it."

"Slate." Bast rolled his eyes and then lowered her gently. "You certainly have a way with words."

"What? Everyone does it."

"Which? Breaking wind or breaking promises?"

"Both. And it's polite not to call either of them out when it happens." Slate patted the dusty man affectionately on his broad arm. "How'd we do?"

"Everyone got away, thanks to you," Bast said.

Coco narrowed her eyes behind her glasses. "Why do I get the feeling there's something you aren't telling us?"

Bast turned to Coco and appraised her and the rest of the group quickly. He seemed to make a snap judgment that they were worth talking to. That was the way of all Vacuans. The fact that they'd clearly just survived a fight, and were bringing back the spoils as well as one of their own people, likely spoke in Team CFVY's favor.

"Slate here saved the lot of us. Again," Bast said.

"Alabaster—" Slate said sharply.

"She never wants any credit for keeping us alive, but you should have seen her. She held off that pod of sand crabs while the rest of us escaped. We got worried when she didn't catch up to us, though."

"Just doing my job," Slate said.

"Are you a Huntress, Slate?" Velvet asked excitedly.

"She's better. She's our mayor," Bast said.

Coco's eyes widened. It wasn't every day that someone surprised her.

"I didn't think nomadic settlements had mayors," Coco said.

"Every group needs a leader," Fox said. "Especially when the group settles down for a while. We need someone who doesn't get complacent, who keeps everyone ready to move on at a moment's notice. That person doesn't always get a formal title."

"Titles are meaningless, anyway." Slate turned her attention to Fox. "You're from here. Who's your tribe?"

"I'm from Kenyte," Fox said. "But it's been a long time."

"No matter how long you've been away, you're always part of your tribe, and your tribe's always part of you," Slate said.

Fox smiled.

"Kenyte is a great distance from here, but last I heard, they're thriving," Slate said.

"As well as anyone can in the desert," Bast added.

"Slate, so you were mayor of . . . Gossan?" Coco asked.

"It doesn't matter anymore," Slate said. She wasn't playing at being humble, or feigning discomfort. She really didn't want the attention.

"Slate is mayor of Tuff. That was the name of our original settlement, and it's what we call ourselves," Bast explained. "Wherever we go, wherever we settle, we call that place by our name—unless we join permanently with another tribe of nomads. We've had to move a few times now. Grimm. They always seem to find us, but more quickly lately. Something strange has been going on."

"Like I said, just doing my job. A job no one else wants," Slate says.

"Including me. I'm glad you're back, Slate." Bast lowered his voice. "Like Gossan, Feldspar has weak leadership. They'll be happy to have you."

Coco looked around. It was impossible to tell apart the recent Gossan refugees from the Feldspar tribe. Maybe some of them were slightly less rumpled and dirty than the others, but that could have just been a matter of personal hygiene.

"The politics here can get interesting. Like I said, most tribes and settlements don't have elected officials," Fox sent. *"As a general rule, we don't like rules. It's even more unusual for a tribe to have a leader that they trust and like, especially after they've connected with a larger group. Slate must be really good."*

Coco licked her dry lips. She was actually starting to like the bitter-tasting sand, but it was no replacement for her favorite lip gloss, which she had run out of a year ago. The boutique that made it had been trashed along with the rest of Beacon.

"I doubt they elected her, but it sounds like no one else was in the running," Coco said. Slate seemed like the kind of person who stepped up when she had to, and most people are naturally inclined to be followers.

"Speaking of jobs," Slate said. "Where are Bertilak and Carmine? They were supposed to be fighting those Grimm."

Coco raised her eyebrows. "There are other Huntsmen here?"

Slate shrugged. "Sort of."

"I'll find them." Bast ran off.

Slate called out to a few boys on the edge of the crowd. "Hans, why don't you and your friends make yourselves useful? This here is fresh sand crab. Take it to the mess and make sure it gets rationed. You three take an extra share for your trouble."

One boy with a dirt-smudged face nodded. "You got it, Ms. Slate!"

"It's just Slate, kid."

Hans and his two friends grabbed the cloth-wrapped bundles of crab meat from Yatsuhashi and Fox.

"Why didn't you mention that you sacrificed yourself to save your people?" Velvet asked Slate.

Slate gave her a penetrating look. "Would it have changed anything? It didn't seem relevant, and you were just as eager to save me when I was some defenseless old woman, which, thank you again, by the way. Fortunately, I didn't end up dying after all. This time."

Slate crossed her arms and looked around. "These aren't *my* people, either. They're just people. Good people. And I believe in helping others when I can. I don't care who they are or where they're from."

She's incredible, Coco thought. She saw why everyone rallied to Slate, and it wasn't just because she helped organize and protect them. It was because she cared more about them than she did herself, and that was a rare quality in Vacuo. As Slate herself had implied back in the desert, it was the kind of quality that eventually got you killed, unless you were also very lucky or very strong.

"Why don't we go to the saloon for a drink and some of that food we brought back," Slate said.

Coco hid a smile. Slate was deft at making an order seem more like a friendly suggestion.

Slate led them to a one-level hut built from sandstone, canvas, and good intentions. It was remarkably spacious and clean inside, and pleasantly warm. The night was gradually getting colder, as it did after the sun went down in Vacuo, but the saloon had a number of roaring fire pits. The laughter, conversation, and music stopped when people spotted Slate.

She smiled and waved. "Can't get rid of me that easily."

Several people called out well-wishes to her, or banged their clay mugs against the long shale tables.

Coco thought Slate would pick a table in the corner for some privacy, but she walked right up to one in the center. CFVY followed her and sat down. The rest of the restaurant soon went back to their business as if they weren't there. Coco figured it was naïve to think they were really being ignored, though; people in Vacuo didn't trust strangers easily, and CFVY had a way of attracting attention wherever they went.

A perky Faunus waitress with a pig snout came over. She rattled off the offerings: "Today's specials are crab burgers, crab steak, crab cake, and crab rangoon. All very fresh."

"This one's on me," Slate said. "I'm gonna need an ale, Topaz. Make it two to start, and keep them coming. And as much as I love crab anything, I've been dreaming about your spicy bat stew for days. Got any of that left?"

"For you? Anything," Topaz said.

"And get these folks whatever they like. They earned it."

"Coffee," Coco said. She madly needed caffeine, and she also liked to stay on brand. "And I'll try the crab burger." *When in Vacuo.*

Yatsuhashi ordered the crab steak and desert lotus tea, and Fox ordered fried crevice worms, lightly toasted cave beetles, and water.

"Cactus tea," Velvet said. "And the gecko cake, please."

"You know it isn't really cake, right?" Coco smiled.

Velvet sighed.

"I'll get those orders right—"

A tall, broad man with a green Mohawk and matching goatee shoved Topaz aside. Coco registered the mace on his belt before she took in the rest of him. A brown hooded cloak made of coarse fabric was draped over his broad shoulders. He wore a green chestplate over a dirty black tunic; his biceps bulged from the short sleeves, showing off a long scar stretching down his right forearm.

"Hey." Yatsuhashi rose and faced him. They were about the same height, but the newcomer ignored him. Meanwhile, Velvet was checking on Topaz.

"You okay?" Velvet asked the waitress.

Topaz nodded. She was shaken, but fine.

"Bertilak, apologize to the girl," Slate said.

"I'm sorry you were in my way," Bertilak growled. "Now run along, piggy."

Fox frowned and fingered the tip of one of his arm blades.

"I apologize," Slate said to Topaz.

Topaz put a hand on Slate's shoulder and then left, casting a scornful look at Bertilak behind his back.

"Well, well. What have we here?" Bertilak stuck a toothpick in his mouth. "Not every day you see new Huntsmen in these parts."

"It's nice to see you, too," Slate said. "You've gotten comfortable in Feldspar already, I see."

"You're tougher than you look. I'm surprised you're alive," Bertilak said.

"No thanks to you," Slate said.

"Everyone got here just fine," Bertilak said.

"Well, thanks for that much, then."

"We didn't do it for you. Thanks for being crab bait." He laughed.

"Bertilak Celadon, this is Coco, Velvet, Fox, and Yatsuhashi. Team CFVY, from Shade Academy."

"Team CFVY, huh? So you're Huntsmen in training?" Bertilak's face registered surprise, and something else Coco couldn't place. Annoyance?

"You attended Shade, too, didn't you?" Slate asked.

"You're a Huntsman?" Coco asked, incredulous.

"Sometimes it's even hard for me to believe." A woman walked up and stood next to Bertilak. Unlike her partner, she was clearly a Huntress—and she was stunning.

Another benefit of wearing sunglasses was people couldn't tell when you were staring, and Coco couldn't take her eyes off the fit, dark-skinned woman. Tinted goggles were perched atop her head, and her wild, unbound scarlet hair reached just past her waist. Freckles dotted her nose and cheeks. A streak of silver hair starting at her left temple shone in the firelight, mirroring the short silver cape draped over her right side. A chain mail crop top exposed her midriff, and she completed the ensemble with a black belt, red mini-shorts, and thigh-high black boots. Holsters on her belt held a pair of long sai.

"Bertilak here barely graduated," the Huntress said.

"Theodore had it in for me," Bertilak says.

"Only because you couldn't follow the rules. I apologize for anything off-color my partner says. If he hasn't offended you yet, trust me, he will."

"I'm Coco Adel." Coco rose and extended a hand.

"Carmine Esclados." She shook Coco's hand firmly, each of them applying just enough pressure to let the other woman know she was holding back.

"You have to tell me where you shop," Coco said. "I love your outfit."

"This old thing? I've had it forever. Picked it up in Mistral years ago. I want your purse. Who's the designer?"

"Coco Adele," Coco said.

"You made it yourself? Must be one of a kind. Careful, or I might have to take it from you." Carmine winked. Then she nodded at Velvet, Yatsuhashi, and Fox. "So, you guys just passing through?"

Coco shook her head. "Someone called Shade asking for help, so Professor Rumpole sent us."

"*Who* called?" Bertilak glared at Slate.

"It's a great mystery," Slate said. "And not the only one around here."

"Well, I want—" Bertilak began; Carmine interrupted him with an elbow jab.

"We're glad to have some backup, of course." Carmine smiled. "We've had our hands full."

"It's strange for someone to send a distress call when there are already Huntsmen around," Velvet said.

"We didn't hire Bertilak and Carmine," Slate said. "They just assist us on occasion. When they feel like it."

"Lucky that you two happened to be close by," Coco said. "What brought you to Vacuo?"

"That's none of your business, sweetheart." Bertilak moved his toothpick to the other side of his mouth.

"We'll be moving on pretty soon," Carmine said.

"The sooner the better," Bertilak said. "I want to get out of here before things heat up again."

"Are you expecting trouble?" Velvet asked.

"Always, darling." He winked.

Velvet crossed her arms and turned back toward Slate.

"Trouble's been following us around," Slate said. "Every few days, something gets people here worked up for no reason. Arguments and fights break out, people get afraid, and of course all that negative emotion brings Grimm. More and more of them every time."

"How long has this been going on?" Coco asked.

"About a month. Half of the folks here have survived three separate attacks at as many settlements." Slate counted them off. "Tuff, Schist, and now Gossan. We've lost a lot of good people along the way."

"Would have been more if not for us," Bertilak said.

"Cool it," Carmine said.

Coco wiped her brow; it was getting a little toasty in the close quarters of the saloon.

Topaz brought over a tray of drinks and food. She gave Bertilak a wide berth as she unloaded the cups and plates on the table.

"Care to join us?" Coco asked, looking at Carmine.

"I'll take a rain check," she said. "And I don't mean that in the Vacuo way." At Coco's puzzled expression, she explained. "It rains so infrequently here, a 'rain check' is kind of their version of 'when pigs fly.'"

"Hey," Topaz said, with a hurt expression.

"No offense intended," Carmine said.

"Where are you from, Carmine?" Coco asked.

"Originally? Atlas, believe it or not. Could you picture me in a uniform?"

Yes, Coco thought.

"A lot has happened since I left. If you have time later, I'll gladly regale you with some hunting stories, but right now I should check on the Caspians."

"They're fine," Bertilak snarled.

"Did you forget we're on the clock? We work for *them*. Let's go," Carmine said pointedly. "Good to meet you. Looking forward to getting to know one another better."

Coco sat down and sipped her coffee. It was scalding hot. They needed to turn down the heat in here.

"Who are the Caspians?" Coco asked when the other Huntsmen had left.

"Edward Caspian and his grandson, August. They seem nice, but they don't socialize much," Slate said. "They're from a village called Sumire."

"Sumire? That's in Vale," Coco said. "That's a long, dangerous journey, even before you hit the desert."

Team CFVY had experienced it for themselves when they had traveled from Beacon to Shade Academy on foot. Along the way, they had encountered an unusually high number of Grimm, which were being drawn to Beacon Tower. They had taken care of as many of them as they could, feeling like they were helping to defend their home even as they were running from it.

"What brings them to Vacuo?" Coco asked.

"Where are they going?" Fox asked.

Slate shrugged. "Good questions. They've never answered them. The Caspians arrived at Tuff with Bertilak and Carmine, in pretty rough shape. Like they'd been running for days. We couldn't turn them away like that. By the time they were back on their feet, the Grimm were at our gates. The four of them have stuck with us ever since."

The group tucked into their food. Yatsuhashi gingerly cut through his crab steak with a fork and knife, the way he did everything when he wasn't wielding his greatsword on the battlefield; he was always afraid of damaging something or hurting someone with his strength.

He took a bite and chewed it thoughtfully. "Not bad. Could use some Mistral spices."

"You think everything could use Mistral spices." Velvet laughed.

Coco thought the burger was maybe too spicy.

Slate took a bite of bat stew, briefly closed her eyes, and sighed happily. "I needed that. And this." She took a big gulp of ale from a frothy mug. She frowned. "Ugh. It's warm."

She gestured to Topaz and then turned back to Coco and the others.

"So you've run from Grimm attacks twice?" Coco asked Slate.

"That's right. I got on this wild ride when we evacuated Tuff. Grimm have been on our heels the whole way. I've never seen anything like it. Sometimes things get tense, sure, and that brings a few stray Grimm. But things always calm down, and life goes on.

"This is different. When emotions start to run high, it just gets worse and worse. And the Grimm come, and they don't stop. So we run. We settle down somewhere else, and pretty soon it all starts again. I don't know what we'll do when those Huntsmen leave with the Caspians."

"*We're* here now," Coco said.

"I was hoping you'd say that. I don't know who summoned you, but we can't pay you. I'm sorry. Even if we took up a collection, it wouldn't be enough," Slate said. "We barter for most of our business, and we've all taken a big hit with the evacuations."

Fox slurped a fried worm into his mouth. "We're doing this for school credit," he said, his mouth full.

"And we'll help because it's the *right thing to do*," Velvet said.

Yatsuhashi nodded, chewing.

"Whatever the reason, we're here," Coco said. "Maybe we can fight the Grimm off without needing to evacuate again."

"Maybe the Grimm won't bother us this time," Topaz said. Coco hadn't even noticed the waitress return to the table.

"Maybe." Slate handed her the mug and explained kindly that ale should be served cold. The waitress looked confused.

Coco realized that Topaz wasn't the only one who had been lingering near their table. A small crowd had gathered around them, the better to eavesdrop on their conversation. No such thing as privacy in Vacuo, not when most of the walls were made of adobe and canvas, and someone else's business usually affected your own.

A crash came from the other side of the saloon, followed by the sound of plates breaking. Two people started yelling. Coco stood and saw two men circling an overturned table, fists raised.

"It's already starting." Slate sighed. She carefully wiped her mouth with a napkin and rose. "This is what I was talking about."

"We'll get to the bottom of it," Coco said. "Just try to keep everyone calm."

Slate nodded and walked toward the impending fight.

"*What can we do here, anyway?*" Fox asked.

"We can start by learning more about what's been

happening here. There has to be a reason for these fights breaking out," Coco said.

"There you go again, making decisions for us," Velvet said.

"Excuse me?" Coco felt a surge of anger. "I'm the boss."

"You're the leader, not the boss," Fox said.

"Whoa," Yatsuhashi said. "Calm down, everyone. We're
tired—"

"I'm sorry. I don't know why I said that! I didn't mean it."
Velvet took a piece of flatbread from Slate's plate and chewed
it quietly.

"*Anyway*. Clearly something is causing people to get . . .
emotional." Coco studied Velvet and Fox. Where had that outburst come from?

"We could interview the nomads." Yatsuhashi was also casting a worried eye on Velvet.

"It's a start," Coco said. "As soon as we're done eating, I'll
find the CCT relay tower and let Professor Rumpole know we
made it and we'll be staying a few days."

She sat back down to sip her cooling coffee and watched
Slate at work. When the brawling men saw the mayor coming,
they lowered their fists and looked deeply embarrassed. Slate
talked to each of them softly. She took a deep breath and let it
out, watched as they mimicked her. Then they shook hands and
picked the shale table back up together.

Slate looked plenty tough to Coco. It was no wonder these
nomads—even the strangers who had joined the group from
other settlements ravaged by Grimm—looked to her as a leader.

Like Slate, Coco hadn't chosen to lead Team CFVY; she had *been* chosen. Sometimes she still didn't know if that had been the right choice. In the beginning, she hadn't particularly wanted responsibility for her team, or now the nomads in Feldspar; she was just trying to do her job.

Coco hoped she'd be as successful at it as Slate one day.

CHAPTER TWO

The First-years had been at Beacon for barely a day, and they were all about to die.

The twenty or so new students were currently flying through the air over the Emerald Forest. More like falling, really. And if they did nothing to slow or cushion their fall, they would certainly go *splat*. In about fifty seconds. Even if they survived the fall, they would be in a forest lousy with Creatures of Grimm, left to fend for themselves.

Fifty seconds was plenty of time to consider the choices that had brought each of them there. Plenty of time to regret them.

Coco Adel had no regrets. She was loving initiation so far. This was why Beacon Academy had been her first-choice school. Professor Ozpin had a reputation for being very mysterious and a bit reckless with his students. Coco liked a challenge.

Besides, Vale had been her home all her life.

She still wasn't sure what to make of Ozpin. The youngest headmaster Beacon had ever had, he had a mischievous streak and a boyish charm that reminded Coco of her younger brother. But at the same time, Ozpin seemed oddly ancient—not just because of his silver hair but because of how he always stood tall, how he talked like he meant much more than he was saying out loud.

Professor Glynda Goodwitch, on the other hand, was the strong leader Coco aspired to be. She might have been Ozpin's second in command, but she gave the sense that she was the one in charge. She was a bit severe, utterly humorless, and her body language said she was all business. And to top it off, she was also hot, with impeccable fashion sense. Her whole outfit worked—with that blouse, the pencil skirt, that cape, those heels!—and she seemed very comfortable with who she was. The fact that Goodwitch clearly respected Ozpin somehow conferred more authority on him than his title.

Coco prepared to land, assessing the tree line ahead and all her options. She yawned. Okay, maybe she had one regret. Even though being flung off a cliff kind of woke you up and got your adrenaline flowing, she wished she'd had a second cup of coffee at breakfast.

Forty seconds.

About twenty feet away from Coco, also falling, Velvet Scarlatina had some regrets.

She couldn't believe that on their second day at Beacon, their headmaster, Professor Ozpin, had catapulted the entire first-year class into a Grimm-infested forest.

Toward a Grimm-infested forest. There was still the little matter of landing in it safely. But more than the falling, more than the Grimm, Velvet was worried about whom she would be partnered with.

Everyone had known they would have a partner for their four years at Beacon, but Velvet had thought she'd have some control over who it would be. Turned out it was going to be completely random.

"Each of you will be given teammates. Today," Professor Ozpin had said. "These teammates will be with you for the rest of your time at Beacon, so it is in your best interest to be paired with someone with whom you can work well. That said, the first person you make eye contact with after landing will be your partner for the next four years."

"What?" Velvet said.

If she had had a choice—which she apparently didn't—she would have chosen Coco Adel. They'd both come to Beacon from Pharos Combat School, so Velvet knew her . . . sort of. Coco probably had no idea who Velvet was, but Velvet knew all about her. Coco had been popular at their school, breaking performance records—and breaking girls' hearts.

Even from twenty feet away, Velvet could see Coco was falling with style. It wasn't only because of the shades, but because of her whole form. She wasn't slowly tumbling in the air like most of their classmates—she had her feet pointed toward the ground, as if she expected to just land like a cat.

As far as Velvet knew, Coco wasn't hiding cat ears under that beret, though. One hand was keeping the hat on her head, the other was at her waist holding on to her purse. And Coco was smiling. Anyone who could look completely confident and happy while plummeting to the ground at thirty-two feet per second was someone you wanted on your side.

Mostly, Velvet knew who she didn't want to be paired with. At the top of her list was the tall dude from Mistral. Less than a day, and Velvet had already been bullied by some of the upper-classmen at Beacon for being a Faunus, and of course, her tormentors were from Mistral.

Velvet loved her ears, which only made it worse when people called her "bunny girl" or made those awful jokes she'd heard hundreds of times before, from the harmless-but-hurtful "hop to it" jabs to the squicky comments that made her feel threatened . . . the boys who joked about hunting rabbits or asked if she could teach them multiplication.

The big kid hadn't said anything like that to her yet, but his people didn't like Faunus and didn't mind letting them know how they felt. Thinking about working with him for four years, Velvet didn't want a partner at all. She'd never had any close friends before, and besides, everyone managed to disappoint her sooner or later.

Thirty seconds.

The "big kid," Yatsuhashi Daichi, knew more about being bullied than anyone could have guessed. He'd always been the big kid growing up, and because of his size most people had assumed he was stupid, or they were scared of him. Other kids didn't want to play with him, thinking he would hurt them, either accidentally or intentionally. Consequently, Yatsuhashi had grown up afraid of what he might do, always self-conscious about his size, his strength, and his Semblance, especially around his parents and little sister, who were pretty much his only real friends.

Yatsuhashi tried to keep his mind free of distracting thoughts like these as he fell, eyes closed and arms crossed over his chest. The wind whistled past his ears, and he blocked that sound out, too, trying to imagine himself floating like a leaf on the wind. That wasn't making him any lighter, but meditation did leave him clear-eyed and ready to handle the situation, which was going to resolve pretty soon, one way or another.

He was always thinking several steps ahead, but until he actually met his partner, he couldn't see his path to the abandoned temple in the forest and the relics that Professor Ozpin had tasked them with finding. Yatsu didn't like leaving anything to chance, and the next four years at Beacon had a big question mark hanging over them. The events of today would have a tremendous impact on his Huntsman training and likely set his course for the rest of his life. He wondered how such a momentous decision could be left to chance.

No.

Yatsu opened his eyes. He had to take control of the situation. This was too important to let the whims of a professor, or Fate, or the gods decide.

Yatsu thought about classmates he had researched and who would make a good partner. He ranked them and then picked out their coordinates as they descended toward the Emerald Forest. He made up his mind quickly, already angling his body into position and considering how to get himself on the ground safely at exactly the right moment.

Twenty seconds.

Today was the day Fox Alistair had been waiting for, not just since enrolling at Beacon but for practically his whole life.

So far it was kind of a disappointment.

Growing up as an orphan in Vacuo, he'd never had a permanent home, or even permanent people in his life. His tribe, the Kenyte—the tribe his parents had belonged to—had taken care of Fox communally. He was grateful for all the sacrifices it took to raise him, but he knew he didn't truly belong there. He had given a lot of thought to the place he would want to call home and the family he wanted one day.

As he had survived the tense, quiet years in the desert, he knew he would become a Huntsman one day. He'd always been drawn to Vale, which seemed to be the opposite of everything he had grown up with. Lush plant life, plenty of water and food, friendly people, fewer things trying to kill you on a daily basis . . . Vale sounded like a nice stable place to settle down and make a life without the constant fear of encountering Grimm—or worse. Vacuo was probably the one place in Remnant where some of the natural wildlife could be considered more dangerous than the Creatures of Grimm.

He figured this whole wild initiation thing must be some kind of ill-conceived hazing for First-years. They couldn't really assign students to each other so randomly—that would be almost as bad as how nomadic tribes and settlements formed back home.

That was probably something the professors said to make the exercise more interesting. And Fox was 100 percent sure Ozpin wouldn't actually put students' lives in jeopardy on their first outing, without any adult supervision . . . not that Fox needed the help, of course. But still, Fox hadn't even signed any kind of liability waiver.

Fox wondered what Ozpin had been thinking when he decided to throw a blind boy off a cliff. He thought it seemed a tad irresponsible, but then again Ozpin also seemed like someone who appreciated a good joke. And that's all this was: a joke.

For his part, Fox liked practical jokes, too, especially when he was the prankster. But on the off chance that some or all of this scenario was exactly as advertised, it was time to get serious.

Fox flipped forward in the air and pointed himself headfirst in the direction he was falling. He tapped the almost-invisible earbud in his ear to activate voice commands on the Scroll in his belt.

"Ada, engage proximity alert. Silent mode."

"Engaged," the Accessibility Dialog Assistant said in its female monotone voice, at its lowest volume.

His Scroll immediately began buzzing in periodic pulses, increasing in intensity the closer he got to the forest.

Fox relied on his Aura for more than just shielding or special boosted attacks like most people; it was one of the ways he could orient himself in his environment without vision. His Semblance allowed him to track where his classmates were in relation to him, at least over short distances. But since they were basically strangers, all he had was a strong impression of their presence. There were very few people Fox had known well enough to pinpoint their locations more precisely, and they were all back in Vacuo, or dead.

His Scroll buzzed steadily. Fox crooked his arms so the blades of his weapon, Sharp Retribution, were ahead and extended to either side of him, just as he breached the canopy of trees. He grimaced with the impact as they sliced through the treetops, but his Aura held and his momentum slowed.

Trees cracked and snapped in his wake as he cut his way through the forest, Ada continuing to send out pulses that helped him feel his way through the canopy. It was exhausting. Around him and in the distance, he heard gunfire, explosions, trees crashing as his classmates found their own methods of arresting their descent.

When he had slowed down enough, he brought his arms up and hooked the blades around a thick tree branch. He spun himself around it several times, stripping away bark and cutting into the wood before he jabbed his elbows downward and launched himself up and over to a higher branch. He grabbed it with both hands for a moment, then let go, falling at a much more manageable speed toward another branch a little lower. As the trees grew wider and closer together toward the ground, he sprung from a branch and kicked off a tree trunk, landing lightly on a lower branch. Drop. Kick. Grab. Spin. Flip.

Fox landed in a crouch.

"Yes! Too bad nobody saw that," he said.

Someone clapped behind him. He felt a nearby presence in his mind, and he smelled chocolate and caramel. He turned to meet his partner for the next four years.

Just before Coco reached the top of the forest, she flicked her purse and it unfolded into her Gatling gun, Gianduja. Coco swung the massive weapon under her and pointed the muzzle down. She braced it between her knees.

She fired Gravity Dust rounds and hoped no one—at least no people or harmless animals—were in the way as the bullets shredded leaves and wood. Enhanced by her Semblance, the Gravity Dust slowed her fall. For a moment she hovered in zero gravity, hanging in midair, and then she began drifting slowly down into the forest.

The world was darker under the canopy, especially with sunglasses on. As she fell and picked up more speed, she yanked her gun up in front of her and angled it toward the ground again, mowing down trees just moments before she would have slammed into them. Her designer shades protected her eyes, but splinters lacerated her face and she tasted sawdust and smoke. The recoil slowed her fall even more.

When she saw an opening in the trees, she pressed the release switch and collapsed the artillery back into a fashionable accessory that no trendy Huntress should be without. Holding on to the strap of the purse, she flung it out and it caught on a branch, forming a slingshot around the limb. The bough bent and then broke, and she was falling again, only slightly out of control.

She used the purse again to lasso another branch, this time spinning herself around the tree trunk, letting go, and repeating the maneuver in the other direction. She slung through and down the trees this way until she was near the forest floor.

Then she opened up the gun again and fired another round straight down, amplifying the Dust's explosiveness. The shock wave from their impact gave her another small boost while also creating a crater in the dirt below. She landed on the edge of the new pit and slid gently down the slope to the bottom.

Coco crouched there for a moment, listening. Someone was slicing through the trees above, sending branches raining down around her. She glanced up and saw a flash of red pass overhead. That had to be Fox Alistair, one of the possibilities on her list of potential partners.

To her left, she saw another classmate, Iris Marilla, float down to the ground. That was a cute trick, and she was cute, too, with those flowers in her hair, but Coco knew Iris also had an annoyingly high-pitched voice that would get old real fast. Besides, Coco wasn't looking for a girlfriend, she was looking for someone who wouldn't hold her back or get her killed on the field. Someone who could keep up.

Coco folded up her gun and sprinted away from Iris, up the side of the crater and deeper into the forest, following the sound of Fox's progress through the trees. Then she couldn't hear him anymore.

She stopped, listening, wondering if he had landed badly—if she needed to save him. She thought that would be a shame, especially because it would mean she had misjudged him. But no, there he was, springing down silently from the trees. He landed ten feet in front of her, catching himself on his hands and one knee. He was facing away from her.

His arm blades looked wicked sharp. People must always be giving him plenty of elbow room.

Fox turned around suddenly and looked straight at her.

"Hello?" he said.

Coco waved. No reaction. She lowered her sunglasses so she could see him better.

"Oh. You're blind," she said. So much for her thorough research.

Fox clapped his hands to his eyes. "Oh no!" he said. "Whyyyyyy?"

Coco put a hand on a cocked hip and grinned. "You are not what I expected. I like that. I'm Coco Adel."

"Fox Alistair."

"I know."

"Do you suppose this counts? 'First person you make eye contact with' and all?" Fox asked. He aimed two fingers at his own eyes, then pointed them at Coco.

"Do you want it to count?" Coco asked.

"You have an absurdly strong Aura, and you smell nice. Uh, don't take that the wrong way."

He can sense Auras? Coco thought. *That's a high-level technique.* Fox was turning out to be even more interesting than she'd first thought. She could work with that.

"There's a right way to take it? Don't worry, Fox. I don't take offense easily," Coco said.

"Then I think this could work," Fox said.

"I was just thinking that. All right. Shall we?"

Fox nodded.

The headmaster's next set of instructions had been:

After you've partnered up, make your way to the northern end of the for-est. You will meet opposition along the way. Do not hesitate to destroy everything in your path, or you will die. You will be monitored and graded for the duration of your initiation, but our instructors will not intervene.

You will find an abandoned temple at the end of the path, containing several relics. Each pair must choose one and return to the top of the cliff. We will regard that item, as well as your standing, and grade you appropriately.

"Let's find that temple," Fox said. "You lead the way."

He and Coco headed off together.

Velvet had the perfect weapon in mind to help her land in one piece. She had surreptitiously preprogrammed her camera, Anesidora, with a photo of a smiling Vega Bleu, a classmate back at Pharos Combat School who had gone on to Atlas Academy.

She was glad she had, because her camera would have been much trickier to program while tumbling through the air. Now it was a simple matter to call up Vega's weapon, a pair of arm-mounted grappling hooks.

As Velvet broke through the treetops, she grabbed the controls of the weapons, accurately reproduced with hard-light using special—and especially expensive—Dust from the Schnee Dust Company. She experienced only the briefest moment of disorientation before her Semblance allowed her to mimic Vega's moves.

And just like that she was firing one grappling hook, swinging on the razor-sharp wire, firing the other hook, releasing the first and retracting it, and so on, swinging effortlessly through the forest like a monkey, or at least precisely like Vega would have. Velvet wondered if her old friend was going through initiation at Atlas right now, and what that was like.

Grappling from tree to tree, Velvet gradually dropped closer to the ground. She kept swinging. A few times she caught a glimpse of dark creatures sniffing around below. She glanced behind her and saw branches breaking and foliage shaking as some of them began following her. Through the leaves she spotted a pack of Boarbatusks, and they spotted her. They gave chase.

So that was about to become her next problem. She picked up speed, trying to stay ahead of them.

But now she had something else to deal with. Her hard-light weapons only lasted for a limited time, and her time had run out;

the grapple lines faded away while she was still a hundred feet above the ground.

She found herself plummeting again, but she managed to twist around and grab hold of a thick branch as she fell. The bough snapped, barely slowing her down, but she held on to it.

She clutched the makeshift staff in front of her and managed to use it to bounce off a trunk that she otherwise would have smacked into headfirst. Her Aura absorbed some of the blow. Jarred by the impact, she dropped straight down the side of the tree, crashing through more branches that broke her momentum. Her Aura continued to protect her from breaking any bones in the process, and she used the branch to push herself away from the tree and out to avoid hitting any more, but now she was falling backward, legs swinging, arms flailing, hoping she could grab hold of something before she hit the ground.

Velvet screamed.

Yatsuhashi felt bad that he and his fellow students were inadvertently destroying the forest, but not bad enough that he let it hold him back.

He drew Fulcrum and swung the sword hard from right to left, twisting his body and using the momentum to start spinning. "Hyaaaah!" he cried.

He held the blade out, flat side up, using it to slice his way through the trees as he spiraled downward. Not so much a leaf on the wind as a helicopter seed, the kind he'd loved dropping from heights as a child.

The forest whirled around him. He burst into a clearing with a flurry of twigs and leaves. He focused on a sturdy tree in his path, seeing it loom larger in flashes as he continued spinning. He tensed his muscles, and at the right moment he flipped the sword around and plunged it into the trunk, blade side down.

"Sorry!" Yatsuhashi mumbled to the tree.

The sword embedded itself to the hilt in the tree and then slid downward. He grunted as he held on, planting his feet against the trunk to slow his momentum further. The wrapped sword hilt grew warm, then hot, then burning under his gloved hands.

He hit the ground hard enough to rattle his teeth and staggered backward, somehow maintaining his balance, even while still dizzy from spinning. When he yanked Fulcrum from the trunk, the tree split in two and fell on either side of him. It screamed.

Yatsuhashi shook his head. Trees didn't scream. Then he looked up and saw a girl falling. He dropped his sword and ran toward her. Leaped into the air. Caught her.

"I've got you," he said.

He landed with her in his arms, more gracefully this time. It was the Faunus with the pretty rabbit ears. He flashed her a goofy smile. She scowled and looked away, shielding her eyes.

"Put me down." She struggled and pushed herself out of

his arms. She opened the box behind her and pulled out a camera.

"You're welcome?" Yatsuhashi said.

She cast her glance downward, rabbit ears drooping over her eyes. Then she sighed and looked up. "Thanks."

"So . . . I guess we're partners?" Yatsuhashi said. He suddenly felt shy.

"This is all a mistake," she said.

Yatsuhashi walked back to the split tree and picked up Fulcrum. He checked it for damage. He knew where every scratch and ding on the blade had come from. He found the new one, a tiny dimple near the hilt that he would forever associate with today's initiation.

"But those are the rules," Yatsuhashi said.

"This isn't going to work," she replied.

"Why?" he asked.

"Because I'm a Faunus, and you're—"

"What?" Yatsuhashi narrowed his eyes. She was looking at him the way people so often did, like she was scared of him, towering above her. His shoulders tightened, and he pressed his arms against his sides, as if he could make himself smaller somehow. Less intimidating.

"You're from Mistral," she said.

Yatsuhashi blinked. "So?"

"Your people don't tend to like my people," she said quietly. She folded her arms against her chest and turned away from him. For her the gesture worked, and she seemed to shrink a little.

"I'm—" Yatsuhashi began. At the sound of his voice, the girl tensed. He lowered his tone as much as he could. "It's clear that people from Mistral have hurt you before. I'm sorry that you had to experience that."

Her shoulders tensed, but she peeked over her shoulder at him.

"I would never mistreat you because you're a Faunus, or for any other reason. It's not who I am or who my mother raised me to be. And if I ever slip up and make a stupid joke or say something insensitive, you have full permission to punch me . . . so I can know how to be better."

The girl looked back over her shoulder at him, uncrossing her arms.

"Can we start over?" He offered his hand.

She nodded, ears bobbing up and down, and turned to face him.

"I am Yatsuhashi Daichi," he said.

She looked up at him—way up—and smiled a little. "Velvet Scarlatina."

"Pleased to meet you," they both said at the same time.

"So if we're partners, I guess there's something you need to know," Velvet said.

"What is it?"

"There was a pack of Boarbatusks on my tail."

Yatsuhashi couldn't help but check. Faunus typically only had one animal feature, but if she said she had a tail—

She blushed, covering her rear. "Excuse you! It was a figure of speech!"

"Oh. Guess that means I've earned my first punch."

Three Boarbatusks suddenly burst into the clearing in front of Yatsuhashi. Their large, curved white tusks and bone masks with four red eyes looked eerie in the dim light filtering through the tree canopy.

"Later, though." Yatsuhashi slowly brought his sword around. "Don't worry, I'll protect you."

A bright light flashed. Momentarily stunned, when the spots in front of his eyes disappeared, he saw Velvet holding a camera.

"What was that for?" he asked.

Velvet pressed something on her camera and a minute later she was holding a glowing, transparent copy of his sword. Yatsu stared, dumbfounded.

"Don't worry." Velvet smirked. "I'll protect you."

"Check out that cave," Coco said.

Fox tilted his head questioningly.

"Right. Well, it has all these drawings around the entrance of stick people attacking a big scorpion," she said.

"So it's a Death Stalker den. Only an idiot would go in there," Fox said.

"Yeah. It just looks interesting."

"I'm more interested in finding the temple."

"The temple should be just up ahead," Coco said as she climbed out into a clearing.

Fox marched forward. It really was hard to tell that he was

blind. Coco watched him carefully, and even when he stumbled on a rock or a root, he quickly adjusted to maintain his balance without missing a beat; you had to be looking to even notice the misstep. Coco envied Fox's complete awareness of his body and how it moved in his environment.

"Four people just left that area, in a hurry. Heading back to the cliff," Fox said.

"How do you know that?" Coco asked.

"I can detect other people's minds, just an impression of their consciousness. And—" Fox shook his head and fell silent again.

"Like when you can feel someone watching you?" Coco asked.

"Sure," Fox said. He found it exhausting, carrying on a conversation, speaking out loud. But it seemed like it was probably necessary for them to bond a little bit. They were supposed to be partners for the next four years, but it would be better if they were friends, too. And they still had to face together whatever was at this temple of Ozpin's.

"Is this it?" Coco asked when they arrived.

Fox waited patiently.

"Oh, sorry." Coco walked toward the small ruin, Fox following. "It's circular, with six pillars supporting a ring of stones above us. Careful, there are two steps up. Okay, we're standing in the middle now. Around us are twenty short pedestals with small stone tablets on them."

Coco walked to one of them. "It's etched like a playing card. This one is the Joker."

Coco moved around the temple, examining the other tablets.

"Here's the King of Hearts. Queen of Hearts. Ace of Spades . . . some cards are missing, so our other classmates must have grabbed them."

She tried to hide her annoyance, but Fox picked up that she was really bothered that they were already behind.

"You like being first," he said.

"And best."

He nodded. "Those aren't always the same thing, or mutually compatible. But maybe we can still beat the others back if we hurry."

Coco folded her arms. "Pick a card, any card."

"Me?" Fox asked.

"Go for it."

Fox turned in a slow circle and then walked purposefully toward a pedestal.

"Um. That one's empty," Coco said. "Try a little to your left."

Fox adjusted his course and reached out to take the stone card: King of Hearts.

"All right, let's go," she said.

Fox tucked the card into a pouch at his belt. Then he held up a hand. "We have incoming." He pointed behind Coco.

Two people were heading toward them fast with a spinning black-and-white ball chasing them. Velvet Scarlatina, whom Coco remembered from Pharos Combat School, and Yatsuhashi Daichi, who generally walked softly and carried a big sword. Only now he was running, waving his sword to get their attention, and shouting a warning.

"I guess we should help them," Fox said.

"I guess we should."

Coco calmly strode to the top of the temple steps and flicked open her Gatling gun. Then she opened fire on the rolling Boarbatusk. Yatsuhashi and Velvet veered out of the way while her bullets rained past them. As the rounds penetrated the Grimm's tough hide, she used her Semblance to boost the volatility of the Dust inside the bullets to blow them up—and tear the creature apart from the inside out.

On her application to Beacon, Coco had named her Semblance "Hype." Her three favorite things in life were fashion, explosions, and killing Grimm, and Beacon allowed her to combine all three.

"Nice hustle, Coco," Fox said. "But heads up."

Coco threw herself back as the Boarbatusk's decapitated head crashed into the ring of stones above her and then onto the temple steps.

"How did you know—" She was cut off as one of the pillars fell to the side. She was getting an idea of how abandoned temples became temple ruins.

The Boarbatusk's head rolled down the steps, and as the red glow in its four eyes dimmed, it evaporated into black smoke.

Velvet looked up at Coco as she hefted her Gatling gun.

"Thanks for the assist," Yatsuhashi said, approaching the temple.

"Sure," Coco said. "But why didn't you just smack that thing with your sword to knock it out of its spin?"

Yatsuhashi rubbed the back of his head. "I didn't think of that. But hey, I did defeat two other ones before. Big ones." He spread his arms wide to demonstrate.

Velvet put a hand on her hip and cleared her throat.

"Velvet got a few of them, too," Yatsuhashi said.

Coco stared at Velvet. She didn't even have a weapon. *How did she—*

Suddenly Yatsuhashi looked past Coco and assumed a fighting stance, sword at the ready. "More company."

Coco turned and saw four Ursai, large bearlike Grimm armored in bony plates.

"I'll hold them off while you get the relic," he called to Velvet.

"But I can help!" she said.

"We don't have to fight all of them. All we have to do is get a relic to the top of the cliff."

"Is that all?" she said. She supposed he had a good point, though. She raced toward the temple, vowing to return to back him up as soon as she had one of the relics. The guy in red with the arm blades sprinted past her, on the way to help Yatsuhashi. Coco remained at the temple, her massive gun locked and loaded on the arriving Grimm.

"Thank you for helping us," Velvet told Coco. "But we totally had that Boarbatusk where we wanted it."

"We just didn't want to miss all the fun," Coco said. "I know you, don't I? From Pharos?"

"Velvet Scarlatina. I saw you around, but we never spoke."

"I wish we had," Coco said. "I'm Coco Adel."

Velvet figured she would just grab the first relic she saw, but when she realized they were all stone tablets fashioned after a deck of cards, she figured it must mean something. She had dabbled in fortune-telling when she was younger, and of the remaining cards, the only one that didn't make her nervous was the Queen of Hearts. She tucked it into Anesidora's box where she stored empty holographic plates. It was a perfect fit.

But while she was busy doing that, Yatsuhashi and Fox had retreated, joining Coco and Velvet inside the temple—which was now surrounded by eight Ursai.

"Can anyone fly?" Coco asked.

No such luck.

"Then it looks like we'll have to fight our way out." Coco grinned and held up her gun.

"It's only eight against four. I like those odds," Fox said.

"I don't believe in luck," Yatsuhashi said. He looked at Velvet. "Got any ranged weapons?"

Coco looked at the box Velvet carried, wondering what was inside.

Velvet shook her head. "What if we attack them one at a time from in here?"

"I'm almost out of bullets," Coco said.

"We could attack them in turn," Yatsuhashi said.

"Dart out, strike, and return?" Fox said.

"That would take all night, and more Grimm will keep coming," Coco said. "I have a better idea."

Velvet hated Coco's idea, but at least it had worked.

It was only later, when the four of them were assembled in
the amphitheater watching replay footage from initiation, that
they realized how outrageous Coco's plan had been. They
watched her open fire with her gun to clear a path through the
ring of Ursai—by blowing one of them into pieces—so Yatsuhashi
and Fox could charge through first. Instead of trying to cut or
stab the Grimm that lunged for him, Yatsuhashi used his sword
to knock it out of the way, while Fox sliced through the creature
in his path with his tonfa blades. Velvet stayed in the middle
while Coco brought up the rear with covering gunfire, preventing the Ursai from closing the gap and attacking them from
behind.

It was fast, and it was dangerous. It also played well for the
crowd.

Velvet knew that she had been keeping track of where all the
Ursai were for the team. Her voice was still hoarse from shouting
warnings and directions to the others while she fired off a hard-
light gun to keep any remaining Grimm off their flank. But on
video, it looked like her three classmates were protecting her the

whole way to the stairs leading up the cliffs. More than one Beacon student commented on that—and her ears.

So while Professor Ozpin announced and named the new four-person teams, Velvet was looking down and feeling sorry for herself . . . until she heard her name.

"Coco Adel, Fox Alistair, Velvet Scarlatina, Yatsuhashi Daichi," Professor Ozpin droned.

Each of them looked up as their faces and names appeared on the screens and rearranged themselves.

"The four of you retrieved the suit of hearts. From this day forward, you will work together as Team CFVY, led by Coco Adel."

"What?" Coco and Velvet said together.

The new team considered one another thoughtfully.

Yatsuhashi looked up at their pictures. "Team CFVY," he said. "I'm a tea drinker, but I like the sound of that."

Velvet did, too.

"This is going to be fun," Fox sent to his new teammates for the first time.

Velvet yelped when she heard his voice in her head. Coco's mouth fell open. Yatsu looked as placid as ever, as if he'd been expecting all of this.

Fox smiled and winked. *"Yeah, that's a thing I can do."*

CHAPTER THREE

Yatsuhashi liked watching Velvet work with the townspeople at Feldspar. He was supposed to be helping her interview them, but he was never much of a talker, so Velvet took the lead while he lent quiet support—his specialty.

Most of the other students at Beacon had the wrong impression of Velvet. She was only shy and reserved around people she didn't know, protecting herself from whatever hateful and hurtful things they might say. When she was with her team or hanging out with friends like Ruby and Weiss, she was more comfortable, more herself.

And when she had a job to do, Velvet was great at connecting with new people.

"What did you feel before the Grimm attacked?" Velvet asked.

The young mother from Gossan, Amaranth, rubbed a hand over her eyes. "I'm not sure what came over me. Ash started crying and crying and crying." She jiggled the infant boy in her lap, who giggled and reached up for Velvet's ears. "And I felt this awful, burning . . . rage. I've never felt anything like it before. I was so scared I was going to hurt him. And then *I* started crying uncontrollably."

Amaranth's hands shook. Velvet put a hand over hers.

"Would you describe it as a 'wave of emotion'?" Velvet asked, echoing the words of many of the other people they had spoken to.

"Sort of." Amaranth shook her head. "It was more like . . . a dam breaking, only it didn't let the feelings in, it let them out. Like all the frustration and fear and anxiety I had been holding in all flooded out at once."

Yatsuhashi gritted his teeth. This sounded like a nightmare.

Amaranth closed her eyes and tears rolled down her cheeks. Ash patted her wet face gently. She opened her eyes and smiled at him.

"It had been going on for a while," she said. "And once the emotions passed, all you were left with was guilt for feeling them—or anger. People argued with one another over things they'd said or done."

Velvet nodded.

"We were always wondering when it would happen again," Amaranth went on. "And it did happen, over and over again, but the next time it was always worse. The feelings got bigger and blacker every time. Jealousy. Regret. Anger. Sadness. Everyone was feeling it, some more than others. Then the Grimm came. We had to run, leave our homes behind. Some of us even left friends and family, people lost in the attack . . . We can never take back our last words or apologize to them again."

Yatsu and Velvet had heard similar stories from all the recent arrivals at Feldspar. Amaranth and her son had come with dozens of others from the Gossan settlement, but some in their group had experienced the same thing in the Schist and Tuff settlements before that.

And as they had seen the night before, whatever was happening was moving with the group and getting more powerful, spreading like an infection. It was at Feldspar now, and Slate estimated they had a few days before their first mass Grimm attack.

It was Beacon all over again.

"Can you think of anything that connected these surges of emotion?" Velvet asked. "Did they happen in a certain place, or at a certain time? Was anyone else around?"

"I'm not sure," Amaranth said. "I think it happened most often at night. But usually I was alone. I mean, with Ash, at home. Once, it happened during the busiest time of day in the market, and everyone was affected at the same time. That was terrible. A Ravager came for us that time. Thank goodness we had those Huntsmen around."

Ravagers were nasty flying Grimm, like uglier, meaner versions of the Nevermores, with dark, leathery wings like bats. Yatsuhashi had seen them circling in the distant sky, but Team CFVY hadn't fought any of them yet. He hoped it stayed that way.

"Bertilak and Carmine helped evacuate?" Yatsu asked.

Amaranth blinked up at him, as if she had forgotten he was there. Yatsuhashi briefly worried that he had accidentally used his Semblance on her, but if he had, she'd have forgotten a lot more than Yatsuhashi's presence. He glanced at the kid on her lap.

No, just like Yatsuhashi's quiet, reassuring presence helped Velvet be more outgoing, Velvet had a way of making Yatsu less intimidating. Seeing someone small like her with a big guy like him put others more at ease—another reason why he hadn't attempted to interview anyone on his own. They made a good team. Perhaps Professor Ozpin had known what he was doing after all when he paired up the teams at Beacon.

"The Huntsmen were leaving, anyway," Amaranth said. "We just tagged along. As long as we kept up with them, they didn't mind. Much."

Velvet frowned.

"I lost my best friend on the way. We lost a whole family. We're cursed," Amaranth said.

Cursed. There was that word again. They had heard it so many times as they talked to people in Feldspar, who now were really people from the Gossan, and Schist, and Tuff tribes—the survivors of numerous Grimm attacks, all the way from the outskirts of Vacuo to here.

Amaranth's huddled posture said she was tired. Defeated. Hopeless. Yatsuhashi wanted to put an arm around her shoulders supportively, but better to leave that to Velvet. He had already made the baby cry when he got too close.

"Thank you," Velvet said. "Don't worry; we'll help figure this out."

Amaranth smiled gratefully. Velvet and Yatsuhashi had told everyone the same thing, and Velvet sounded so convincing that even he believed her. But they'd spoken to more than forty people already, and they weren't any closer to figuring this out. He wasn't, anyway. Velvet was making *charts*.

"Would you mind if I took your picture?" Velvet held up her camera hopefully.

"Really?" Amaranth wiped the tears from her face. "I'm such a mess."

"You look perfect." Velvet peered through the viewfinder and focused.

Ash's face scrunched up. By now Yatsuhashi knew that meant he was about to start bawling. Was it another one of those emotional outbursts? No, just him being a normal baby.

"Shhh . . . ," Amaranth said soothingly.

Yatsuhashi held up his index and middle fingers in a V behind Velvet's head, between her ears. Ash's eyes lit up. He clapped and burbled happily. Velvet snapped the photo.

Yatsuhashi quickly pulled his hand back to his side and tried to look casual. Velvet turned and looked at him suspiciously.

"What were you doing?" she asked.

"Nothing," he said innocently.

Amaranth caught his eye and smiled.

The next five interviews went much the same. They talked to young newlyweds, Opal and Jasper, who had to marry in secret because it was too dangerous to gather so many people in one place. Cursed.

Celestine was a schoolteacher from Schist, who was too afraid to go back to work when her classroom erupted into a violent argument. Cursed.

A weaver named Beryl lamented the loss of her home and business, then tried to sell Velvet a new cloak to keep the desert dust off her. Cursed.

Exhausted, Yatsuhashi and Velvet joined Coco and Fox to share their findings with Slate. They found the mayor in a small tent near the center of town. Ten other people were waiting to talk to her, but when CFVY joined the end of the line, she waved them forward.

"Give us a few more minutes, folks," Slate told the waiting settlers. They didn't seem as annoyed at the delay as Yatsuhashi would have expected.

"What's this?" Coco asked, gesturing to the small crowd.

"People like to tell me their problems." Slate shrugged. "Even if I can't do anything about them. It's either me or a therapist, and my ear is free."

By now, Yatsuhashi knew most of the people in Feldspar and those who came with Slate from Gossan.

"The people in Feldspar seem to have embraced you as their mayor," Yatsuhashi observed. "I thought Vacuans don't like authority."

"They don't. But there's a difference between being a leader who tells their people what to do and a leader who cares about what they want. My job is to convince them that, more often than not, those are the same thing," Slate said.

Coco nodded. "Didn't Feldspar have its own leader before you arrived?"

"Every settlement and tribe has a person, or several people, who end up being in charge. Your natural organizers, those who can motivate others to do more than just scrape by day to day, looking out for themselves and their families." Slate glanced behind the team at the people waiting in line. She lowered her voice. "The fella before me didn't want the job any more than I do. But someone's gotta do it, and I'm just being honest when I say I know I'm the right one for it."

"How's everyone doing?" Coco asked.

"Absorbing a bunch of new people always takes time. Right now, most folks are worried about Grimm. The Feldspar tribe have started to hear about what happened to everyone from Gossan, Schist, and Tuff, and they aren't so sure they want us to stay here."

"Understandable." Coco took in the line of people, then looked around the settlement.

"Have you learned anything helpful yet?" Slate asked.

"We've interviewed almost all the refugees. Their stories are similar, but other than the shared fits of uncontrolled emotions, the Grimm, and the evacuations, we don't know what else the incidents have in common," Coco said.

Velvet thumbed through a spreadsheet on her Scroll. Slate looked interested, so she tilted the screen toward her.

"I compiled the info from all our interviews. The data suggests that the emotional outbursts happen to everyone at the same time, but not necessarily with the same force."

Velvet held up a graph showing a line rising from left to right. "They're also happening with more frequency, with greater intensity, and lasting for longer periods of time."

Velvet showed a couple more charts illustrating the progression and then stared at her Scroll thoughtfully.

Slate blew out a breath. "I don't need a fancy chart to tell me that."

"We need more time," Coco said.

"I'm afraid we're running out of it," Slate said.

"If the trend continues, this is just going to get worse," Velvet agreed. "It won't be long before everyone will have to migrate to another settlement again."

"It's also going to get harder to find settlements to take all these people." Coco twirled a finger in a long lock of her caramel-colored hair. "Feldspar had more than a hundred people before you guys showed up."

"The next settlement certainly won't roll out the welcome mat," Slate said. "Even with casualties along the way, we'll probably bring more mouths and bodies than they're willing or able to accommodate."

Yatsuhashi was surprised at how dispassionately Slate spoke about losing people to Grimm, but that seemed to be the reality here. Not feeling every death personally was one of the hardest things he had to learn in his Huntsmen training—or at least not letting that loss paralyze him.

Yatsuhashi was simply determined not to lose anyone ever again, but he knew all too well that one day he might fail, whether it was a stranger or one of his friends. Enough of Beacon Academy still stood as a testament to their greatest loss.

Velvet's ears perked up.

"What?" Coco asked.

"I just realized. There *is* a common element linking all these incidents," Velvet said.

The group waited. And waited.

"Well?" Slate asked.

"I was being dramatic," Velvet said.

Coco turned a hand over, telling her to get on with it.

"The common element is the four people who came from Vale," Velvet said. "They've been there for every attack."

Fox facepalmed. *"Of course,"* he sent.

"The Caspians, Bertilak, and Carmine?" Slate frowned.

Velvet spread her Scroll wider and leaned over it, zipping through her notes. "How long after they arrived did you start experiencing periods of heightened emotion?"

"I don't know. We didn't think anything of it at first. It was only when it got really bad that we realized something unusual was happening, and even then it didn't become suspicious until we had relocated to Schist and it all repeated again. But if I think back . . . maybe a few days?"

"That's hardly conclusive, but it's a start," Coco said.

"Are you suggesting one of them is causing all this?" Slate asked.

"I don't know," Velvet began. "But Yatsu and I haven't interviewed them."

"Neither did we." Coco glanced at Fox. "Clearly we need to talk to them, see if they have any idea what could be causing the emotional surges."

"Good luck with that," Slate said. "They aren't the sharing type. The Caspians hired Bertilak and Carmine for protection, and whatever their faults, those Huntsmen are serious about protecting them—from everyone."

"Isn't that a little paranoid?" Coco asked.

"You tell me. You're Huntsmen. I figured it was part of your training." Slate leaned back. "Either that, or they're worried about thieves. Edward Caspian is obviously loaded, though money doesn't do you too much good out in the desert." She pressed her lips together.

"Vacuans have a reputation for being dishonest," Fox explained telepathically. *"It's misplaced, particularly since it's the other kingdoms who stole from us."*

"The downside of keeping to yourself is that other people are free to tell your story," Yatsuhashi replied to the group.

Fox tipped his head in acknowledgment.

"Where can we find them?" Coco asked.

"They're staying in a sand shed on the north end of Feldspar. Like I said, they keep to themselves."

"Thanks, Slate," Coco said.

Slate spread her hands. "See? I didn't do anything. I just listened, shared a little information, and you figured it out for yourself. This job isn't so bad." She waved them off. "Next!"

They left Slate to her supplicants and huddled together in

the night market. The moon was high in the western sky, a sprinkle of debris just visible on its edge. This should be one of the busiest times at the market. The fruit stand behind them could have been closed because fruit was scarce, especially with all the extra people to feed. But most of the flimsy wooden stalls were shuttered and empty . . . clearly business wasn't booming.

Yatsuhashi gazed at the boarded-up stalls. He suddenly really wanted to bite into a juicy breadfruit.

"What do you guys think?" Coco asked in a low voice.

"Either Bertilak and Carmine aren't team players, which is odd for Huntsmen, or they're hiding something," Fox sent.

"I agree, we should be careful about trusting them," Coco said. "Slate seemed a bit down on them herself, and she appears to be a good judge of character."

"You're just saying that because she likes us," Velvet teased.

"That's how I know she's a good judge of character. So here's what we'll do: Fox and I will approach Bertilak and Carmine, while Yatsuhashi and Velvet hang back a bit—"

"Of course," Velvet muttered under her breath. Coco gave her a look but ignored the remark. Yatsuhashi placed a hand on Velvet's shoulder. He felt the tension there, and then she relaxed.

"Wait for our signal, and then try to talk to the Caspians alone," Coco said. "I'd like to see if their stories match up with what we've been hearing from the Vacuan nomads."

Yatsuhashi and Velvet trailed a bit behind Coco and Fox as they walked north. Fox pointed out that the northern section of the brick wall separating Feldspar from the desert was taller than the rest and reinforced.

"Not many people live on this side of settlements because of the Wasting Winds," Fox sent.

Velvet shuddered. "What are those?"

"Forceful sandstorms that come from the north. Even with the wall, this section gets hit pretty hard."

Vacuans had exciting names for every natural phenomenon, most of them destructive or deadly: Misery's Kiss (sunstroke). Lasting Regret (food poisoning). Sudden Demise (a sinkhole spontaneously forming, which occasionally swallowed whole settlements).

"Hang on," Velvet said. She patted Yatsuhashi's arm and then dashed away. "Keep going, I'm right behind you."

Yatsuhashi whirled around in confusion, but Velvet was gone. He didn't like losing sight of her; what kind of trouble was she getting up to now?

Ahead of him, Coco and Fox reached a sand shed that was conspicuously standing alone on the edge of town. Yatsuhashi leaned against the rough stone wall of a house a hundred feet away and watched as Carmine came outside and began talking with Coco.

Then Velvet was at Yatsuhashi's side again. Her sudden appearance made him jump.

"Here." She held out a skewer with a brown gooey mess on the end of it and looked at him expectantly.

Yatsuhashi raised an eyebrow. The thing in his hand seemed to be food. "Uh. What is this?"

"Breadfruit," she said.

"What happened to it?" he asked.

"It was candied and caramelized."

His eyes lit up. "For me?" He took the stick from her.

"I thought you might want to share?" she said hopefully, steepling her fingers.

He broke off a piece of the sticky ball and handed it to her. Velvet nibbled at it.

"This is better than it should be," Yatsuhashi said, licking his fingers as the sweet and salty flavor exploded in his mouth. "Thank you. How did you know?"

"I don't have to be a mind reader when I can see you drooling at the fruit stands," Velvet said with a giggle.

"I don't drool," Yatsuhashi said.

Velvet pointed to the corner of his mouth. He swept the back of his hand to the same spot on his mouth and then wiped it on his trousers.

"That was sweat," he said.

"You guys are up," Fox sent. *"Make it quick."*

Coco and Fox were following Bertilak and Carmine away from their sand shed.

"How did you get them to leave?" Yatsuhashi sent back.

"Coco said she wanted to help secure the perimeter, set up guard against Grimm. Bertilak and Carmine are going to show us how."

Yatsuhashi imagined how frustrating that had to be for Coco and Fox; they'd covered—and mastered—that exercise in Professor Greene's Stealth and Security class in their second year at Beacon.

"*That's it?*" Velvet sent.

"*Coco also implied that guarding the Caspians here wouldn't do them much good if the Grimm breach the town. She basically volunteered us to do the guarding. Bertilak and Carmine support the idea. But I don't think we can keep them away long.*"

"*Just let us know when you're on your way back.*" Yatsuhashi gobbled down the rest of the breadfruit.

As Fox and the others disappeared from view, Yatsuhashi and Velvet hurried to the Caspians' door, which was covered by a dirty old blanket. Yatsuhashi looked for somewhere to knock, but the doorway was made of adobe, so he said, "Knock knock."

A moment later, the curtain pulled aside and a boy said, "Is everything okay?" Then he realized he didn't know them and said, "Oh."

He was tan, maybe eleven or twelve years old with short, curly black hair, dressed in jeans and a baggy T-shirt from the Thirty-eighth Vytal Festival Tournament in Vacuo.

"Hi," Velvet said. "I'm Velvet and this is my friend Yatsuhashi."

"Hello," Yatsuhashi said.

"You're those new Huntsmen," the boy said.

"And you are . . . ?"

"Gus Caspian."

"Can we come in?" Velvet asked.

He shifted his weight from one foot to the other. "Um. I'm not sure."

"Is your grandfather here? Can we talk to him?" Velvet asked.

Gus's expression turned serious. "Now isn't a good time." He started to pull the blanket back over the entrance.

"Nonsense!" An older man came to the doorway. He was hunched over, but at his full height, he would have been almost as tall as Yatsu. He was slender, but not frail—he still had some muscle on him. His thinning silver hair was pulled into a short ponytail, and he had several days' growth of gray stubble. Yatsu thought he looked familiar, but couldn't place him.

"We're about to have tea and play Gus's favorite game. Why don't you join us?" the man said.

"Yes, please!" Velvet said.

"Grandpa," Gus said. "It's almost time for your nap. You know how you get if you don't sleep."

The man waved his hand. "I'll be fine. Come in, come in. I'm Edward Caspian, and fellow Huntsmen are always welcome in my home."

Fellow Huntsmen, Yatsuhashi thought.

The man ushered them in and directed them to a woven mat in the sand with a porcelain tea service set on a bronze tray. A deck of cards lay beside it. Yatsuhashi sat and folded his legs, trying to make himself smaller in the enclosed space. Velvet sat down cross-legged beside him.

"Go get cups for our guests, Gus," Edward said.

Gus glanced at his grandfather nervously, but then he scurried off.

"You used to hunt?" Yatsuhashi asked. "Grimm?"

Edward smiled. "I *used* to do a lot of things. I haven't hunted Grimm in a long time, but once a Huntsman always a Huntsman. Until you die . . ."

He trailed off. His face went slack and his eyes lost focus. Yatsu had seen that look before, and it made him anxious.

"Sir? Are you all right?" Yatsuhashi leaned forward and touched Edward's arm. He wished he could give people back their memories as easily as he could take them.

"Don't touch him!" Gus said.

Yatsuhashi flinched and withdrew his hand.

"Is he . . . all right?" Velvet asked.

"It happens sometimes," Gus said. "Like part of him goes away for a little while. But he always comes back."

Gus put the cups down in front of Yatsuhashi and Velvet. He watched Edward's face worriedly, then poured some tea.

Velvet picked up her cup and breathed in the steam. "What kind of tea is this?"

"Cactus leaf. It's the best we can do."

Velvet sipped her tea. "It's perfect," she said. "Thank you."

"How old is your grandfather?" Yatsuhashi asked.

Gus slurped tea from his own cup. "He'll be seventy-one next month."

It wasn't common for Huntsmen to live that long, certainly not with all their body parts intact. But it seemed as if Edward's mind wasn't quite intact. He was in no condition to be traveling long distances, certainly not in a hostile environment like Vacuo. What could have driven them into the desert, and where were they heading?

"It's just the two of you?" Velvet asked.

"Yes." Gus stared into the bottom of his cup. Yatsu found it strange that the Caspians had been toting things as delicate as a teapot and these cups from town to town. It was almost more remarkable that the tea service had survived all those Grimm attacks. There were a couple of leather chests in the small room, and in the corner was a buckler, a small round shield with a sharp metal edge. The kind of weapon a Huntsman would carry.

"It's been just us since my parents were killed by Grimm." Gus swallowed hard.

"I am so, so sorry," Velvet said.

Gus blinked back tears and nodded.

Yatsuhashi was surprised to see that Velvet was crying. He was even more surprised to realize that his own cheeks were wet. He felt sorry for the kid, too, but he didn't cry often.

It's happening again right now, Yatsuhashi realized.

Tears were also streaming down Edward's face.

"Velvet," Yatsuhashi cautioned.

Velvet was typing on her Scroll, likely trying to capture the firsthand experience. Anything to help the tribe get to the bottom of what was going on.

"Is this how it always is?" Velvet asked.

"The mood bomb?" Gus asked.

She paused. "I haven't heard anyone call it that yet. But yes, I suppose that's accurate."

Gus sighed. "It usually goes this way. Whatever you're feeling gets sort of . . . amplified. You can't control it. If it hits critical mass . . ." Gus opened his fingers and made a whooshing sound. "Boom."

"And then the Grimm," Yatsuhashi said.

"The mood bombs started back in Sumire, right?" Velvet said. "That was the first Grimm invasion, and you escaped into Vacuo with the Huntsmen."

Yatsuhashi looked at Velvet. They hadn't heard about any Grimm attacks in the Vale village. He quickly realized she was bluffing that they knew more than they did.

Gus craned his neck to see what was on her screen. "Who told you that?"

Velvet's gamble was paying off. She'd obviously hit a nerve.

"Can you think of anything suspicious or out of the ordinary that started triggering these bombs?" she asked.

Gus opened his mouth.

"Anything at all would be helpful," Yatsu said.

Gus closed his mouth. Shook his head.

He's hiding something, Yatsuhashi thought.

Maybe if they tried a different approach. "You met up with Bertilak and Carmine in Sumire?" Yatsu asked.

"We were lucky they were passing through," Edward said. The old man had snapped out of whatever fugue he'd been in and was carrying on as if nothing had happened. "They defended the village from a Grimm attack, when I lost my girl and her husband." He paused and composed himself.

"Grandpa," Gus said.

Edward kept talking. "They heard us talking about wanting to leave, going somewhere to be on our own, away from people. Carmine said she knew the perfect spot: an old lighthouse on the western shore of Sanus. She said she and Bertilak could guide us there and protect us along the way."

"But to get there, you have to cross the entire desert," Yatsuhashi said.

Gus picked up the deck of cards. "We playing or not?"

Edward nodded. "Set it up, Gus."

Yatsuhashi and Velvet exchanged a look.

Gus laid out the cards facedown in an eight-by-eight grid. Yatsuhashi tasted his cactus tea—it was a little weak, but still refreshing.

"Even with a couple of Huntsmen, it seems dangerous to risk a trip like that," Yatsuhashi said.

"Especially with Grimm following you from Sumire," Velvet said. Once again, neither Edward nor Gus corrected her.

"You think I'm an old fool," Edward said. "But better to have protection in Vacuo than no protection in Vale. Besides, the way things have been going, Vale isn't much better off these days."

Edward leaned in and turned over one of the cards, which showed a picture of a Death Stalker. He turned over another: a Beowolf.

Yatsuhashi used to play a matching card memory game like this when he was a kid, only the cards had been different varieties of flowers, not different types of Grimm.

"We don't think you're foolish, sir. We're just trying to understand why you're here," Yatsuhashi said.

"Why are *you* here?" Gus asked.

"I ask myself that every day," Velvet said. She glanced at Yatsuhashi with a guilty expression on her face.

Gus turned over two cards to reveal a Nevermore and a Death Stalker.

Velvet turned over the two Death Stalker cards and claimed the pair. "Did you notice the mood bombs in Sumire, too?" she asked.

Edward looked around in confusion. His eyes began to glaze over.

"Grandpa! Your turn," Gus lied.

Edward slowly reached down and turned over the same card he'd had before, a Beowolf. Then he stared at the board, frowning. "What was I saying? Oh yes. Vale's having Grimm trouble these days, too. At least in Vacuo, it's harder for them to track you because of the shifting sands."

"Vacuo still seems a bit extreme," Velvet said.

"Not if you want to get away from other people just as much," Gus said softly.

"Then why are you hanging out here?" Velvet asked. "Why haven't you moved on with Bertilak and Carmine?"

"Grandpa won't let us," Gus said bitterly.

"Why is that, sir?" Yatsuhashi asked.

"We can afford to hire Huntsmen for protection," Edward said. "The settlements can't. As long as we're together, it's the same thing."

Gus threw down his cards. "But that's stupid when we're—" He stopped himself. He seemed shocked at the outburst. Or afraid.

"Gus?" Velvet asked. "When you're what?"

"When we're taking extra time to cross the desert." He sighed. "Grandpa also can't travel as well as he used to. The desert's hard on him. He needs these breaks." He gestured at Edward again, who was muttering to himself with his eyes closed.

"You should try harder to get him to listen," Velvet snapped.

Gus looked stunned.

Yatsuhashi's eyes shot up. "Velvet?"

"Don't start, Yatsu."

"Okay. Calm down." Yatsuhashi raised his hands in a soothing gesture.

"*You* calm down," she said. Then she looked at him and started laughing. "That's funny. You're the chillest person I know." She began laughing hysterically.

Yatsuhashi wasn't sure if that was any better. But it was pretty funny, and suddenly he was laughing, too.

"Wait, this isn't normal," he said. Tears were pouring from his eyes, but this time not from sadness. Even as he was feeling the lightness and joy of laughter, Yatsuhashi hated losing control of his emotions this way. He abruptly fell silent while Velvet carried on.

Edward was chuckling to himself, but his eyes were vacant. Who knew what he was thinking at that moment? Gus was crying again, but his teeth were gritted and he clenched his hands on his knees.

"This is bad," Yatsuhashi said sadly.

"Are you guys all right?" Fox sent.

"It's getting worse," Yatsuhashi sent.

"It's hilarious!" Velvet said.

"You'd better come outside. We need your help," Fox said. *"Hurry!"*

CHAPTER FOUR

"*It doesn't look like much, Fox, but I wish you could see it. Hardy palm trees arching over a clear blue oasis, bright green leaves reflected in the still water. There's grass on the shore, lush green grass, dotted with pink and white flowers. Bees lazily drift over them, collecting pollen. Do you hear them buzzing? This is the center of town, where everyone gathers to talk, eat, conduct business at the market. Around us are burlap tents and lean-tos built by the traveling merchants, beyond are the huts, squat shelters made of mud brick and straw where our people dwell.*"

Every settlement in Vacuo was pretty much the same, not from lack of imagination, but because of the building materials available—anything they could find, especially sand and stone—and practicality.

It didn't make sense to commit much time and energy to building structures that could be abandoned or wiped away by a sandstorm at a moment's notice. Vacuans lived extemporaneously, with little attachments aside from the people they cared about—and even then, many just weren't into commitment.

With commitment came responsibility, and responsibility often made you weak or vulnerable. In Vacuo, there were two kinds of people: those who were selfish and those who were fully dedicated to their community, and, in time, Fox came to understand that the latter usually had a better chance of survival.

Copper hadn't been much older than Fox, more a big brother than an uncle, but the Vacuan honorific also included mentors. Uncle Copper had done more than keep Fox alive in those early years; he had also trained Fox to fight when everyone else thought a wiry blind boy was just another liability.

Fox remembered Copper's strong, calloused hands on his shoulders as he leaned over and whispered descriptions in his ear. He knew how much Fox hated loud noises.

"Fox, it's beautiful. Though our homes are simple and inelegant, they stand as a testament to our sheer will to survive. The fact that anything can live in the desert is a miracle. And when the desert winds knock all this down, we'll just rebuild. When the monsters run us out, we will move and start anew elsewhere. Always remember that. Every life is precious, even the mole crabs and the carrion hawks and the slowworms . . . all the more so out here where there is so little of it."

Uncle Copper had been killed shortly after that conversation, not by the Grimm but by one of those loners who wanted what he had, and was subsequently killed by the tribe himself as punishment.

Then Fox had been alone, yet not alone, again, raised by the various kind souls of the Kenyte community. He moved with them until he was old enough to go to Beacon Academy; his one and a half years at Beacon were the longest he'd ever spent in one place, and the happiest. Now that it had fallen to Grimm, he was sticking with the family he had made there, and looking forward to rebuilding. To the others, Beacon may have seemed like a lost cause, but within its ruins was the foundation for something new. Believing that was a gift Vacuo had given him.

Coco, Velvet, and Yatsuhashi had struggled with the way of life in Vacuo, and provided Fox with some perspective on his culture—which had also benefited from his time away. Living from moment to moment instead of planning for the next day, week, or year seemed strange to many outsiders, but it also made Vacuans appreciate things in those moments far more—every meal, every conversation, every joke was a celebration of life, and even the sad and painful moments carried greater significance.

And this was one of those terrible moments.

So this is how it happens, Fox thought.

After hearing about the explosions of emotion that had been plaguing these poor people, and feeling some mild effects themselves in the last day, Fox and Coco were now in the middle of a full-blown panic. If they didn't act quickly, this chaos would escalate and draw Creatures of Grimm from miles around.

The nearby Grimm had to be on their way already. Even if the townspeople calmed down now, the amount of time CFVY had to solve the problem here was growing significantly shorter.

"Calm down!" Bertilak shouted. "You fools are going to get us all killed!"

"Cool it, Bertilak," Carmine said. "Put that mace away. You're only making this worse."

"The hell I am," Bertilak said.

Fox searched for Coco. He knew her well enough to pick her out of a crowd, and it was even easier because she was *above* the crowd, on a rooftop at the edge of the square. He leaped up lightly and joined her.

He heard chaos down below. People shoving and fighting in the alleyways, fists hitting flesh, bodies hitting the ground. Out of the mess of minds clustered below, on top of one another, Fox noticed some of them heading away from the crowd. Heading out of the settlement. Not a bad idea if the Grimm were on their way, though they would be more exposed outside the village walls.

"Are those people running away armed? Do they have supplies?" Fox asked.

"No," Coco said.

"Then they'll die in the desert, or come crawling back later," Fox sent. And since they had fled instead of helping defend their settlement and people, they might not be welcomed back so warmly.

"If there is a later," Coco said.

Fox heard groups of people sobbing, arguing, shouting. Shouting everywhere. And they were so worked up, their thoughts so unguarded, he was even being flooded with snatches of their thoughts, impressions of their feelings carried telepathically to him and then amplified by whatever was causing this. As if his own feelings weren't enough to try to control.

We're going to die was the most common thought, from people all around him.

We'll be together again soon, Mariah, came another stray thought. *Why aren't they doing anything?*

Where's Slate?

My kids. I have to save my kids.

We're going to die.

"Shut up!" That thought was Fox's, and it wasn't until he heard momentary quiet in the square that he realized he'd inadvertently mentally shouted at everyone in his immediate vicinity. They were probably more confused than cooperative, though.

"Ow," Coco said. "Thanks for the headache. But that was good, Fox. What else you got?"

Fox put his fingers to his lips and whistled. The sharp sound cut through the still square.

"Okay, that works," Coco said. "Everyone, please calm down." She stepped forward, right to the edge of the roof. "As long as we keep our heads, we'll have nothing to worry about. Many of you have gone through this before, and you know that what you're feeling will pass soon."

Murmurs of agreement from the crowd as the latest wave of emotion subsided.

"Everything will be all right. Short of Shade Academy, this is probably the safest place in Vacuo right now—you've got six Huntsmen here to protect you," Coco said.

"Seven!" a man shouted in a shaky voice. People laughed, the situation defused.

Fox focused on the man. His mind was bright, burning brighter than most people's, but it was also flickering, like it was struggling not to go out. Through familiarity, Fox recognized that Velvet and Yatsuhashi were standing near him, and there was another presence close by that was harder to pin down. It was almost as bright as the man's, but with dark spots on it, and in constant turmoil.

That had to be Edward and August Caspian.

But then someone shouted, "Look!"

Fox sighed. "What is it, Coco?"

Coco didn't answer him. More people were shouting, and some people were screaming in abject terror. Fox heard feet pounding on the ground and sensed everyone scattering in different directions quickly.

"Coco," Fox sent.

"I've got this." Fox heard Coco's handbag transform into her Gatling gun.

"Isn't that overkill?" Fox sent. His own panic was rising out of control. He hadn't felt this nervous since their mission in Lower Cairn.

"I think it's just the right amount of kill," Coco said.

Then Fox felt it—an *emptiness* of thought and spirit—just over their heads. A Grimm.

"Everyone down!" Yatsuhashi shouted.

Coco opened fire. Fox covered his ears and turned away, wincing at the loud gunfire right next to him. Then, distantly, he heard the sound of her Semblance-enhanced bullets hitting their target and exploding, high above them. A Grimm wailed as it was torn apart.

The crowd cheered and clapped. Then a moment later the cheers turned to surprised shrieks, followed by the thump and squelch of flesh hitting the sand all around them. It was raining Grimm gore.

"What was that?" Fox sent.

"Ravager," Yatsu sent back.

"This is even grosser than the mole crabs," Velvet said.

"The Grimm parts are already fading," Coco said.

She folded up her gun. "Now that we have your attention. As I was saying, we'll keep you safe. But you have to help us out, too."

Fox felt the surging anxiety of moments ago subside, like an outgoing tide on the beach.

But where did those hidden feelings come from? And where did they go when they weren't being forced to the surface?

"She's right," Bertilak called out. "We're here to protect you."

"But the best way to keep safe," Carmine said, "to keep *everyone* safe, is to stay in your own homes when one of these mood bombs hits."

Bomb is a great analogy for what happened, Fox thought.

"Gathering in crowds like this only causes more conflicts, which makes the situation even more volatile," Carmine said.

It might not be good but it was only natural to seek out other people when you were scared and alone. And even under the best circumstances—when your feelings weren't being manipulated or magnified by some unknown force—it was hard to manage your emotions. Incredibly sensitive people like Yatsuhashi had mastered the art of keeping their feelings under control, while others, like Coco, could channel them into action. Velvet sometimes let her feelings get the best of her, Fox thought. And Fox? His lonely upbringing meant he was still getting used to showing any feelings at all.

"But what if there are more Grimm out there?" a woman called.

"There are definitely more Grimm, you can count on that," Carmine said. "But we just need to work on keeping them out there while we're staying calm and collected in here."

"Maybe we should leave now," someone suggested. "Instead of waiting for them to attack."

"Then they'll just attack us out there," Carmine said. "And we'll die."

"Well, most of *you* will," Bertilak said.

"It's better if we keep trying to figure out what's causing these emotional surges," Coco said. "We're getting close, I know it. We've spoken to a lot of you already, but if anyone can think of a cause for these mood bombs, please speak up. Anything could be helpful. Anything can help us save lives."

Coco waited. "No one?"

"This probably isn't the time or place for this," Bertilak said. "The bottom line is we need to keep the group in mind. What's best for everyone, not just ourselves. Right?"

"Right," Carmine said.

"I have an idea." Slate's voice carried easily across the square without the need to shout. It didn't hurt that everyone was inclined to listen to her.

"First of all, thank you, Ms. Adel, and thank you, Huntsmen, for keeping us safe. I'd rather have pieces of a Grimm stuck in my hair than find myself stuck in its craw."

That got a few laughs. She went on. "It certainly seems like there's good cause to believe that something among us is causing emotions to run wild. It's like we're carrying a disease and we keep infecting new towns with it as we spread out."

The crowd murmured in agreement and alarm. Slate held up a hand and they quieted. "Now that we have six able Huntsmen—no offense, Mr. Caspian—maybe we should consider breaking up into smaller groups, each one guarded by one of you. Then we spread out a bit. All of us can survive out in the desert for a couple of days, right?"

Everyone made sounds of agreement.

"That's not such a bad idea," Carmine said.

"Thanks," Slate said wryly. "In smaller groups, maybe we could isolate whatever is affecting emotions."

At first, Fox agreed that the proposal seemed worth considering. They had figured that one of the refugees from the first settlement, Tuff, might be responsible for the strange incidents that had begun there and spread to subsequent settlements. Splitting into smaller groups, each assigned to a Huntsman or Huntress, could narrow down the search. But even if it would save lives and end the cycle of Grimm attacks, Fox didn't think Coco would go for it in a million years.

"I don't like the idea of using people as bait," Coco said.

"We would be minimizing risk for everyone. If the Grimm go after one of the groups, they can call for help," Slate said.

"As long as we all stay in range of a CCT support tower," Coco said. "And if we're all in range of it, we're probably still close enough for everyone's emotions to be affected."

"However, it wouldn't affect everyone equally," Velvet said. "Distance does seem to be a factor in the intensity of the experience."

"It seems risky," Yatsuhashi said.

The tension was thick in the air, maybe thick enough to pull in more Grimm.

"We should all stick together," Coco said. "Isn't that what you do in Vacuo? Even a large group with six Huntsmen is going to have better odds than a group of thirty with only one Huntsman or Huntress."

"Well, it's our call—" Carmine began.

"Actually, it's my call," Edward Caspian said. "Since you work for me."

"Now's not the time to develop a spine, old man," Bertilak said.

"Grandpa," Gus said. "Hear them out."

"I've heard enough," Edward said. "I'm with the young lady with the big gun. Separating the town would be a mistake— we're more powerful united. That's the way we did it back when I was an 'able Huntsman.'"

"Okay, then," Slate said.

"There are likely more Grimm in the area," Coco said. "My

team will start patrolling the borders and sound the alarm if any of them get too close."

"Much appreciated," Slate said. "And what will you two do?"

"Watch Edward and Gus, like we were hired to," Bertilak grumbled.

The people in Feldspar might have slept less well if they had known that one of the Huntsmen on night watch was blind.

On the other hand, darkness was no problem for him. Fox felt the tiny, faint presence of assorted animals out there, dotting the landscape much like he was told stars pinpricked a black sky. Most of them were in burrows just under the surface, sheltering deep where the sand was still warm, as the night air dropped to below-freezing temperatures. Fox was wrapped in his cloak and a thick fur blanket as he slowly patrolled the outskirts of the settlement. He was searching for . . . Well, nothing. An absence of feeling, the lack of a soul, the yawning void that heralded a creature of Grimm.

Then he noticed another mind out there. A person. No one should be wandering in the desert alone, especially at night. Whoever it was, their consciousness was dim; it could have been someone sleepwalking, a deadly habit in these parts, if no one was looking out for you. Fortunately, Fox was looking out for everyone tonight.

And it seemed he wasn't the only one. He picked up another consciousness, following the first. One he knew very well.

"*Velvet,*" Fox sent. "*Where are you going?*" Fox was already heading for her position.

"*I'm following Edward,*" Velvet said. "*I think he's sleepwalking or something.*"

"*You didn't think to say something to the rest of us?*"

"*How?*"

Fox's Semblance came in handy, particularly with his team, giving them a unique strategic edge in combat. But the drawback was that no one could communicate with Fox until he initiated contact and kept the connection open.

"*How about your Scroll?*" Fox sent.

"*Oh, right,*" Velvet sent. "*I forgot we could do that since we're close to the relay tower.*"

"*Uh-huh,*" Fox sent. "*What are you really doing?*"

Velvet was silent for a moment, but he kept waiting for her response.

"*I've got this,*" she said. "*I can see in the dark better than anyone, and I know how to talk to him. We'll be back before you know it.*"

"*I hope you won't mind a little backup.*" Yatsuhashi and Coco would kill him if he let anything happen to Velvet. "*Just me, okay?*"

"*Thanks,*" Velvet sent.

He understood why Velvet wanted to strike out on her own, to prove herself not only to the team but also to herself. Growing up, Fox had been the outsider, the orphan, the little blind boy. His people had meant to be kind, but their overprotectiveness was stifling. Everyone but Copper had underestimated his abilities and treated him as fragile, unable to take care of himself.

Besides, if he told Coco that Velvet was out here, Coco would come charging out on her own. And she needed to stay where she was, keeping guard in town in case anything got past Fox—and keeping an eye on Bertilak and Carmine, who they worried might try to ditch the settlement, job or no job. As much as the pair seemed to prevent CFVY from taking charge, they also had seemed relieved to have the team draw the attention of the belea-guered townspeople.

Fox hurried in the general direction of Velvet and Edward, noting that Edward's mental impression was becoming faint, which probably wasn't a good sign. And on top of that, Fox began to sense . . . nothing. That really wasn't a good sign.

"Grimm," Fox sent to Velvet. *"Moving in on Edward."*

"I'll meet you there," Velvet responded.

Fox noted Velvet picking up speed, closing the distance between her and Edward. She could move *fast*.

Edward's consciousness nearly blipped out. Fox started run-ning. He could move fast, too.

"Trouble!" Fox sent.

He reached Edward just behind Velvet. He could barely sense Edward now.

"How is he?" Fox sent.

"He isn't sleepwalking anymore. Now he's just sleeping," Velvet said. "And breathing, thank goodness. He's out here in just his pj's."

Fox was surprised the old man had made it this far before passing out from the cold, without any protective clothing. He pulled off his blanket and bundled it around the old man. He was heavy.

"I'll take him." Fox draped Edward over his shoulder. *"Let's get him out of here before—"*

Velvet shoved Fox and Edward out of the way as something fast and large struck at where he'd been standing. Fox grunted and spat out sand and blood; he laid Edward on the ground behind him.

"It's a King Taijitu," Velvet said. "We'll need to lure it away from Edward." Fox heard her activate a hard-light weapon and then a heavy *thwack* as she hit the massive viper hard with whatever it was. The snake hissed and its scaly skin rasped against the sand as it drew back.

Fox oriented himself toward the Grimm and crossed his arms in front of him, making an X with his blades. He relied on his hearing in the still night and the gentle vibrations of the sand to follow its movement.

"Can you see all of it?" Fox asked.

"Just the white half," Velvet sent. She knew better than to speak aloud when he was listening in the middle of a fight. Being able to communicate quietly, especially around Grimm, gave them a nice advantage—even if it drained Fox and weakened his Aura over time. *"The rest of it must be under the sand."*

That explained why Fox felt movement below his feet, while it seemed the snake was withdrawing aboveground.

"It's coiling to strike," Velvet said. He heard her snap a photo of

him and then activate another weapon. He grinned, knowing she was now armed the same way he was, with his own fighting techniques.

Fox took in a deep breath, then darted forward, arms up, blades out. As he reached the King Taijitu he ducked and pushed himself forward even faster. He felt a breeze as the snake's head passed just over his own. He lifted his arms, cutting down the length of its body toward the trunk. Then he locked his arms in front of him, brought the blades forward, and fired their guns behind him for an extra boost—and sliced clean through its body.

"Great!" Velvet sent. *"The white end's gone, but the other end is—"*

The ground beneath Fox caved, sucking him under. The sand filled in around him, pinning his arms to his sides. He felt hot breath from the remaining half of the Taijitu rearing up in front of his face.

"My turn," Velvet sent.

The King Taijitu shifted to attack her, giving Fox his chance to dig himself out. He still couldn't budge his arms, since the sand was packed in tightly, so he fired his blade guns. The explosive force cleared enough space for him to drag himself out of the pit. He rolled onto his back and squinted as sand blew into his face. A dust devil?

No, it was just Velvet zipping by him and then up the length of the snake. He heard the familiar sound of Sharp Retribution— an echo of his own weapons—cutting through its steely scales.

"Heads up!" Velvet sent.

Fox scrambled to his feet, waiting for his cue.

"And now it's coming down!" Velvet sent.

The ground shook and sand blasted over Fox as the King Taijitu's head slammed into the ground just in front of him. He dashed around to its right side and slashed a blade at the eye while it was stunned, then vaulted up to move to the other side. While he was on top of its head, the snake suddenly reared up and Fox nearly lost his balance. He jammed his arm blades into its skull and held on.

It did not like that.

The snake thrashed around, trying to dislodge Fox, as it raced around the desert.

Bullets from Coco's Gatling gun followed it around.

Coco was here?

A bullet whistled just past Fox's ear.

"Sorry!" Velvet said.

Velvet again. But without Coco's ability to enhance the strength of her bullets, her hard-light gun couldn't do much damage on the King Taijitu.

Fox twisted his left arm blade and the snake veered left. He twisted to the right, and it turned right. He could steer the Grimm! The question was, where should he take it?

Away from Feldspar, obviously, but he didn't know how long he could keep this up, and he just wanted to finish the Grimm off.

"The quarry!" Velvet sent.

"What about it?" Fox asked.

"I meant the nearby Dust quarry, not the Grimm," Velvet sent. *"The stone pit just north of here. Isn't it weird when the same word means two wildly different things?"*

"So weird," Fox sent. *"I'm gonna ditch our quarry in the quarry."*

He was already steering the half-blinded, half King Taijitu toward the great stone pit near the town. Quarries like this one could be found all over Vacuo. Once upon a time, about a century back, they had all been part of a major mining operation. Once the corporations had leeched the land of the Dust that made it so valuable, they up and left—having helped the desert claim more of the land, and leaving giant holes like this one.

The snake didn't see the pit coming until it was already slipping over the edge. It flailed around, but it was falling down the side of the man-made crater. Fox pulled his tonfa free, turned, and ran up the length of the King Taijitu toward the edge of the cliff.

Just as he leaped off, the tail end of the snake lashed out and wrapped itself around Fox, pulling him down with it.

"What?" Fox sent.

He and the King Taijitu tumbled down the canyon. Fox's arms were free so he jammed them into the stone wall. Metal and stone screamed against each other, sparks flew, and Fox thought his arms were going to be yanked out of their sockets. But the blades held, and Fox's descent slowed and then stopped.

The only problem was he had half a Grimm snake hanging from his waist, and it wasn't giving up without a fight. Fox couldn't hold on forever.

"*Uh, Velvet?*" Fox sent. "*Help?*"

"*I can't get a clear shot from here,*" Velvet said. "*I'll have to come down there.*"

"*Never mind,*" Fox sent. "*How far is the drop?*"

"*Don't even think about it,*" Velvet said. "*I can't see the bottom, so it must be a long way down.*"

Fox gritted his teeth. He yanked the blade on his left arm out of the rock face and then aimed his gun at the snake wrapped around his chest and legs. His right arm was on fire as he supported the weight of both him and the King Taijitu.

He fired several rounds into the snake at point blank. The snake spasmed and squeezed tighter.

That didn't work as planned, Fox thought. The air was pushed out of his lungs and blood pounded in his head.

He fired again, and slowly, incredibly slowly, the Grimm loosened its hold on him. The coil around him slipped free, and the snake fell, spitting and hissing all the way down. It was a long time before he heard a distant crash of impact.

Fox swung his left arm back up and grabbed hold of a crevice in the rock wall. His shoulder joint popped and he felt a stab of pain, losing his grip.

A hand grabbed his.

"Got you," Velvet said.

"I told you not to climb down here," Fox said.

"Good thing I did it anyway."

Velvet tied a loop of rope around Fox and then scampered up the rock wall. That was the last time he would under-estimate her.

She pulled on the rope, helping him climb back up to the top of the abandoned quarry.

"You okay?" Velvet asked.

"Yeah, thanks to you. Hope there are no more Grimm like that out there," Fox said, knowing that there were—and likely worse. King Taijitu were just faster than many other land-based Grimm, especially in a desert terrain. They were running out of time. The increasing frequency and strength of the mood bombs were gathering Grimm for another major attack.

"How's Edward?" Fox asked.

"Awake," Velvet said.

Edward's mind seemed stronger now, but it was still fuzzy around the edges.

"What am I doing here?" Edward asked. His voice sounding smaller and more frail than it had back at Feldspar. "Velvet? I want to go home."

"We're taking you there," Velvet said.

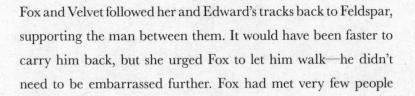

Fox and Velvet followed her and Edward's tracks back to Feldspar, supporting the man between them. It would have been faster to carry him back, but she urged Fox to let him walk—he didn't need to be embarrassed further. Fox had met very few people

Edward's age, especially in Vacuo, but when you got to be that old, you had earned a certain amount of respect, and sometimes your pride was all you had left. Edward could walk, and though he was freezing in his pajamas under a dusty old blanket, he deserved to return to Feldspar on his own two feet.

"Someone's coming," Fox sent.

"It's Bertilak," Velvet murmured.

Edward stumbled and nearly fell. He grabbed on to their arms more tightly.

"There you are!" Bertilak bellowed at Edward. "What are you playing at, old man?"

"Easy," Fox said, holding up a hand.

"He's all right," Velvet said. "That's the important thing, right?"

"The important thing is not going off on your own without telling us," Bertilak said. "Especially not into the damn desert in the middle of the damn night."

"I don't think he did this on purpose," Velvet said.

"The hell he didn't," Bertilak said. "This is the third time he's pulled a stunt like this."

"I'd run away from this ass, too," Fox sent to Velvet.

She giggled.

"You find that funny, girl?" Bertilak asked.

Velvet cleared her throat. "Sorry, I just swallowed some sand."

Fox hid a smile.

Bertilak reached for Edward, but Edward pulled away. Fox caught him.

"We've got him," Velvet said.

Bertilak was quiet for a long while. "Fine." Then he stomped back toward Feldspar. It was even more childish considering how futile it is to stomp in sand.

Fox wiped his brow. It was warming up out here in the waning dark, though dawn was still an hour away.

"He's a bit hotheaded," Velvet said. "Something to keep an eye on."

"I'll let you do that," Fox sent.

Velvet laughed.

All of Feldspar was awake by the time they returned with Edward. Carmine, Gus, Coco, and Yatsuhashi hurried over as soon as Bertilak, Velvet, and Fox arrived.

"I found him!" Bertilak said cheerfully.

Fox felt Velvet stiffen, but she didn't correct the Huntsman.

"Grandpa!" Gus cried. Edward brushed off Velvet's and Fox's helping hands and embraced the boy.

"Gus, I'm sorry, my boy!" Edward said.

"He seems okay now," Fox sent to Velvet. *"Think he was pretending to be in worse shape than he is?"*

"I think he's pretending not *to be,"* Velvet sent. *"He's trying to be strong for Gus."*

"What were you guys doing out there on your own?" Coco asked.

"We had it under control," Fox sent.

"Well?" Coco said. "Someone say something."

"Coco?" Fox sent. *"Velvet?"* he tried.

Neither of them reacted. Then Fox realized he couldn't sense their minds, either, or anyone else's.

"That's strange," Fox said in a shaky voice. "My Semblance isn't working."

"You're probably drained from the fight," Velvet said. "We both are."

"*What* fight?" Yatsuhashi asked. "Are you all right, Velvet?"

"What's going on here? Carmine and Bertilak woke up the village to help search for Edward, but you two were out taking him for a walk?" Coco said.

"We were worried," Carmine said. "The desert is no place for an old man."

"Which is why it's an interesting choice to take him there," Fox said. Everyone looked at him. "Oh, did I say that out loud? I meant to use my inside voice."

"Edward wants to cross the desert, so that's where we're taking him," Bertilak said. "And I'm tired of you young punks acting like you know better than us. We've been Huntsmen for a long time, ever since you kids were in diapers."

"Hey, I'm not *that* old," Carmine said.

"*There's something weird going on with those two,*" Fox sent. He sighed when no one reacted. His Semblance was still on the fritz. It often weakened after extensive use, after pushing himself in battle. All he needed was some sleep and food. And a shower, but he wasn't likely to get that until they got back to Shade Academy.

"I'm just saying, we have a lot of experience. And I'd be

happy to show this brat just how little he knows about fighting and survival in Vacuo. I don't think he's got what it takes to be a real Huntsman. None of you do."

"Oh, really?" Coco said.

"Please stop this! I'm just glad my grandfather is back," Gus said.

"No thanks to Bertilak," Fox said. "Isn't it your job to keep Edward and Gus safe?"

"We're being spread a little bit thin here, trying to keep over a hundred people alive," Bertilak said. "But you're right. It's time we got back to basics. We'll take the Caspians out of here in the morning."

"No," Edward said. "We're staying with these people."

"He just gets this way sometimes. He wanders off," Gus said.

"This won't happen again," Edward said.

"That kind of behavior gets you killed, one way or another. Especially in Vacuo. He would have frozen to death or been killed by a King Taijitu if we hadn't been there. If he keeps it up, one day he's not coming back," Fox said.

Silence fell over the group, abruptly broken by Gus bursting into tears.

"He's not wrong," Bertilak said. Fox heard a slap and then Bertilak said, "Ow!"

"Fox," Velvet said softly. "That wasn't very nice."

Fox folded his arms. "*Nice* gets you killed out here. *Nice* doesn't belong in the desert. These two don't belong in Vacuo." He gestured at Gus and Edward.

"Neither do we," Velvet said, but so softly Fox thought only *he* heard it. Then she had knelt beside Gus to pat his shoulder comfortingly.

"Don't worry," she said. "We'll help keep you safe. We'll get to the bottom of this before there's another attack."

"I didn't mean to upset you, Gus," Fox said. "But you did need to hear that."

"I'm sorry," Gus sobbed.

"Nothing to be sorry about," Coco said. "Just try to keep better track of your grandfather."

"No." Gus sucked up snot. "I mean . . . I'm to blame for this."

"Blame for what?" Velvet asked gently.

"Everything," Gus said. "The Grimm attacks. The evacuations. The mood bombs. It's all my fault."

CHAPTER FIVE

"My fault! I'm so sorry, Weiss!" Ruby Rose trailed behind Weiss Schnee in the ballroom, holding a napkin and an empty glass. "I'll get your dress cleaned."

Oh no, Coco thought. *This is a crime.*

Red fruit punch, the prior contents of Ruby's glass, was all over Weiss's white dress. She looked like she had a mortal wound in her side.

"Do you know how much this dress cost?" Weiss whirled around to face the pest who was following her.

Ruby stopped short. "I don't know. Maybe . . . twenty Lien?"

Coco snorted, but the other girls didn't notice.

"Twenty Lien?! Where do you shop?" Weiss folded her arms.

"I made this myself." Ruby looked down at her black-and-red dress and corset. "You can't find a cape like this in a thrift shop."

Coco definitely liked the girl's ensemble. She only really trusted people who knew how to dress, which wasn't as much about what was fashionable or expensive but finding the outfit that suited them. And, of course, it had to function well and look damn good while fighting. Check, check, and check.

"I certainly don't go to *thrift shops*," Weiss snapped. "And it was a rhetorical question. They were *all* rhetorical questions, because I don't really care about anything you have to say. Listen, don't worry about it. I just want to go back to my room and get some sleep. It's been a long day."

"*Our* room," Ruby reminded her. "We're roomies now, remember?" She punched a fist in the air. "Team RWBY!"

Weiss sighed. "For a brief, blissful moment, I had forgotten. See you later, Ruby. Don't wake me when you come in. Even better, don't come in." Weiss turned sharply on her heel and stalked off.

Ruby stared after her sadly. Then she noticed Coco watching her.

"Oh, hey. Did you, uh, see all that?" Ruby asked.

"Nice moves back there, kid," Coco said.

Ruby held up her glass. "I'm so clumsy sometimes. And by 'sometimes,' I mean all the time."

"I didn't mean spilling the drink. That was hilarious, though. I mean, an honest mistake." Coco tilted her head after Weiss. "Don't beat yourself up over it. I doubt it's the only dress Ms. Schnee owns. And I can guarantee she was overcharged for that one."

"I've only ever seen her wear the one dress, though," Ruby said. "It's probably her favorite, at least."

"Or she has a closet full of the same combat skirts," Coco said. "You always need backups. I'm Coco Adel, by the way."

Coco strode toward Ruby and held out her hand. Ruby glanced at her full hands and tossed the napkin and glass behind her back. She winced when the glass shattered and then laughed nervously. She awkwardly shook Coco's hand.

"I'm Ruby Rose," Ruby said.

"I know. The whole school knows about Beacon Academy's hotshot new team. Team RWBY. RWBY and Ruby. I bet that's gonna get confusing."

"Which is your team?" Ruby squinted at Coco.

"Team CFVY," Coco said. "Last year's hotshot new team."

Ruby's silver eyes widened. "You're Team CFVY!"

"Our reputation precedes us yet again," Coco said. "Let me get you a new drink, and some unsolicited advice, from one leader to another."

The two of them walked back to the refreshments and Coco poured Ruby another glass of punch. She tossed in a cocktail umbrella and gave it a little spin.

"A tiny umbrella! It's so cute," Ruby said.

"I thought you'd like it. And the cup is plastic. Please don't spill it on me. This is *my* favorite outfit, and I'd fly into a murderous rage if anything ruined it." Coco smiled sweetly.

"I . . . can't tell if you're joking or not," Ruby said uncertainly.

"Good," Coco said. "Listen, we were all impressed by your moves out there in the forest, Ruby. Kind of a rough start, but they all are, am I right?"

"Oh . . . that was nothing." Ruby slurped her punch noisily.

"Taking down a Nevermore isn't nothing. Especially putting on a show like that for everyone," Coco said.

"Putting on a show?" Ruby looked surprised. "What do you mean?"

"The way you toyed with the Grimm instead of going for the quick kill. Mugging for the camera."

"You can kill them *quickly*?" Ruby asked.

It had taken the combined efforts of her, Blake, Weiss, and Yang to kill the giant flying Grimm that had attacked them among the ruins during their initiation. It had probably been luck as much as skill, and it was just a matter of circumstance that Ruby had dealt the killing blow, severing the Nevermore's head with her scythe, Crescent Rose. And she certainly hadn't been worried about making it look good while she did it—she was just trying to survive.

"If you have the right weapon." Coco patted her handbag. *And the right Semblance*, she thought. "I do like your scythe, though."

"Thanks. Hold on, you were watching our initiation?" Ruby asked.

"The whole school was. Every moment," Coco said. "And you should remember that, because your team is also going to be watching you all the time, following your example. Following your orders. As good as you are, Ruby, you have to try to be even better—for them. You can't show weakness. You can't be weak, because they're depending on you to keep them safe."

"I don't know if I can be that for them," Ruby said. "Maybe

Professor Ozpin had an off day, mixed up his files or drank too much coffee or something."

"There's no such thing as too much coffee," Coco said.

Ruby laughed. "CFVY and coffee. I bet that gets confusing, huh?"

"Not really," Coco said. She didn't mention that Professor Ozpin only drank hot chocolate.

"Okay." Ruby tried to drink her punch, realized her glass was empty, and then occupied herself pouring another. At this rate, she was going to have to hit the bathroom soon.

"The headmaster knows what he's doing. Everyone here is on the right team, with the right role, for the right reason. It just takes a little while to figure out how you fit in, and what those reasons are," Coco said.

"Well, it still seems completely random to me," Ruby said.

"Professor Ozpin told me something once," Coco said. "When I asked him if I was supposed to be leading Team CFVY." She recalled his words as she repeated them for Ruby, a moment she would never forget.

"He said, *The world is chaotic. We try to assert order on it, try to make sense of it. We organized into four kingdoms, four schools . . . teams of four. But what if the only way to fight the chaos is to give in to it? All your planning, all your preparation, can be undone in a moment of bad luck. Or a split second in which you make the wrong decision, or miss your mark* just so.

"*Thus, I believe that we need to embrace randomness as well, try to harness it and turn it to our advantage. We have to plan for the unexpected, prepare ourselves for situations we never could have anticipated or trained for. You and I are having this conversation because of a lifetime of choices and seemingly unrelated occurrences that nonetheless shaped who we are and led us here.*

"The fact that two people met by chance and fell in love and had a daughter named Coco Adele is remarkable, don't you think? I do. Make no mistake, there is a higher power guiding our actions. Call it Fate. Call it Destiny. Call it the gods. Or maybe it's simply the randomness of existence. Whatever it is, I have to trust that we are here for a reason, and while my methods might be unorthodox, they haven't failed me yet."

Ruby took a breath. "Deep," she said. "I feel like I should have been writing that down."

"When Professor Ozpin talks to you, it's important to take note. Something tells me he'll be talking to Team RWBY a lot."

"If we're supposed to be a team, shouldn't we actually want to spend time with one another?" Ruby said. Weiss had gone back to their room. Yang was probably partying with her Signal friends somewhere. And she could almost guarantee Blake was curled up with a book. Ruby suddenly felt lost and alone.

"It takes time to become a team," Coco said. "But when it clicks, there's nothing like it. And nothing will be able to stop you."

Ruby grinned. "You have any more advice for me, Coco?"

Coco took off her glasses. "Number one. Stop apologizing all the time for minor stuff."

"Sorry!" Ruby covered her mouth.

"Save it for when you really screw up." Coco sighed and looked down. "Number two. Don't screw up. If you fail, you fail your team and the people you're trying to protect. Failure is not an option." She put her glasses back on. "Three. It never hurts to fight with a little style. Have some fun with it. Being a Huntress is the best feeling in the world."

"Have fun," Ruby said. "Got it!"

"That's the only part of my advice you remember?" Coco asked.

"Don't be sorry, and don't fail!"

"You got it. If there's ever anything you need, feel free to ask," Coco said.

"Thank you," Ruby said. "I only have one question so far."

"Shoot," Coco said.

"Can you really see with those shades on?" Ruby waved a hand in front of Coco's face. "We're indoors! Isn't it too dark?"

Coco laughed.

As Yatsuhashi and Fox rounded a corner in the hallway, someone crashed into Yatsuhashi at full speed and went sprawling backward.

"Are you all right?" Yatsuhashi leaned over and offered the girl a hand up. She shoved it aside and scrambled to her feet. "What happened? Is that blood?" He pointed to the red stain on the side of her white dress. "I can't stand the sight of blood."

"No, it was *Ruby*," she said.

Yatsuhashi's brow furrowed in confusion. Then his eyes lit up. "Team RWBY?"

"Apparently," she said.

"Right, we saw you guys in action. Initiation can be wild, but you were great."

"Thanks, but I'm still waiting for an apology," Weiss said.

"Wow," Fox sent to Yatsuhashi.

"Wait—from me? But I didn't do anything wrong," Yatsuhashi said.

"You're saying it was my fault I bumped into you?" Weiss asked.

"We were just walking, you were the one running without paying attention to where you were going."

"But you . . . take up so much space!" Weiss said.

Fox shook his head.

"And *you* act like you own the place." Yatsuhashi started to get angry. He closed his eyes, went to his happy place, and took a deep breath. He opened his eyes.

"It's really not a big deal. Let's start again. I'm Yatsuhashi Daichi, and this is Fox Alistair." Fox held up a hand in a half-hearted wave.

"So?" Weiss said.

"Someone needs to learn a few manners," Fox sent to Yatsuhashi.

Yatsuhashi laughed. *"This looks like a job for Team CFVY,"* he sent back.

The laughing only made Weiss angrier.

"Am I missing something?" She hated being left out. "What's so funny?" She scowled at Fox. "And what are you looking at, Red?"

"Nothing," he said mildly.

"Excuse me?" Weiss's hand went to the hilt of her weapon, a wicked-looking rapier.

Yatsuhashi held up a hand. "Hold on. He means 'nothing' literally. Fox is blind."

"Oh." Weiss studied Fox's face. "I see."

"Go on, rub it in." Fox smirked.

Her face turned pink. Yatsuhashi noticed a scar over her left eye. She wasn't so perfect as she liked to think, he figured, and maybe that was why she had such a huge chip on her shoulder.

"Well, it was nice running into you, but I have to get out of this dress. Uh." Her face reddened. She slipped between Yatsuhashi and Fox and hurried down the hall. Then she stopped and turned.

"Sorry, what team did you say you were with, again?" she asked.

"Team CFVY," Yatsuhashi said.

"Team CFVY?!" They were kind of a big deal at Beacon. Weiss should have recognized the big guy and the skinny guy in red, but she had been so annoyed with Ruby. Weiss had been planning to join the best team of first-year students at Beacon, and have Pyrrha Nikos as her partner. Weiss would have been leader of the group, of course, and she was gonna become besties with Coco Adel and get pointers on being the best Huntress she could be— and then blow all of Team CFVY's records out of the water.

Instead, none of that had happened. None of it *would* happen, unless she could convince Professor Ozpin to change his mind and put Weiss in charge of Team RWBY. She wondered what they would name the group. Team WRBY. Team Warby? That didn't have the same ring to it.

"Oh, you've heard of us?" Yatsuhashi asked casually.

"Now you're just being mean," Fox sent to him. *"This party is more fun than I thought it would be. Thanks for making me stick around."*

Weiss covered her eyes with a hand. "I am such an idiot."

Velvet tried to ignore the boys following her as she hurried away from the party in the amphitheater.

"Hey, where are you going?" one boy asked.

"Not much of a party animal?" They both laughed.

Velvet walked faster.

"I don't know; she looks like she knows how to have fun," his friend said.

"Yeah, you know what they say about bunny girls."

Velvet hurried up so she didn't have to hear that one again.

"Uh-oh. I think we're making her hopping mad," his friend said.

Blake Belladonna looked up from the book she was reading as Velvet passed her table. She had been deeply engrossed in *The Boy Who Fell from the Sky*, but she couldn't tune out the abusive behavior of the boys following the Faunus girl. As a Faunus herself—albeit one in hiding, with a bow covering her cat ears— and as a Beacon student and a Huntress in training, she was disgusted by the ugliness her fellow classmates were showing.

When the boys approached, she put out a foot and casually tripped one of them. He went down hard, face-first. Blake calmly resumed reading as his friend balled up his fists and turned on her.

"What was that for?" he yelled.

Up ahead, Velvet stopped and turned around, instantly taking in what had happened. She hesitated, wondering if she should go help the black-haired girl or take this opportunity to slip away.

There wasn't really a choice. Velvet went back.

Blake sighed and put down her book again. She stood up.

"I don't like your blatant racism," she said.

"What's it to you?" the boy asked.

"You had something to say to me?" Velvet asked.

The boy clamped his mouth shut.

"No more big words, huh?" Blake asked. "Typical cowards."

"Who do you think you are?" he said.

"Blake Belladonna," she replied. Then she smiled. "Team RWBY."

The boy's face paled. "The ones from . . ." He turned and looked at the big screen on the wall, which was playing highlights from the initiation earlier that day. His mouth fell open as he watched Blake swing on her ribbon through the Emerald Forest ruins, land on a giant Nevermore, and bury her blade ferociously in its back, her eyes gleaming.

"Uh, sorry to bother you." The boy started backing away.

"Not so fast." Blake's ribbon wrapped around the boy, holding him in place.

"Hey." He squirmed. "I don't want to fight you."

"Good. That wouldn't be much of a fight," Blake said. "What should we do with him?" She looked at Velvet.

Velvet looked surprised. She stared at the boy. "Um. Let him go?"

"Thank you!" the boy said.

Blake pulled him toward her with her ribbon, then kicked him in the back, sending him spinning away into his friend and releasing him from her ribbon.

Blake calmly sat down and opened her book. Velvet watched her quietly for a moment. She approached, one hand on an elbow. "Um. Thanks."

"Sure." Blake kept reading.

"Okay." Velvet started walking away.

"Why did you let him off so easy?" Blake asked.

Velvet looked back. "What?"

"You let someone like that go with a slap on the wrist—not even that much—and they'll just keep repeating the same behavior."

"I don't believe in fighting prejudice with violence," Velvet said.

Blake wrinkled her nose. "You don't like fighting?"

"I'm here, aren't I? I like fighting Grimm fine, but not other people."

"Even when those other people don't treat you like a person?"

Velvet shook her head. "Roughing him up wouldn't have changed his mind. It would have only made him angrier. Maybe next time he would try to hurt me with more than words. Or worse, he might just go pick on someone else. Maybe if I treat him with respect, he'll learn to treat me with respect."

Blake shook her head. "That's not how we deal with people like him where I come from."

"Where's that?"

Blake closed her book and smiled. "Hi, I'm Blake. And you're Velvet Scarlatina."

"That's right." Velvet didn't hide her surprise as she sat down across from the girl. "Have we met?"

"Just now," Blake said. "Let me ask my question another way. Why is a member of the legendary Team CFVY running away from two losers who were barely able to pass initiation?"

Velvet's eyes darted to the floor. "I didn't want to attract attention."

"They don't belong here. You do," Blake said. "People like that need to be shut down, or they'll go on harassing other people. We should at least report them to Professor Ozpin."

"He has more important things to worry about," Velvet said.

"Professor Goodwitch, then. She'd teach them a lesson."

"It really isn't worth my time. That's the best way to fight back—by not letting them get to me."

"It's your call, but I think you should stick up for yourself. Those guys aren't even a fraction as scary as Grimm, and I know you can handle yourself in the field." Blake pushed her book over to Velvet. "Here, I think you'll enjoy this."

Velvet flipped through the book. "Really?"

"Just don't fold the pages over. I hate dog ears," Blake said.

Suddenly someone deposited three glasses on the table between Blake and Velvet.

"Hey, did I miss anything?" Yang asked. "Hi! I'm Yang Xiao Long."

"Velvet Scarlatina," Velvet said, looking up at an extremely badass blonde. She had seen her fight Grimm with amazing gauntlets that really packed a punch. Velvet couldn't wait to try them out for herself. She had to leave tonight with pictures of these two girls and their weapons. "Three drinks?"

"Always carry an extra," Yang said. "But since you're sitting with us, you can have it. I'm telling you, Blake, you're gonna love this Strawberry Sunrise."

Blake sniffed it. "Nonalcoholic, right?"

"Do I look like someone who breaks the rules?" Yang sat down. "Don't answer that." She sipped her drink. "Speaking of breaking bones—"

"Rules?" Velvet asked.

"Rules, bones, sometimes they're the same thing." Yang shrugged. Coco was going to like her, Velvet thought. "Anyway, these two idiots pushed past me on my way over here, made me drop my drinks. That's why I'm late."

"They had to get you new ones?" Velvet asked.

"No, I had to beat them up." Yang laughed and held up her glass. "Banzai! I love it here!"

Blake and Velvet clinked glasses with Yang.

"Here's to a great year," Blake said.

Velvet sipped her drink. Surprisingly, it tasted exactly like strawberries and sunshine. She raised her glass in another toast. "To new friendships."

CHAPTER SIX

Back inside the Caspians' shed, Velvet sat next to Gus, hoping it would help him relax. He seemed to trust her, and he was clearly nervous with all the Huntsmen plus Slate watching, waiting for him to explain himself.

"How can it be all your fault, Gus?" Coco asked.

"Give him some space, Coco," Velvet snapped.

Coco crossed her arms. "We don't have time to coddle anyone, *Velvet*."

"What do you mean by that?" Velvet said.

"Guys," Fox sent. *"Can . . . not . . . fighting?"*

Velvet and Yatsu glanced at each other. Yatsu tapped Fox on the shoulder. "Didn't get all that. You okay?" he whispered.

Fox's shoulders slumped. It looked like his Semblance was still malfunctioning.

"Well, get on with it, boy," Bertilak barked.

Gus flinched.

Velvet hated bullies. She put her hand on Gus's shoulder.

"You can do this," she said.

He took her hand and squeezed it. Velvet felt a blip of

happiness, a feeling she'd almost forgotten ever since they'd lost Beacon and come to Vacuo.

Gus took a deep, shaky breath. Then he sat up straight. "It's my Semblance. I'm able to . . ." He glanced at Edward. "I'm able to block other people's Semblances."

The group was silent for a moment.

Then Fox whooped. "That's what's wrong with me! You've been blocking my Semblance!"

Gus's eyes went wide. "I'm sorry! I can't control it very well. It's kind of all or nothing."

"That kind of Semblance would be a big advantage in a fight," Coco said. "If you know how to use it. Have you thought about training to be a Huntsman?" Coco asked.

"No way," Gus said.

"Now's really not the time to be discussing the kid's life goals," Bertilak said.

"Hold on," Slate said. "I still don't get how blocking Semblances is linked to unleashing emotions."

Gus nodded and swallowed. "I've been using my Semblance to keep my grandfather's Semblance in check. *His* ability is to manipulate other people's emotions."

"What?!" Bertilak jumped up. "You're the reason the Grimm keep attacking us?"

"Bertilak," Carmine said in a warning tone.

"You should have said something," he went on. "It's important to share this kind of information with the people you hired to keep you alive!"

"Sit down, Bertilak," Slate said.

"You aren't the boss of me," he said.

"No, but I'm in charge here," Slate said. "You can leave anytime."

"You'd be in charge of corpses and empty homes if it weren't for us. Sand and ash, you get me?"

Carmine grabbed Bertilak's arm. "Sit down."

Sweat trickled down Velvet's forehead and stung at the corner of her left eye. She squinted. It felt like it had gotten five degrees warmer in here in the last minute; dawn must be breaking outside.

He yanked his arm away from his partner and sat. "You aren't the boss of me, either, Carmine," Bertilak said in a warning voice.

"But you did sit down." She smirked. "Now, Slate makes a good point. Maybe we *should* leave. Now that we know Edward is drawing the Grimm, we should take him away from here as soon as possible."

Velvet looked at Edward to see what he thought of all this, but he didn't seem to even be aware that they were talking about him. She leaned forward and talked to Gus.

"So, your grandfather is no longer able to control his ability?" she asked.

"He can't even stop himself from wandering around the desert in his pajamas." Bertilak gestured at Edward. "See what we're dealing with here?"

"Bertilak," Carmine said.

"As he's gotten older, he's been losing control of it," Gus said. "Now he just magnifies whatever emotions people already have. Not all the time, but when he's agitated or distracted. When he's sleeping sometimes. It's unpredictable, and it's getting worse. Um, harder for me to block. I'm not strong enough."

Carmine stared at Edward. "It's been you all along. No wonder you wanted to avoid other people."

Fox leaned forward, a puzzled expression on his face.

"Do they seem suspicious to you?" he sent. Then he smiled because his Semblance was working again. Slate looked at Fox curiously but then turned her attention back to Bertilak, Carmine, and the Caspians.

The other Huntsmen had always seemed suspicious, but now that Fox mentioned it, their reactions to Gus's confession didn't seem genuine.

"Their behavior does seem odd," Velvet sent. *"Like they're acting?"*

"You should have mentioned this when you hired us, Edward," Bertilak growled. "You've put countless lives in jeopardy."

"Bertilak is overdoing it a little. If I had to bet, I'd say they already knew Edward was causing the mood bombs. Probably even before he hired them. But if that's the case, why did they keep that info to themselves?" Coco sent.

"Maybe they're just trying to avoid getting in trouble?" Yatsuhashi sent. *"Because we'd be angry at them, too, if we knew they knew all along?"*

"Let's settle down," Slate said.

"I told you, it isn't Grandpa's fault," Gus said. "It's mine."

"It's no more your fault for not being strong enough to block him than it is Edward's fault for losing control," Coco said.

"Definitely," Velvet said.

"Running someplace you could avoid other people is very noble of you, Edward," Carmine said.

"But why Vacuo?" Fox asked.

Velvet realized she and Yatsu hadn't briefed Coco and Fox yet, and it seemed they hadn't discussed this with Bertilak and Carmine, either.

"We're heading to the western shore," Gus said.

"It's remote, on the edge of CCT range, when the system was working. Guess it's moot now. But for a couple of people who don't want to be bothered? Bliss," Carmine said.

"But it isn't much safer there than in the desert," Fox said. "There's a reason more people haven't settled there."

"And that's a long, dangerous journey through Vacuo." Slate shook her head. "Damn tourists."

"Well, you know what? It's none of your business where we're taking them." Bertilak sneered.

"Guys," Yatsu said. "We have to calm down."

Velvet had rarely seen Yatsu like this. Sweat beaded his face and he looked pale and wobbly. He must be struggling to keep his emotions in check. *Poor Yatsu,* she thought.

Velvet looked at Gus. "Can you try harder to block Edward's Semblance now? This has to be another mood bomb. We aren't acting like ourselves."

"It's hard. Sometimes, when I'm upset . . ." Gus bent over and placed his face in his hands. Velvet patted his back.

"We need to get out there and check on everyone else. We'll sort out what to do later," Slate said.

"We need to leave the settlement, now," Carmine said.

Carmine, Bertilak, and Slate started arguing.

"Isolating Edward isn't the answer. We may as well kill him ourselves and be done with it," Fox sent.

"Fox!" Coco sent.

"I'm just making a point. The Caspians will die on their own. I think they'd be better off in civilization—but not a small, defenseless settlement like this one."

"I'd hardly call Feldspar defenseless," Coco said.

"You know what I mean. We should take them to a big city, with lots of Huntsmen."

"You mean the capital?" Velvet asked.

"From here, it's about as far north to Vacuo as it is to go west to the shore," Fox sent.

"But what effect would a mood bomb have on a population that size? I don't know, Fox," Yatsuhashi said.

"What do *you* want, Gus?" Velvet asked softly. "It's time to speak up for yourself."

"It doesn't matter," Gus said.

"It does. It has to." Velvet knelt in front of him. "If you want to survive in the west, or anywhere in Remnant these days, you have to stick up for yourself."

Slate held up a hand to silence Bertilak and Carmine, who

seemed to be arguing as much with each other now as with the rest of them.

"So what is it?" Velvet asked. "Where do you want to go, Gus?"

"With an ability like yours, you could be a Huntsman one day," Fox said. "All you need is some training. We could take you to a combat school in the city. I bet Headmaster Theodore would recommend you."

"The boy doesn't want a life like that," Carmine said. "Look where it left his grandfather." She flung a hand in Edward's direction. He looked oblivious to everything that was happening around him.

"That had nothing to do with being a Huntsman," Yatsu said. "Memory is fragile, easy to lose, especially in old age."

Gus drew his shoulders in even more, practically curling into a fetal position.

"Being a Huntsman can be just as dangerous as living alone in the wilderness, especially if you don't have the instincts," Coco said.

"Now you're seeing some sense," Bertilak said.

Coco's glasses flashed as she turned to stare the larger Huntsman down. "But Gus does need training, and Edward needs help. They won't get either of those living in the middle of nowhere."

"We'll try the city of Vacuo first. If no one there can help your grandfather, I bet the hospitals in Atlas could," Velvet said. "And if you wanted to, they also have schools that can teach you to control your Semblance and better manage Edward's. Would you like that?" she said to Gus.

"We're responsible for the Caspians," Bertilak said, "and we're taking them where Edward asked us to take them—to the western shore. You four *trainees* stay here and defend Feldspar if you want, but we're out."

"That's a death sentence," Coco said. "You can't drop them off and leave them undefended."

"We're being paid to get them there. Once we do, the job is done." Bertilak laughed.

"This is just about money?" Coco shook her purse and her Gatling gun appeared.

What are you doing, Coco? Velvet thought.

"I've been wanting to tell you, I think you're a terrible Huntsman," Coco said. "A disgrace to our profession."

"You don't have what it takes to be a Huntress," Bertilak said.

"Nope. We're not doing this. Let's go, kid." Carmine stood and grabbed Gus's arm. He held tightly on to Velvet's hand.

"Hey!" Velvet said. She felt the fury build in her. It may have been magnified by Edward's unchecked ability, but it was all hers, and she was ready to own it. "Back off, lady. Gus hasn't said what he wants yet."

Gus muttered something under his breath. Velvet heard him.

Fox heard him, too, because he responded telepathically, *"There we go, then."* But everyone needed to hear it, in Gus's own voice.

"Louder," Velvet said.

Gus repeated himself, only marginally louder. The whole room fell quiet.

"One more time, Gus," Velvet said. "Speak loud and clear. This is your choice."

Gus looked up, a fierce expression on his tear-streaked face. "I don't want to split up!"

"Edward is paying for our services, and until he tells us otherwise, we're following his order." Bertilak grabbed Edward's arm.

"Get your hands off him," Coco said.

"Let me make this perfectly clear." Bertilak drew his mace and extended its chain. Spikes popped out of the steel ball at the end of it. The handle also seemed to have a pistol grip. The black metal was scratched and cracked, and there were specks of rust— Velvet hoped they were rust—on the spikes. "The old man will not be going with you, no matter what it takes."

"Bertilak," Carmine said.

The air was practically boiling in the room, and it was getting hard to breathe. It was hard to see, with a hazy shimmer making everything all wavy, like none of them were real, this was all a mirage. But it was getting very real.

Yatsu drew his sword. Fox brought his arms up into a fighting stance. Coco idly swung her handbag.

"Guys," Velvet said. "Put your weapons away." Even as she said it, she pulled her camera box around to her front, thinking about what weapon would end this most quickly, without anyone having to get hurt. She had to defuse the situation. Give the mood bomb time to wear off. Let everyone cool down and come back to their senses.

There was a tense standoff, no one willing to make the first move. And then they heard a shout outside. A scream. More screams. Running. Gunfire.

"Too late," Slate said. She leaned on the table with her arms locked, looking utterly exhausted and resigned. "The Grimm are here."

CHAPTER SEVEN

At eight years old, Yatsuhashi unlocked his Semblance when he accidentally made his dad forget that he'd already given him his allowance and got another three Lien.

It had taken him a while to figure out how his Semblance worked, and whenever he told his parents and grandfather what it was, they immediately forgot about it. For years, it was a way for him to get out of trouble when he did something wrong, or to get an extra serving of dessert.

At first, Yatsuhashi had excused this mischief as "experimenting" and it seemed mostly harmless. Over time, he learned that it was easiest to get someone to forget something they didn't care much about. A fleeting thought or a stray remark, made without much intent. But if an idea was more firmly fixed in a person's long-term memory, he could only make them lose it for a short period of time.

Then one day it had gone from funny to scary. Yatsuhashi's mother had recently given birth to his little sister, Hiyoko, and he was jealous of all the attention the baby was getting. One morning, his sleep-deprived, stressed-out mother had told him to go clean his room, one of his least favorite chores. So he decided to make her forget about it so he could go play instead. All it took was a little mental nudge, get her to think about something else, like the baby. That shouldn't be too hard.

His mother lifted her coffee to her lips and then paused, blinking. Then she put the cup down without taking a sip. She glanced at Yatsuhashi with a glazed expression.

"Good morning, Yatsu. What was I saying?"

Yatsuhashi grinned. "Good morning! You told me to 'run along and play.'"

She frowned. "I thought there was something else . . ." Then the fog passed. "Run along and play, then." She smiled.

Yatsuhashi pulled on his shoes and was about to go outside, when Hiyoko started crying. He slid open the door, but he waited when his mother came out to the living room, looking confused.

"That sounds just like a baby," she said.

Yatsuhashi froze. "It's Hiyoko," he said.

"Hiyoko? Do the neighbors have a new baby? I must have forgotten."

"It's Hiyoko," Yatsuhashi repeated.

"That's such a pretty name."

Yatsuhashi was sweating now. "Your baby, Hiyoko. My sister."

His mother laughed. "That's a good one."

All the while, Hiyoko kept crying.

"I do wish she'd stop crying," his mother said. "Where are her parents?"

Yatsuhashi hurried into the nursery and picked up the red-faced girl. He cradled her against his chest, supporting her fragile neck, the way his parents had shown him. He'd only held her once, but he simply hadn't been interested in more contact than that. It was bad enough that everyone else had been catering to her needs every moment of every day.

He was surprisingly touched at how she snuggled into his shoulder and how she had calmed down when he picked her up. She only did that for his mother and grandfather—and really made his dad work to soothe her— jiggling her up and down, rocking her, singing, until he or the baby or both of them was worn out.

She was so light and warm and she smelled nice.

Yatsuhashi went into the living room, where his mother was reading a book, something she hadn't been able to do since she had come home from the hospital. Yatsuhashi had been annoyed that she didn't have the time or energy to play with him anymore, but he'd missed the fact that she didn't have any time for herself, either, including a moment to drink her morning coffee while paging through a book.

"Who's this?" his mother asked.

"Hiyoko," Yatsuhashi said, looking for even a slight glimmer of recognition. Nothing. Yatsu knew almost nothing about caring for a baby, but his grandfather and father were out fishing, so it all came down to Yatsuhashi.

"When did you start babysitting?" his mother asked. "That's so sweet of you."

"Just now, but I should have started a long time ago," Yatsuhashi said.

Little Hiyoko wasn't content resting in Yatsuhashi's arms for long. When she started snuffling again, he checked her diaper—thankfully clean—and then got her a bottle of milk. He asked his mother to show him how to feed her.

"I haven't done this since you were a baby," she told Yatsuhashi, "but it feels like only yesterday." He took over for her while she went to go get a shower. Then he played with Hiyoko for a little while, which mostly involved tickling her and making funny faces. When his mother came back, she still didn't remember her daughter. Yatsuhashi was starting to get worried, but either she would remember or his dad would come home, and he could try to explain what had happened . . . maybe this time they would remember what he told them about his Semblance.

Yatsuhashi ended up spending the whole day with Hiyoko. When she wouldn't go to sleep, he cradled her on his chest and she dropped right off, and so did he.

His mother woke him as she took the sleeping baby from his arms. It was dark outside.

"Thank goodness you were here, Yatsu," she whispered. "I don't know what happened. It was like I forgot about Hiyoko . . ." She was distraught.

"It was my fault," Yatsuhashi said.

She gave him a puzzled look. When she had placed Hiyoko back in her crib, she found Yatsuhashi in the kitchen. He had been so busy with his sister, he hadn't even eaten all day. He grabbed a slice of cake, and his mother didn't question it.

He told her about his Semblance, what he had done. She was quiet when he finished, and there was a frightened look in her eyes that haunted him to this day.

"Why didn't you tell us about this earlier?" she said.

"I have. You never remember it when I stop talking. So I stopped trying."

She shook her head. "This explains a lot. We all noticed we were getting more forgetful, but we didn't know why.

"This is an incredible discovery, Yatsu. You have an amazing ability." She took a deep breath and looked at him warily. "But you know you have to stop using it on us."

Yatsuhashi realized he was crying. "I'm sorry," he said. "I didn't mean to make you forget about Hiyoko."

She pulled him close, and her arms around him made him feel better. He stopped crying. He rested his head on her shoulder.

"Shhh. I know, sweetie. But you did the right thing to keep her safe. Thank you," she said.

When his father and grandfather came home, Yatsuhashi went through the story again, with his mother's help. This time, the news stuck in their memories.

His father cradled Hiyoko with a dark expression, half anger, half fear. "Even if you thought you weren't causing any harm, you shouldn't have been doing that to us, Yatsuhashi! What were you thinking?"

Yatsu lowered his eyes and remained silent.

"You have to respect the minds of others," his mother said. "When you affect people like that, you take away more than memories. You take away their right to make their own choices."

Yatsu's grandfather nodded. "All we are is what we remember. If you erase the wrong memory, you erase our identity."

"You are not to use this ability again, do you understand me?" his father said.

His grandfather held up a hand. "Not until you have learned to control *it. With the proper training, you can find a way to use your Semblance for good."*

Yatsu's dad turned away, bouncing Hiyoko in his arms. "It's dangerous," he muttered.

"This is still our Yatsu. He's a good boy. And now that he's told us about his Semblance, we can help him learn to use it appropriately," his mother said.

Just before bed, Yatsuhashi checked in on Hiyoko. He watched her sleeping peacefully on her back, arms and legs sprawled everywhere, mouth open. She wasn't really that bad. He might even be starting to love her.

On his way to his room, he heard his parents talking quietly to each other. His grandfather caught him sitting on the floor in the hallway, arms crossed over his knees.

"I'm a monster," Yatsu whispered.

"Only if you choose to be. The person you become will be defined by all the choices you make along the way, good and bad." His grandfather put a hand on his head. "It'll be all right, Yatsu. You don't have to deal with this on your own anymore. We're here for you."

Monsters. Everywhere.

Yatsuhashi felt a knot in his stomach at the sight of the Feldspar townspeople fleeing from Grimm. He had only seen some of these Grimm species as drawings on Professor Port's walls, but there was no mistaking the black, red, and white markings on the demons—or their base hatred for people as they stalked among the tents and homes.

For the moment, Bertilak and Carmine were no longer interested in fighting Team CFVY—now that there was a clear, common danger.

"We'll take Edward and Gus out of here to the north while your team evacuates Feldspar," Carmine said to Coco.

"North?" Fox asked.

"The Grimm aren't attacking on that side because of the wall," Carmine said.

Coco hefted her Gatling gun. "You heard Gus. He doesn't want to split up, and now isn't the time to settle this. Grimm are already here, and emotions are gonna run high whether Edward is here or not."

Yatsuhashi drew Fulcrum and bounced lightly on the balls of his feet. This was no time for talk. They needed to get out there to fight and defend and evacuate.

"Together, we can fight our way through on the western border of the settlement," Velvet said. "If we hurry before the Grimm head us off."

"We stick with your original plan," Coco said. "Head west, fast, try to get out of the desert. Once we're out, we can move faster on firm ground and stay ahead of the Grimm. If Gus wants to try combat school, it'll be safer to loop around and reenter the desert farther north. We can even deliver the Caspians to the city for you, since we'll be heading back to Shade ourselves."

"You'll like the city of Vacuo," Fox told Gus. "It's rougher than Vale, but there are few more welcoming places in Remnant, or livelier. Anyone who makes it through the desert to the city has already proven they belong there."

Yatsuhashi wished Shade Academy were more like the city Fox described. It felt like every day at the school was a test to see how good you were, to prove that you deserved to be training to be a Huntsman. Survival was more important than teamwork, and it was more competitive than Beacon Academy—even within your own team—placing CFVY at a unique disadvantage. Although they had quickly risen in the ranks and earned the respect of their peers, that admiration only lasted until their next mission. If the combat schools in Vacuo were anything like that, he honestly wondered if Gus would thank them for getting him there.

"I agree with Coco. If you two won't come with us, then we'll come with you—make sure you get the Caspians where they want to go," Slate said. "It's the only way the tribe can make it with this many Grimm attracted to the area."

Carmine considered and then nodded. "Seems sensible."

"Fine," Bertilak said. "You win."

"Hold on," Yatsuhashi said. "Gus. You understand what we're saying? We're going to take you someplace safe for now, where we can talk more about what you and your grandfather want to do. You don't have to deal with this on your own anymore."

Velvet smiled up at her partner.

Gus looked surprised. His eyes were suddenly wet.

Yatsuhashi knew what it meant for a kid to hear something

like that and realize they didn't have to carry a heavy burden alone.

Gus wiped his tears away with his arm.

"I trust you," Gus said. "Let's stick together."

Yatsuhashi might have been imagining it, but with that finally settled, he felt lighter, more positive—which didn't match up with the Grimm horde advancing through town. Or maybe he was just looking forward to dealing with a problem he could more easily solve. But the moment was short-lived.

"Great. You don't want anyone else to get hurt, and this is how to save as many of them as possible," Coco said.

"You know, Theodore won't thank you for bringing more Grimm to his city," Slate said. "Or an old man who attracts them."

"I think the headmaster will be fascinated by Edward, and understand why we brought him. And there are more than enough Huntsmen in the city and at the Academy to defend Vacuo."

"Isn't that what you thought about Beacon?" Bertilak said.

The anger flared up in Yatsuhashi faster than he could swallow it. He threw a punch at Bertilak, but the Huntsman saw the blow coming and leaned away so his fist only scored a glancing hit.

"Yeah! I've been waiting for this." Bertilak gestured Yatsuhashi forward. Yatsuhashi lunged for him, but Velvet grabbed his arm.

"Yatsu! No!" she said.

"He has it coming," Yatsuhashi growled.

"Yatsuhashi, stand down. Right now we need to fight the Grimm, not each other," Coco said. "When everyone's safe, you can sort this out with Bertilak—but you'll have to take a number."

"I'm ready anytime," Bertilak said.

"She's right," Carmine said. "Let's focus on surviving this attack instead of killing each other, or we'll all be dead."

"Carmine, Bertilak, you protect Gus and Edward. You've been through this before, so work with Slate and Velvet to organize an evacuation," Coco said.

"Oh, come on," Velvet said.

"Not now, Velvet." Coco looked at Yatsuhashi and Fox. "We'll hold off the Grimm."

"We don't take orders from kids," Bertilak growled.

"It wasn't an order. It was a suggestion." Coco lifted her gun and turned away from him. "A strong suggestion."

"Bertilak," Slate said. "We need you."

Carmine drew the sai from her belt. She clicked their hilts together and then pulled them apart to extend them into a long bō with bladed ends. "Locked and loaded."

Coco tapped Fox on the shoulder. "Can you push a message to everyone at once, like before? Tell them the plan? Try and get them to calm down."

Fox hesitated and nodded. He lowered his head, and a moment later, Yatsuhashi heard his voice in his mind, while Fox spoke aloud, slightly out of sync.

"Attention. Please try to calm down. Your emotions will only draw more

Grimm to you. Make your way to the west end of Feldspar as quickly as possible. Slate is organizing an evacuation. Bertilak and Carmine will keep you safe, and we'll keep the Grimm busy to cover your escape."

Fox pitched forward and Yatsuhashi caught him. Using his Semblance to that extent took a lot out of him.

"Okay?" Yatsuhashi asked.

"I can fight," Fox said.

"Not what I asked, but it's good enough for me."

"You have what you need, Velvet?" Coco nodded to the camera in Velvet's hands.

Velvet gave her a thumbs-up. She locked eyes with Yatsuhashi for a moment.

Yatsuhashi nodded. He turned and ran toward the screams.

Fox and Coco were just behind him. Up ahead, Yatsuhashi saw a Ravager beating its wings over the heads of a red-haired woman and her child. He recognized them as Amaranth and Ash.

These people weren't just strangers. He had spoken with many of them, heard firsthand about all they'd been through. He didn't know how people could live this way. Maybe people in the other kingdoms had gotten spoiled with their home's relative stability, since this was just how things were in Vacuo.

He and his team had been upset about losing Beacon for the last year, but the desert nomads never even had homes for long. Their whole existence was centered on picking up and moving on. And it was the other kingdoms that had created this situation for them. No wonder they didn't want to get involved in Remnant's politics.

Yatsuhashi ran toward the huddled mother and son, yelling to draw the Grimm's attention. It flapped up and turned to face Yatsuhashi, shrieking back at him at an ear-piercing pitch. Yatsuhashi winced and gripped his sword tighter. The creature flew up, up, up, and then it dove, moving far more quickly than he'd expected.

It opened its mouth, still blasting him with sonic waves and baring four wicked sharp teeth, each the size and shape of Fox's arm blades. Yatsuhashi clenched his jaw and readied himself.

Just before the Ravager reached him, he vaulted up and over it, twisting in midair and slashing down with his sword, slicing the bat diagonally in half. The two pieces fluttered down on lifeless wings before the Grimm evaporated into black smoke.

Yatsuhashi landed on his feet, planting his sword tip in the ground to get his balance. Ash gaped at him with his eyes and mouth wide open.

"Head west. Look for Velvet," Yatsuhashi said. "She and the others will get you out of here."

"Thank you!" Amaranth picked up Ash and ran toward safety.

Yatsuhashi saw Fox battling a Dromedon, delivering swift kicks to the monstrous pitch-black camel's head to prevent it from spitting venom at him. He delivered a punch to the Grimm's misshapen hump, which expanded like a balloon before it burst with a soft boom.

Coco was protecting a group of children from a Jackalope, a huge four-legged beast with black fur, branching red-and-white antlers extending from its bone mask, and powerful hind legs that could propel it a great height and allow it to run fast. She couldn't get a clean shot with her gun, so she was fighting it with her bag and fists at close range. Finally having enough of that, she grabbed the Grimm by its horns and flipped it over her head.

It landed on its leg and kicked, flying toward Coco and ramming her with its antlers, knocking her down. It scrambled onto its feet and snapped at her with slavering teeth. The inside of its mouth glowed as red as its eyes.

Coco held her ground. She shook out her gun in one smooth motion, planted her feet, and reduced the Grimm to smoky black shreds with her Aura-charged bullets.

The group kept advancing deeper into Feldspar. As they went, they checked every shack, tent, and stall for survivors. Checking every body they found. Yatsuhashi knew many of their names, too, and recalled the conversations they had shared only days before. Each fallen person spurred him on to reach the next tent while he could still help them.

Yatsuhashi had seen the long-necked Ziraph advancing quickly through town toward them. Its three heads bobbed above the short roofs, while it kicked anyone and anything that crossed its path.

"You want to handle that?" Coco asked Yatsuhashi.

"You're asking me?" His eyes tracked it as it strode toward them on four long legs covered in razor-sharp, bony plates. Its skin was black with glowing red spots like a leopard's with two short but pointed white horns over its fiery red eyes.

"It's tall. You're tall." She reloaded her gun with Dust bullets. She frowned and he realized she was already running low on ammunition.

Yatsuhashi thought back to Professor Port's lesson on the desert-type Grimm. He wished there was more information about the creatures that gravitated toward Vacuo, and that he'd paid more attention at the time.

"We can't get too close to the legs, but if you can bring it to its knees, Fox and I can go for the necks." The five-story-high heads made a large target, and he had a large sword.

"You got it." Coco braced her Gatling gun on the ground and took careful aim. She fired a short burst and the Ziraph pitched forward as its front right leg gave out.

"Great shot." Yatsuhashi ran toward the Ziraph, Fox keeping pace with him. It went down on its back knees as Coco continued firing, trying to be conservative with her bullets.

Fox picked up speed and reached the Ziraph first, jumping up and springing off its body with one hand and somersaulting his way up its side. He then ran up the Grimm's central neck, making quick slashes along the way with his tonfas. When he reached the head, he stabbed his blades into either side of it.

The Ziraph bellowed and bowed its neck, shaking its head to knock Fox off. Another head snapped at him, while the third tried to gore him with its horns.

As the creature came in range, Yatsuhashi leaped, pushed off one of its knees, and flew toward the right-hand neck. He brought Fulcrum down hard. At the same moment, Fox flipped toward him and landed on the top edge of Yatsuhashi's sword, providing enough extra weight and momentum to help drive it clean through the Ziraph's neck.

A long, dark tongue wrapped itself around Yatsuhashi. He waited until the Ziraph drew him back to one of its two remaining heads, then lopped off the tongue and stabbed into the neck as he fell, splitting it open. The head fell, lifeless, to the ground, while the last head swiveled around, to face Yatsuhashi. It opened its mouth, its grotesque tongue emerged—

And a black line appeared across the neck, just before the head tipped forward and tumbled down. Fox waved from his position where the head had been a moment before he had sliced it off. He jumped down as the Grimm collapsed onto its side and dissipated.

Coco guided more townspeople to the evacuation in the north.

"Can't be too many more of them." Coco whipped the beret from her head and wiped sweat from her forehead. She slicked her limp hair back and restored her beret. It was getting on toward noon, the hottest part of day. The worst time to be marching in the desert, especially without adequate time to prepare and pack food and water.

"I hope not," Yatsuhashi replied. A moment later he wasn't sure if she was referring to the people or the Grimm. But there were still plenty of the latter to fight, and they needed to buy time for the evacuees to get away.

Surviving the Grimm was just the first step. The desert could just be a slower death, if they didn't reach the western shore quickly. But the Vacuans could handle the heat, hunger, and thirst; all Team CFVY could do was fight to give them a chance to live.

They pushed through to the eastern end of the settlement, where the invading Grimm were thickest, still flooding into the town. But without the high emotions of the townspeople to draw them, they were wandering around looking for prey—which was exactly what the Huntsmen were doing.

They rescued a couple of stragglers from a trio of buzzing Lancers that had cornered them in their shack.

"Anyone else, Fox?" Coco asked.

Fox slowly turned in a circle, his face strained with concentration and fatigue. He'd been pushing himself hard for too long. They all had, but he, Velvet, and Coco had been up all night on watch duty with little opportunity to rest. And Fox and Velvet had already been out in the desert, fighting a King Taijitu.

"That's everyone," he said. "The Grimm are starting to thin out a little, too, but some of them are still following the evacuees."

"Damn," Coco said. "I didn't think of that."

"We can't rejoin the others yet," Yatsuhashi said. "We'll just lead even more Grimm toward them."

Fox knelt on the ground, head bowed. "So we draw them somewhere else," he said softly.

It showed how tired he was that he'd simply spoken aloud rather than use even a little of his Semblance to communicate. Yatsuhashi gathered he didn't have much to spare. He didn't have to check an Aura monitor to know that all it would take was one heavy hit and Fox would be down for the count.

Yatsuhashi looked around. He would make sure no Grimm even got close enough to breathe on Fox until he'd regained some of his strength.

"How many people do you think made it?" Coco asked.

How many people did we lose? she meant. But she was always the optimist.

"Most of them got out of town," Yatsuhashi said. "Maybe one hundred and twelve?" He couldn't say whether everyone who escaped would last. Several of them had been injured, some grievously, and there wouldn't be much opportunity to stop to treat them, or even supplies to treat them with, in the open desert.

Coco nodded. "Not bad." She took off her sunglasses and pinched the bridge of her nose, eyes closed. Yatsuhashi noted the dark circles under her bloodshot eyes before she slipped her mask back on. "Could have been better. We could have avoided all of this."

"We can only do our best," Fox said.

"I want my best to be better." Coco shrugged. "We're still on the clock, so let's go."

"Where to?" Yatsuhashi asked.

"They're going west, so we go northwest," Fox said. "Get as many of them off their trail as we can. Then we lose them in the desert and rendezvous with the others at the shore. Then hopefully we bring the Caspians back home with us to Vacuo."

Team CFVY had been living in Vacuo for a year, but none of them had yet called the city or Shade Academy home. It wasn't Beacon, but even so, Yatsuhashi would be glad to be back there.

"We can do this," Coco said. "Hang in there, guys."

"Aye, aye. Hanging in there, chief," Fox said.

"I hope they're okay." Yatsuhashi looked to the west thoughtfully.

"Velvet's with them," Coco said. "They'll be fine. As long as everyone sticks together and sticks to the plan."

CHAPTER EIGHT

"Let's just review the plan one more time before we go," Velvet said. She looked around at the others gathered in the ballroom: all the members of teams RWBY and CFVY. They were standing around a large round table scattered with Weiss's notes on what was going where, who was doing what, and what was happening when.

Team CFVY had been tasked with planning the Beacon Dance, a formal affair that students anticipated with a mixture of eagerness and dread. Velvet had been excited about getting to mix with teams from other schools, and having the chance to plan a really fun event for everyone, but then Coco had volunteered them for an optional extra mission that had just come in. Coco assured them they'd wrap things up with plenty of time to fulfill their duties, but Velvet wanted to have a backup just in case, and she couldn't think of anyone better than Yang and Weiss, who respectively brought the enthusiasm and the stubbornness necessary to get the job done.

"A Bullhead's waiting for us," Coco said.

"This is important!" Weiss said.

Coco's expression didn't change, but Weiss pointed at her.

"There! You just rolled your eyes, didn't you?" Weiss demanded.

"It's just a dance," Coco said. "It's no big deal."

"No big deal?" Yang threw her hands up in the air. "This is *the* social event of the season!" She put her hands on her hips. "Aside from, you know, the Vytal Festival itself. But this is going to be fun!"

"Fighting is fun," Yatsuhashi said.

"True," Yang said. "But this is different. Dancing is like fighting—with music! And, uh, hormones?"

Ruby sighed. "I'd rather fight with *weapons*. You guys are so lucky to get assigned to an important mission."

"Yeah, we're *lucky*," Velvet said glumly.

"Hey! Here's an idea." Ruby held up her hands, fingers wide. "Picture this. Instead of the Beacon Dance, it could be . . . Beacon Battle Club! It would be good practice for the tournament. We could play music while we *actually* fight! All the best fight scenes on TV have awesome rock songs playing that reflect the themes of the episode and the hidden yearnings of the characters."

"Which would be terrible if real life was anything like that," Weiss said.

"Oh? What are you hiding, Weiss?" Ruby asked.

Weiss rolled her eyes. "I just rolled my eyes at you, Ruby."

"I know! I can see your eyes."

"I just wanted to make sure you knew."

"I appreciated that courtesy," Fox said.

"Thank you," Weiss said.

"Fine, but let's hurry it up, okay?" Coco paced.

"We will not turn the dance into a fight club," Velvet said.

"Cage matches?" Ruby asked.

"No."

"Rock, paper, scissors?"

"No." Velvet shook her head. "The decorations are pretty straightforward. Streamers, tablecloths, flowers."

"And doilies, of course," Weiss said.

"What was that, Grandma?" Yang asked.

"Doilies are very refined." Weiss sniffed.

"Doilies are absurd and elitist," Yang said.

"What did you call me?" Weiss asked.

"I didn't say anything about you. But your taste, on the other hand . . ." Yang held out a hand, indicating that it spoke for itself.

Fox leaned close to Ruby. "You guys do like each other, right?" he asked. "I'm picking up on a lot of tension here."

"Things have been sort of . . . stressful lately," Ruby said. She slumped over with her elbows on the table, chin on hands.

"Sounds like our first year here," he said. "It gets better, though. We had some rough patches early on, too, and now look at us. The important thing is to talk to one another."

Ruby sat up and smiled at Fox. "That's great to hear. Thank you. And I think that's the most words I've ever heard you say at once. For a while there, we wondered if you ever talked." She covered her mouth. "And now *I* should stop talking," she said with a muffled voice. "Ah! Shut up, Ruby. Idiot."

"You'd be surprised how chatty I can be." Fox grinned. "But I'm about to use up my word quota for the—" He stopped.

Ruby waited and then prompted him. "Day? Week?"

He winked.

"Oh!" She laughed. "I get it. I didn't know you're funny, too."

"Every team needs some comic relief. Right?"

Ruby nodded. Then her eyes widened. "Am *I* the comic relief?" She shook her head. "No! Impossible! Yang is funny, too. Funnier than me! She's always saying goofy things like, 'Let's start things off with a Yang!' I don't do that. And Weiss. Weiss is always joking with me."

"Or is she making fun of you?" Fox asked.

"You think so?" Ruby rubbed the back of her head and frowned while thinking about that. "Hey . . ." She glared at Weiss. "We'll talk about that later."

Fox laughed.

"Stop laughing! I am not funny." Ruby pouted. "I'm the leader. Leaders can't be the comic relief."

Fox raised his eyebrows. "Jaune."

Ruby looked stricken. Then she put her head on the table and hid her face in her arms. "I *am* the comic relief!"

"Coco can be very funny, too," Fox said with a straight face.

"Right, Fox?" Velvet said. Everyone turned to look at him. Startled, he stood bolt upright.

"What?" he asked.

"The music. For the dance?"

"Right. Got it covered," he said. "You're gonna love the DJs."

"Great." She pointed across the room. "My photo booth is going to be over there. We'll get everyone to take silly pictures."

Weiss took the list from Velvet and ran down the rest of the items. "Yatsuhashi has already taken care of the desserts. Coco is . . ." Weiss looked up. "You aren't on the list."

"Yup," Coco said. "Are we almost done here?"

Weiss started to argue, but then she thought better of it. "Yang will greet guests, and Blake . . . Blake?"

The bow disguising Blake's cat ears was all that was visible of her behind the large book propped on the table in front of her, *Hidden Remnant*.

"Blake?" Weiss asked again. Then she stalked over and yanked the book up, revealing a second book: *My Sweet Samurai*. And behind that book . . . Blake had fallen asleep. She had dark smudges under her closed eyes from too many nights awake patrolling the warehouses for Roman Torchwick and the White Fang.

"She must have needed a catnap," Yatsuhashi said.

"Shhh!" Velvet punched Yatsuhashi on his arm. "Bad, Yatsu! Bad!"

"What?" he asked. "Oh, sorry. Was that inappropriate?"

"Yes, it was."

"I'm sorry. I didn't mean it that way," he said.

"You just have to choose your words more carefully. Blake trusted us with her secret. Don't make her regret it with your insensitive jokes."

Yatsuhashi's face fell.

"So that's everything, then. Let's go." Coco hoisted her bag.

"Hold on," Yang said.

"What? Are we missing something?" Weiss asked.

Yang looked around slowly. "We're only missing an opportunity. What about . . . a fog machine?"

"A fog machine," Weiss said.

"A fog machine?" Velvet asked.

Coco picked up her bag. "It's time to say good-bye."

Velvet and Yatsu looked at each other and shrugged.

"Well, thanks, guys," Velvet said. "We appreciate the help. We'll see you in a couple of days."

"You can count on us!" Ruby said cheerfully.

"You haven't signed up to do anything!" Weiss said.

"And you can count on me to follow through—on absolutely nothing."

Fox pointed at Ruby. "Comic relief."

"Ha!" Weiss folded her arms. "You totally are."

"Be safe, guys." Ruby waved.

"And think about the fog machine!" Yang called after Velvet, Yatsuhashi, Fox, and Coco as they left the ballroom.

Blake sat up with a splutter and looked around. "What'd I miss?"

Coco stuck her head back into the ballroom. "No fog machine." Then she left again.

CHAPTER NINE

A blanket of rolling white mist covered the desert sand as far as Coco could see.

"Where's this fog coming from?" she asked. Her voice was hoarse from shouting during the evacuation and Grimm fight, and from heat and dehydration. "Not that I'm complaining."

The air was still warm, but the tiny water droplets condensing from the fog felt refreshing against her skin. She breathed in and her parched throat started to feel better. She licked water from her cracking lips.

"The west winds blow moisture in from the ocean," Fox sent.

Coco thought Fox was lucky that he didn't have to open his mouth to talk. Their special teamspeak was a big asset that they had managed to keep from everyone else at Beacon, except Professor Goodwitch, who knew everything about her students, and Professor Ozpin, who seemed to know everything. But now that they were at Shade, no one—not even Headmaster Theodore—seemed to know.

She took advantage of the open channel. *"But that has to be dozens of miles away,"* she sent back.

"Life may be slow in Vacuo, but things can move fast," Fox said. *"The fog will burn off soon."*

He was right. Not long after, as the afternoon stretched on and the day got hotter, the mist disappeared and they were once again at the mercy of the sun. They trudged onward, the landscape around them shimmering so much in the heat that it felt like they were walking through a dreamscape. But it was more like a nightmare.

"Hold up." Yatsuhashi raised a hand to stop them.

"What is it?" Coco asked.

He pointed north. "Tracks."

Coco examined the sand. They had been following the path Velvet and the rest of the evacuees had taken, which was easy to spot—even with the desert's habitually shifting sands—because the sand had been disturbed so much by the feet of nearly a hundred people. Fortunately, they hadn't encountered any bodies along the way, though they easily could have been claimed by the desert or its wildlife before they passed by.

Yatsuhashi was right: Another set of tracks was heading off to the north, but they were obscured so it was hard to tell if it was one person or multiple travelers.

"Someone is trying to hide their trail," Yatsuhashi said.

Coco pulled out her Scroll to try to contact Velvet, hoping they were still between relay towers. NO SIGNAL flashed on her screen.

"Can't reach Velvet," she said. "Fox?"

"I'm trying," he sent, *"but I'm not getting through, either."*

"I hope nothing happened to them," Yatsuhashi said.

"Gus is probably blocking your Semblance again," she said.

"Or they're too far away." Fox turned his head toward the north. *"I'm sensing someone out there, but it's very faint."*

"And what's that ominous cloud on the horizon?" Yatsuhashi asked.

"It's definitely not fog," Coco said.

"Describe it," Fox said sharply.

"It looks kind of like giant cauliflower lying on the ground."

"Cauliflower?" Coco squinted in the distance.

"How would you describe it?" Yatsuhashi asked.

"Steam blasting from an espresso machine," Coco said.

Yatsuhashi squinted. "Oh yeah, I can see that. So what is it really?"

"Trouble," Fox said. *"It's a sandstorm."*

"At least it's really far away," Yatsuhashi said. "Probably fifteen miles."

"Like I mentioned, things move fast in the desert. The desert was formed over centuries, but that's one of the things that does the shaping. It's powerful, swift, and deadly." Fox rarely looked worried, but his concern was plain on his face. *"We're all in danger. It will probably be here within the hour. We have to find shelter."*

"Let's hurry and catch up to the others. The storm's going to erase all these tracks," Coco said.

"What about whoever is out there?" Yatsuhashi asked.

Coco was torn. Whoever it was wanted to be out there if they had covered their tracks so carefully. But it seemed suspicious, and she didn't like to leave anyone behind.

"I'll check it out," she said. "Meet up with you guys later."

Fox swept his hand in front of him. "Nope. I'll go after them. You need to see tracks to follow them, but I don't." He tapped his right temple. "As soon as I get close enough, I'll be able to find you."

"Fox, if you get caught in that storm, you'll be—"

"Blind?" He crossed his arms. "Exactly. I also know the desert better than both of you. And I travel faster. And I have—"

"Okay, okay, no need to give Yatsuhashi an inferiority complex," Coco said.

Yatsuhashi rolled his eyes.

"I saw that," Coco said.

"Even I saw that," Fox said.

"You clearly know exactly what you're getting into, so if you want to volunteer on a suicide mission, I guess I won't stop you," Coco said.

"I didn't say anything about suicide," Fox said. "I'm coming back."

"Sure you will," she said. "It's been nice working with you. I hope we don't get stuck with a weird acronym after you're gone. Come on, Yatsuhashi."

Yatsuhashi paused, then reached down and grabbed Fox in a bear hug, lifting him up off the ground.

"Ow!" Fox said. "I need my ribs and spine to walk, you big dummy. And I'm coming back."

"Sure," Yatsuhashi said.

"Guys," Fox said.

"Good luck." Coco waved a hand behind her as she walked off with Yatsuhashi, on the path of the evacuees.

Stupid, she thought. *He can't see you.* Even after all this time, she could still slip up, but Fox had a way of putting people at ease, cracking jokes to defuse the tension while people were tripping over themselves to apologize. He had once joked that he should be the one with the sunglasses.

But I look cooler in them, Coco had told him.

I'll have to take your word for it, Fox had responded. *But I bet you're wrong.*

She glanced to her right and saw Fox was running and had already gotten a good distance away; he really was built for the desert, but she couldn't imagine running in this heat. Walking was hard enough.

The desert was almost enough to make her regret her dark outfit, but her clothes were more comfortable and cool than they looked. The fabric breathed well, and she made a point of treating them with UV protection and lathering herself in sunscreen to preserve her fair complexion.

Even so, after a year in Vacuo, she was more tan than she'd ever been in her life. Beaches and Coco went together like milk and lemon, and she had somehow ended up on the biggest beach in Remnant. It had been a tough decision to go there, and not always a popular one, but she was still convinced it had been the right choice. Vacuo was the only place outside of Vale where every member of Team CFVY would be welcome—at least, as welcoming as a place like Vacuo could be.

In some ways, it had an advantage over Beacon. Coco hadn't known the best way to help Velvet with the bullying members of their class—since the school's rules expressly forbade fighting other students outside of school-sanctioned sparring matches. That was one of the reasons Coco had looked forward to the Vytal Tournament so much, and then they'd gone and lost their match against Mercury and Emerald. Just another one of the failures as a leader and a friend that Coco carried around, like an out-of-season accessory.

"You okay?" Yatsuhashi asked.

"Just thinking about our classmates," Coco said. "At Beacon," she clarified.

"Yeah," Yatsuhashi said.

"Sometimes I wish I could just forget what happened." She grimaced. "Sorry, didn't mean that."

She was in rare form today. In truth, she'd been off her game since that mission at Lower Cairn, and she kept waiting for the others to see it. Professor Ozpin may have had high expectations for her as a leader, but he couldn't have predicted this. The world was testing all of them, and she wasn't sure she would be ready to step up when the time came. All she could do was try to keep it together from one day to the next.

"Believe me, I know what you mean," Yatsuhashi said. "But we need to remember the bad along with the good. It's what makes us who we are. Making mistakes, carrying their lessons with us, makes us stronger. It's the only way we can become better than we were."

"That's deep," Coco said.

"I got it from the back of a Pumpkin Pete's cereal box," he said.

"Really?"

"No, just kidding. That cereal isn't very good for you. I always wondered why Pyrrha . . ." He trailed off. "Anyway, it goes back to something my grandfather told me once. I've been thinking about him a lot lately."

"Because of Edward," Coco said.

Yatsuhashi kicked some sand ahead of him. A tiny crab scuttled away and burrowed back into the cooler sand below. It was nowhere near the size of a mole crab, but Coco still shuddered involuntarily. They hadn't been much of a threat, as it turned out, but she didn't like the idea of countless enemies burrowing beneath her feet.

"When I first unlocked my Semblance, I did some bad things with it. Some by accident, some on purpose. I was jealous of my little sister, and one day, I made my mother forget she even existed." Yatsuhashi squinted and looked off into the distance. "That's when I told them about my ability. They were . . . afraid of me." He shook his head. "No, they were afraid of what I might become."

"That must have been hard for you," Coco said. "Is that why you don't like using your Semblance?"

"Yeah. I've learned to control it, but it still doesn't feel right, messing with other people's memories like that. It's too invasive. Even when I'm doing good with it, it feels . . . wrong."

Coco peered over the top of her shades at him. "So what was it your grandfather said to you?"

"That our choices make us who we are. The good ones and the bad ones." Yatsuhashi placed a hand on her shoulder. "No one is perfect, not even you."

"Thanks. I was already painfully aware of that."

"I mean, it's okay that you aren't. Because you're always trying to be better. You're always trying to do the right thing. I think our intentions matter just as much as the outcomes."

Coco hid her eyes behind her sunglasses again. "Thank you. I . . . I needed to hear that."

"That's why I said it."

"But I'm really *close* to perfect, right?"

Yatsuhashi put a hand behind his head and laughed. Then his eyes widened and he pointed behind her. "Do you see that?"

"Trying to change the subject?" Coco turned, and on the wavy, hazy horizon, she saw a makeshift settlement of dune buggies, wagons, and tents.

"I see it," she said. "I wonder why they stopped."

She checked her Scroll again, but there was still no signal. She sighed and walked faster, Yatsuhashi huffing alongside her as they approached the group.

They reached them half an hour later. The sun was directly overhead, leaving no shadows on the sand. It was hot enough that they weren't even sweating because it evaporated instantly.

Velvet bounded out of the settlement and launched herself at Yatsuhashi. He caught her, laughing, and spun her around.

"I'm glad you're all right, V," he said.

"You too, Yatsu. And Coco." Then she looked worried. "Fox?" Her voice caught in her throat.

"He's okay," Coco said. *As far as I know,* she thought. "Why did you guys stop here?"

"We thought we should get organized and make sure we know everyone who escaped Feldspar with us."

"Smart," Coco said.

"We already lost two people along the way. Bertilak and Edward," Velvet said.

"Lost as in—"

"They aren't dead. We don't think, anyway. We just don't know where they are."

"Edward I could understand wandering off, but Bertilak?" Coco said.

"Maybe Bertilak noticed Edward was gone and went after him?" Velvet asked.

"Without telling anyone? What does Carmine say?" Coco asked.

"She's as concerned as we are."

"We only found one set of tracks out there," Yatsuhashi said. "It looked like whoever it was tried to cover them up so we wouldn't be able to find them. If that was Edward . . ."

"He might be trying to sacrifice himself to save the tribe," Velvet finished.

"Don't worry. Fox is following the tracks; he'll find him."

Velvet looked relieved. "He'll be back soon," she said. "But

Slate says we have another problem. There's a sandstorm coming from the north, and we need to find shelter. She says there are some slot canyons just north of here, if we can get to them in time. The high walls should reduce our exposure to the windblasted sand."

"Oh good," Coco said. She hated closed spaces.

"It's the best option. Otherwise, we're liable to lose our vehicles and equipment, not to mention a lot of lives," Velvet said.

"Do you ever get the feeling that the desert is trying to kill us?" Yatsuhashi asked.

"Every second," Velvet said. "I would much rather fight an Atlesian Paladin again or a regular villain like Torchwick."

"That sounds heavenly," Coco agreed. "I'll take a human opponent over this nature nonsense any day."

Velvet led them into the camp, which was surrounded by a circle of wagons and covered with stitched-together tarps, tents, robes, and what seemed to be the shirts off people's backs. Vacuo wasn't a shirt-and-tie kind of place, but a number of men were walking around bare-chested and even the women were down to halter tops.

Focus, Coco, she thought.

The makeshift roof may have lowered the temperature by only a few degrees, but at the hottest time of day in the desert, it made a huge difference.

"How has it been here? They all seem pretty calm now."

"We've had a few rough moments, but the mood bombs have been relatively mild," Velvet said. "Maybe because Edward is getting farther away from camp."

Slate emerged from a small tent behind Velvet. "Welcome back. I knew you'd be along soon enough, but you're a sight for sore eyes." She smiled at Coco and Yatsuhashi. Then her smile faded. "What happened to Red?" she asked.

"Fox is going after Bertilak and Edward; at least we assume that's whose trail he went to follow."

The flap of the tent flew open and Carmine stepped out, ducking through the low entrance and rising to her full height. Gus stepped out gingerly after her.

"You found them?" Carmine asked. Her skin glistened and she smelled like aloe, a common sunscreen cream in Vacuo. Very nice. Coco blushed.

"We think so. Fox will bring them back," Coco said. "Any idea why they went off on their own?"

"Grandpa probably just got confused again. I'm sorry." He looked pale, sweat dotting his brow. He was shaky on his feet, like he needed to go lie down for a while. Understandable with his grandfather missing.

Carmine patted the boy on the head awkwardly. "Not your fault, kid. Bertilak must have noticed and hurried after him. Bertilak kind of does his own thing a lot of the time, if you hadn't noticed. Too often, if you ask me," Carmine said. "That's one of the drawbacks when it's just the two of you hunting Grimm, instead of a team with a strong leader to keep everyone in check. You'll see one day."

Coco looked at Velvet and Yatsuhashi. She hadn't given much thought to what would happen after they graduated. Funny how quickly she had gone from being a loner—albeit a popular one—to a leader, and now she couldn't imagine not being part of a team with her three friends. Even Shade Academy hadn't weakened their bond, despite the focus on survival and results rather than teamwork and studies. Once upon a time, she was the type of person who would flourish at Shade, but she depended on the rest of Team CFVY too much now—and she cared too much about their well-being, even over her own. They didn't teach you that sort of thing at Shade.

She wondered how Team JNPR was holding up now without Pyrrha. What was Jaune doing after losing a member of his team, a friend . . . someone he clearly cared about.

"It's time to pack it up," Slate said. "Get in the vans and drive as fast as we can. We have a storm to outrace."

"But how will Fox, Bertilak, and Grandpa find us if we start going north?" Gus asked.

"Fox has his ways," Coco said. She was more worried about him catching up to them on foot. Even in vehicles, she wasn't sure if they'd make it to these canyons in time.

She also hoped she was wrong, but she was worried about Fox out there with Bertilak and the old man. Something about all this just wasn't adding up yet.

CHAPTER TEN

The wind was rising, a hot wind, rustling Fox's hair and rushing by his ears. It seemed to be speaking to him in a whisper, and it howled in the distance. At the same time, he was finding it harder to breathe. The air felt heavier, thicker. The breeze, for the moment, felt good against his skin, and the intensity of the midday sun weakened.

He marched on, pebbles and sand rising from the desert floor and pelting his legs. He had been caught out in a storm only once before, with his uncle Copper, who had described these moments like the sand waking up. It rippled like muscles under the skin, rose in waves like an ocean tide. And like the tide, it could threaten to swallow you up, killing you and burying you all in one gesture. It would be a slow, painful, panicky death. A suffocation, nose and mouth filling with sand as you were buried alive.

Somewhere in the distance, a bird squawked a warning before it flew off in search of shelter from the sandstorm. Fox was running out of time. Edward was running out of time.

Fox couldn't get a good fix on Edward; he was tired, spurred on by desperation and adrenaline. There was definitely a mental presence ahead of him, coming in and out of Fox's awareness.

He was fortunate that he could keep his eyes squeezed shut against the sand blasting into his face, rubbing the skin raw. Even being able to see wouldn't have been much help right now, with the rising wind wiping out the trail Coco and Yatsu had spotted, as well as his own footsteps.

With his team split up and far away, with no way for them to find him, Fox suddenly felt vulnerable. It wasn't a good feeling; it reminded him too much of his childhood and the life he'd left. He hadn't been alone—really alone—a single day since he had enrolled at Beacon Academy and gone through his initiation.

At least Fox had his Scroll. He used it on a daily basis to get around whenever Coco and the others weren't in close proximity, and to mask the fact that he could sense others and place them in his mind as well as in the space around him.

He plugged Ada's tiny earpieces into his ears and switched on the Scroll.

"Tap to unlock," the Accessibility Dialog Assistant said in her mechanical, vaguely feminine voice.

Fox tapped. He slid his thumb along his most common apps on the home screen, and got it on the second try.

"Compass activated," Ada said.

"Thanks, Ada," Fox said.

"You're welcome, Fox."

Fox kept walking forward. The sand kicked up around his shins now, and the wind tugged at his clothing and hair. He raised his hands to protect his face and pressed his mouth tightly shut.

Each time he picked up a blip of consciousness ahead, he adjusted his course and tapped the screen to lock in a trajectory. So when he went several minutes without another signal from the person he was following, he instructed Ada to beep softly if he strayed too far to the left or right as he pushed on.

Beep. He heard a gentle tone in his right ear. Fox angled himself slightly left and continued.

Beep, in his left ear. He turned two degrees to the right. He just hoped whomever he was following was sticking to the same course.

And then he tripped over a pile of sand. Only when he reached down and dug, he realized it was a man huddled on the ground, his head buried in his knees. The sand had a way of quickly covering anything that wasn't moving.

"We have to keep moving," Fox said, getting a mouthful of sand in the process. He realized the wind in his ears had gotten louder, so he tried his Semblance, but it failed him. He shouted instead. "Are you all right? Can you get up? We have to keep moving."

Fox's fingers danced over the man's head. Thinning hair, tied into a ponytail. The beginnings of a beard, dusted with sand. Deep lines in his face, filled with sand. Lips dried and cracked, coated in sand.

"Edward," Fox said. "Get up. Please. We have to find shelter."

And I don't know where that is, he thought.

They were screwed.

Edward jolted awake and knocked Fox backward. Metal scraped against metal as the old Huntsman removed a weapon from his belt.

"Hyaaah!" the man shouted, coming closer to Fox. Fox lifted his arm and just deflected Edward's weapon with a spark and a ringing sound.

"Hey!" Fox shouted. "Stop! I don't want to hurt you."

He leaped lightly to his feet and backed away. It was difficult without a good bead on Edward's mind, but he paid attention to the sound of his footsteps, the way the wind sounded as it moved around an object—in this case, a person, as Edward circled Fox.

"You dragged me out here, but I'm not as weak as you thought, eh?" Edward coughed.

Fox needed more assistance. "Ada, run Cyrano protocol," he shouted. "Battle mode!"

"Activating battle mode," Ada said. It had to be his imagination, but the limited artificial intelligence sounded excited.

"Describe," Fox said.

Ada used the Scroll tucked into his belt to analyze the environment, with the help of the Scroll's camera and his earbud transceivers. "One opponent, about seventy years old. Weapon: Buckler, a small hand shield with a sharp metal edge. Update: Outer ring is removable. Update: Outer ring has been removed."

"Engage proximity alert," Fox said.

"Engaged."

Fox had to disarm Edward, preferably without injuring him.

He dashed forward. Ada's beeping let him know how close he was to his opponent, and used other audio cues to update him on the position of Edward's weapon, head, fists, feet, all on a projected x- and y-axis that extended in a five-foot radius of Fox.

Cyrano was a sophisticated program out of Atlas, experimental tech the kingdom granted older academy students access to for field testing. It had made Fox's life tremendously easier to navigate, though he often got more useful information from his teammates' running commentary when the situation allowed for it. It was designed to adapt to Fox just as he adapted to it, and they were a pretty effective team—as long as he remembered to charge his Scroll.

Fox dashed forward. When he heard a steady tone in both ears, he knew Edward was directly in front of him, and a low thrumming pulse told him where his hand holding his disc-blade was. Fox jabbed his right elbow toward it and hooked Sharp Retribution on the weapon. He pulled and twisted, yanking the disc away, but Edward held on with surprising strength.

Fox heard a gunshot and the emergency tone in his left ear made him jerk his head back. A bullet whizzed by his forehead.

"Update," Ada said. "Weapon has projectile capabilities."

"You mean it's also a gun."

Imagine that.

"Correct. Proceed with caution."

"What do you think I've been doing?"

Fox swept his leg forward and knocked Edward to the ground. The old man grunted. A fist connected with Fox's chest, but he pulled back just in time so it only made a glancing blow. He reached with his left hand, grabbed Edward's right, and pulled downward. Edward lurched forward as Fox lifted his left knee. Edward's skull cracked against it, and Edward went down.

But he didn't stay down. His weapon came up, and Fox parried it. Once, twice. Fox then took a chance and fired a shot of his own. He heard a bullet strike metal and Edward cried out in surprise. The weapon fell a few feet away and landed in the sand.

Edward dove for it. "Where is it? Where is it?"

"Sorry," Fox said. "Are you all right?"

Edward lifted his head and started to cough. "I know you, don't I?" The wind whipped his feeble voice away.

Fox breathed a sigh of relief. "Yes." Finally.

"Yatsuhashi, right?"

Fox's shoulders fell. "Close. I'm Fox Alistair. Can you stand?"

"Yes." Edward got to his feet, but only with Fox's help.

"I'm sorry about that. I hope I didn't hurt you."

"You're a formidable opponent."

"Warning: Sandstorm imminent," Ada said.

"Thank you, Ada. Disengage battle mode," Fox said.

"Who's Ada?" Edward said.

"She's the voice in my head," Fox said. "We need to find shelter."

"There were some big rocks up ahead. They were weird shapes. The big one looked like a rubber ducky Gus used to have." He paused. "Gus! Is he all right?"

"I'm sure he's fine. Do you think you can find those rocks?"

"Hold on. You can't see," Edward said.

Fox usually feigned surprise whenever someone mentioned that, as though they were telling him something he didn't know. But they didn't have time for that now.

"How did you even find me?" Edward asked.

"Just my lucky day." Fox grimaced. They were really being buffeted by the wind now. He held on tight to the old man's arm, as much to keep him close as to help steady him. "Lead on," he said.

Fox gently nudged Edward forward; he kept his hand there as pressure to keep moving, and they gradually made their way across the desert.

The wind abruptly died down and Fox felt the temperature drop.

"The sun's gone," Edward muttered.

Then, a short while later, Edward said, "Here they are," just as Ada's proximity alarm dinged softly to let Fox know he was about to walk into something solid. He moved forward slowly, hands outstretched. His fingers grazed a hard surface in front of him. He pressed his hand against the cool stone. Limestone. Patches of it were rough, others worn smooth, and it seemed to curve inward into a natural sort of lean-to. Sandstorms like this one had likely eroded it over hundreds of years; fortunately the wind was blowing from its opposing side this time. But that wouldn't matter much when the storm descended on them in earnest.

"Where are we?" Edward asked. "How did I get out here?"

"You wandered off again from the group. After evacuating Feldspar, remember?"

"That doesn't sound right. Where's Gus?" Edward asked.

"He's back with Velvet and the others. I'll get you to him as soon as this storm dies down." Fox just hoped it was one of the brief sandstorms. Some of them were known to last for days.

"No. We can't wait a moment longer." Edward stood and started to venture out. Fox grabbed his arm.

"Hold on! You have to stop doing that."

"I have to get back to them. They're all in danger."

"Everyone is in danger all the time here," Fox said.

"No," Edward said. "He can't control his ability. He'll bring them again. I can't stop it."

"His ability?" Fox frowned. Then he realized what the man was saying.

Oh no, he thought.

"You mean, *Gus* is the one who's amplifying people's emotions?" Fox said.

"Yes." Edward slumped back into Fox's arms, as though he was exhausted and all his strength had suddenly left him.

Don't lose it now, Edward, Fox thought.

"That means *your* Semblance is to block other Semblances," Fox said. Which was why he'd had a hard time tracking Edward's consciousness in the desert, and couldn't sense his mind even now.

"I've been blocking his ability since he was a small boy. But after his parents died, it became more powerful, more difficult to control. More . . . negative. And my own Semblance has been weakening. I can't keep him in check anymore. Especially when he's stressed."

"Which is all the time out here," Fox said. "Why did you two lie about this?"

"It was my idea, to protect Gus," Edward said. "If anyone figured out we were the ones causing the mood bombs and drawing the Grimm, I made him agree to tell them it was my fault."

Fox understood. If someone decided to try to stop the bombs in the most expedient way, Gus likely would have been killed. Besides, it wasn't always a good idea to reveal your Semblance to strangers. Lots of Huntsmen, like Velvet, tended to keep that information secret, to give them an edge in combat. Others, such as Yatsu, weren't proud of their ability, or didn't want others to judge them for it. And with a Semblance as dangerous as Gus's, it made sense for Edward to paint a target on his own back instead of the kid's, until they got someplace far enough away from people that it wouldn't matter anymore.

But what kind of a life could they live out there in voluntary exile? It was a waste of potential. A waste of life.

Edward was right, though. They had to get back to the evacuees. They were under a tremendous amount of stress, and with his grandfather missing, Gus was bound to lose it and set the Grimm back on their trail.

"We can make it," Fox said. "The storm's just beginning. We'll have to hurry." Maybe it wouldn't be too bad.

Edward pulled himself up again and groaned.

"Won't we get lost in the storm?" Edward asked.

Fox stepped out from the rock into the driving winds. "I never get lost," he said.

Then someone large and heavy dropped down on him from above. The proximity alarm whined in Fox's ears as he stumbled to his knees in the sand, ham-sized fists beating the side of his head.

CHAPTER ELEVEN

"Well, I'm lost," Fox sent.

Coco tossed her hands up in the air. "Fantastic." She put her gun down and sat on a rock. She leaned forward with her elbows on her knees, hands clasped, and tried to think of a plan.

They'd already had a plan. The village of Lower Cairn had sent a distress call saying they were being attacked by Grimm. They were escaping, but they needed protection. CFVY was supposed to go in, find the survivors, and bring them back to Vale. It should have been straightforward, nothing they hadn't handled before, but there had been too many Grimm. More Grimm than any of them had ever seen in a single place before. And Lower Cairn . . . it was just *gone*.

Usually when a village was attacked, even destroyed and abandoned, most of its buildings remained: houses, shops, restaurants. Ruins of temples and cities persisted all over Remnant, enduring signs that people had lived there. But Lower Cairn had been flattened. All but a couple of stone buildings on the outskirts had been reduced to rubble and splinters, like a great hand had come down and swept it aside as easily as a child knocking down a block tower. It was shocking in its implied malice and brutality, and they couldn't imagine what could cause such devastation.

That had shaken the team, of course, but it was the sight of the dozens of Ursai and Beowolves roaming the trampled streets, in broad daylight—dark parodies of the townspeople who had lived there only days before—that had really unnerved Coco, Fox, Velvet, and Yatsuhashi. Fox didn't even have any jokes that could lighten the situation.

Coco had ordered them to avoid engaging the Grimm, which felt like a defeat in itself. They were Huntsmen in training, they were supposed to fight these things. But if they began fighting, they could quickly be overwhelmed. Even so, their low spirits and anxiety had drawn the attention of some of the demons. So as they hiked toward the mountains and searched for survivors, they were harassed by an increasing number of Grimm; it was just a matter of time before there would be too many of them and they would have to abandon their mission.

So far they had only picked up fragments of a trail toward the mountains—broken branches, footprints in the mud, threads snagged on brambles in the underbrush. Then the trail ran cold and it looked like they would have to give up, but Fox had insisted that he could find the villagers with his Semblance.

"I don't get it. They should be right here." Fox sat down next to Coco.

"I guess you slightly oversold your ability to track the survivors," Coco said.

He shrugged. *"I know someone's out there, but the signal's weak. I think the mountain passes are causing interference, like the buildings back in Vale. Either that, or . . ."*

"What?" Velvet asked.

"There aren't enough survivors to get a good fix on them," Fox sent.

"The longer it takes to locate them, the fewer there'll be," Coco said.

"Maybe we should call it in," Fox said.

"Not yet," Coco said.

"We've been out here for ten days. We should have been back by now."

Professor Port had finally contacted them and chewed Coco out for not reporting in. She had snapped that they were in a precarious position, with Grimm all around them—it wasn't exactly convenient to talk. And as if to punctuate her point, CFVY had been attacked by a pair of Beringels, incredibly strong and vicious ape-like Grimm. They had to cut off the call with Port, with barely enough time for Velvet to ask him to tell Yang and Weiss that they were going to be too late to set up for the Beacon Dance. He had spluttered and told them to keep their minds on the job, that there were more important things than a dance. If they couldn't handle it, he would be sending an extraction team.

Velvet and Yatsuhashi looked around. They looked up into the sparse trees and the rocky terrain rising on either side of the narrow passage they were in. There was no place even a single person could hide, let alone a large group of people.

Suddenly a Creep rounded the corner and rushed for Velvet. She was so startled she stepped backward, stumbled over a rock, and went down, barely rolling out of the way of its attack. She scrambled up into a crouch as the two-legged Grimm skidded, turned, and faced her. There was no time for her to pull a weapon. She squinted, estimating the best time to jump to clear it on its next charge.

It barreled toward her, faster than she had expected, faster than it should be possible for something like that to move.

"I hate these things!" Yatsuhashi shouted. Then his great-sword smashed into it, with enough concussive force to not only definitively obliterate it but to make the ground shake and fracture the bedrock in an eight-foot radius around it. The blast sent Velvet tumbling back head over heels. A flying piece of stone or skull smacked her in the forehead. She lay on her back, winded and dazed.

"Velvet!" Yatsuhashi dropped his sword with a heavy clang and rushed to her side.

"I'm okay!" she said.

"I'm sorry," he said. "I'm just . . ." He frowned. "This is starting to get to me."

She put a hand on his cheek. "It's all right." None of them had had much of a chance to rest, let alone sleep. The constant barrage of Grimm was getting to her, too. She knew Yatsu needed time to re-center himself, to take control of his anxiety.

"It's not all right. You got hurt," he said.

"I'm more annoyed that you took my kill. Again," she teased.

"I wanted to help."

"I know."

Yatsuhashi stood and reached down to pull her up.

"Seriously? What was that?" Coco asked. "Velvet, pay more attention!"

"What?" Velvet said, shocked.

"Have you noticed we're in hostile territory?"

"Of course, but—"

"Then how did you let a Creep sneak up on you like that?"

"Hey, go easy," Yatsuhashi said. "We're all right."

"And you," Coco went on. "You went a little overboard on that kill. Save your strength. There's no one to show off for out here."

"He didn't do that on purpose," Velvet said.

"Then he needs to control himself better," Coco said.

"He knows that." Velvet's nostrils flared. "He spends every moment of every day trying to control his strength. He doesn't need you to tell him what to do. None of us do. Look where it's gotten us!"

A stunned silence fell on the group.

"I'm your leader," Coco said.

"Leading means more than bossing us around," Fox sent. *"Or getting on our cases when we fail to live up to your absurdly high expectations."*

"It's not like you guys have come up with any better ideas," Coco said.

"How can we when you never even offer us the chance?" Yatsuhashi said. "If you want us to trust you, then you need to trust us."

Velvet nodded. "We're a team, aren't we?"

"Yeah, but I'm responsible for keeping you alive," Coco said.

"We're supposed to keep each other alive," Fox sent. *"And we share the re—"* He held up a hand. *"Shhh. Listen."*

"What is it?" Coco sent back.

Fox started walking down the mountain path, so softly his footsteps didn't make a sound. Velvet's rabbit ears twitched and rotated, orienting on the sound. *"I heard it, too,"* she sent. *"Follow us."*

As they went deeper into the passage, the others heard it, too—faint voices, calling for help. The voices led Fox to a narrow crevice in the side of the mountain, maybe one and a half feet across.

"Hello?" Velvet called inside.

There was quiet for a moment, then several voices, accompanied by cheering and sobbing.

"One at a time," Velvet said. "We can't hear you."

"Thank the Brothers that you found us," a man's voice called. "We're trapped underground. Part of the tunnel caved in a minute ago."

Coco glared at Yatsuhashi. He rubbed the back of his head sheepishly.

"Are you from Lower Cairn?" Coco asked.

"Yes! The Grimm attacked, destroyed the village. It was so fast."

"How many are with you?" Velvet asked.

There was no answer.

"Hello?" she called again.

"There's only six of us." More sobbing drifted up from the cave.

"Only six." Coco slumped to the ground beside the crack in the mountain.

"Over two hundred people lived in Lower Cairn," Velvet said.

"My gods," Fox sent.

"Maybe there are more survivors . . ." Yatsu looked away down the mountain path. It was enough of a miracle that they had found these. But that made it even more important to come to them.

"Are you hurt?" Velvet asked.

"My wife sprained her ankle, and my son needs his medicine," the man called. "And we're very hungry and thirsty."

"We're coming to you," Velvet said. "We'll get you out."

She removed her camera and started to lower herself through the opening.

Coco put a hand on her shoulder. "Hold on. What are you doing?"

"We can't waste any more time," Velvet said. "This is what we came here for."

Coco shook her head. "Velvet. You're hurt," she said softly.

"I'm fine." Velvet briefly closed her eyes as a wave of nausea and dizziness washed over her. "No one else can squeeze through this opening."

"I can make it wider." Yatsuhashi reached for his sword.

"You're more likely to finish the job and bring the tunnel

down the rest of the way," Coco said. "I'm just as small as you, Velvet. Shorter if you don't count the ears. Maybe a little thinner, too."

"Hey," Velvet said.

"Besides, the team will need you and Fox's hearing to find another entrance and locate me and the survivors. I'll go. This is all my fault anyway, right?"

"I didn't mean that," Velvet said.

"You did, and you were right." She looked around. "Your Semblance led us right, Fox. The survivors were exactly where you thought they were, only they were under us. I'm sorry for doubting you."

Fox nodded.

"When we get out of here, we should probably all have a long talk," Coco said. "We have some things to work out."

Velvet crawled out of the crevice. Coco peered inside. She took off her sunglasses.

"Sure is dark down there, isn't it?" She hoped no one heard the trembling in her voice. The others pretended they didn't. She put her glasses on Velvet. "Hold on to these for me. Don't scratch them."

Coco scraped, pushed, and pulled her way through the tiny opening, sucking in her stomach and holding her breath. She slid down a steep slope, sending rocks and pebbles falling with her, and dropped down, much farther than she had expected. She looked up at the sliver of light about ten feet above her head. There was no getting back up there.

"The only way out is through," she said. Her voice echoed eerily around her.

The light disappeared briefly, and a second later Coco caught her bag. She immediately felt better.

"You all right?" Fox sent.

Coco's hands shook as she fumbled with her Scroll. She'd had a phobia for dark and enclosed spaces ever since she was young. She and her brothers had been playing hide-and-seek, and Coco had hidden in a small cabinet under the sink. After she had waited a long time for one of them to find her, she tried to crawl out to see what had happened to Mate and Toma—but the door wouldn't budge. It had gotten stuck, and they didn't hear her calls for help or the pounding of her bare feet against the door as she tried to get it open. Her father eventually found her after she had begun banging on the pipes under the sink and the sound traveled down to his workshop. Later, she found out her younger brother, Mate, *had* looked for her in that cabinet, but he'd given up when he couldn't open it and assumed she had run off in the middle of the game.

Coco's Scroll lit up. "Weak signal," the screen read. She turned on the flashlight function and light flooded the cavern. Now it wasn't quite so dark, but the space was only a few feet across. She couldn't tell how far along it went. It was cool and wet down there, and dust drifted down from the ceiling with the occasional pebble dropping and clattering against stone.

"Over here!" the man's voice called. The echo bounced around her and magnified, making it difficult to pinpoint the source.

"That was a one-way trip," Coco sent, allowing Fox to broadcast her words to Velvet and Yatsuhashi. *"I'll have to find the survivors and another exit."*

"We'll look from outside, and make a new opening if we have to," Fox sent.

"Drop my pack before you go."

It once again got darker and then Coco's backpack landed on the rock in front of her. There wasn't much food and water left, since they'd been here longer than planned, but it was more than the survivors would have eaten in days.

Coco moved down the passage, trying not to think about how much closer the walls were getting the deeper she went. She splashed through shallow pools and water dripped on her face. Water must have carved these caves out over centuries, which meant there must be another opening in the other direction, which let water flow in during heavy rains. Maybe it even opened onto the river.

She found the Lower Cairn survivors in a hollowed-out dead end.

"I'm Coco," she said. "I'm from Beacon Academy."

"Oh, you're a student?" the man asked. "We thought you were a Huntress."

"I'm a Huntress in training," Coco said. "But we're the best at Beacon."

"Thank you for coming." He introduced himself as Linus Gray, and the other survivors: his wife, Rhea; his son, Leander; and his three daughters, Phoebe, Helen, and Clio.

One family was all that was left of Lower Cairn, Coco realized. She and CFVY had heard of worse outcomes in their history lessons with Dr. Oobleck: Some of her classmates had been the lone survivors of a Grimm attack. A common motivation for people to train as Huntsmen was for revenge, because they had nothing more to lose, or because they wanted to make sure no one else had to suffer the same fate.

Linus and his family eagerly ate the meager supplies Coco had brought and finished the water in her canteen. Then it was time to move on. As she led them past the crack she'd come through, she kicked herself. She shouldn't have been using the light the whole time—the screen's glow was dimming. But she hadn't wanted to go without it, either, worried about what might be waiting in the darkness. Now she didn't have a choice; she would have to push on, fears or no fears. Knowing the family of six was depending on her and her team helped keep her moving.

"We found a way in and we're on our way toward you," Fox said.

"Great," Coco said. "My friends are coming," she told the family.

They sped up, until the battery on her Scroll died. Then they preceded more slowly along the passage. Coco was glad it was dark, because the family couldn't see how scared she was, stumbling and helpless in the cavern.

"How are you doing?" Fox asked.

"Fine." Coco was glad she didn't have to speak aloud; he definitely would have heard her voice shaking. *"Lost our light, but there seems to be only one way to go. Shouldn't we be meeting up soon?"*

"Can you try making some noise so we know how far you are?" Yatsuhashi sent.

Coco saw a soft orange light ahead. *"Oh, never mind, I see your light,"* she said. "Come on," she called over her shoulder.

They hurried toward the light. The path opened up into a larger cavern. Somewhere, water plopped rhythmically into a pool.

"Light? We don't have a light," Fox said. *"Yatsu's following Velvet, and I'm using my Semblance."*

Coco froze. "Go back!" she whispered urgently to the family.

But it was too late. The light above their heads, like a golden lantern, was joined by two glowing red slits in the darkness.

"A Death Stalker!" Coco shouted.

Rhea screamed and her children began crying.

"We hear you," Fox said. *"Did you say 'Death Stalker'?"*

"Yes! Hurry!"

The orange light moved farther away, then it zipped toward Coco. She was mesmerized by it, enough that she didn't move, until someone pushed her aside and she fell into the cavern wall.

Linus grunted and cursed. The Grimm scorpion's tail had pierced his leg, pinning him to the ground. Rhea grabbed his arm and pulled as the Death Stalker advanced, claws clacking.

"Damn," Coco said as she opened up her gun and tracked the Death Stalker. Then she fired.

The gunshots were deafening. The tunnels shook, dirt and stone raining down around them.

"Stop!" Rhea shrieked. "You'll bring it all down on top of us!"

A rock slab fell a foot in front of Coco. She stopped firing and stumbled backward, coughing. If she had boosted the impact of their bullets, they would probably all be dead. She didn't even think she'd hit the Death Stalker—she had been firing blindly out of panic.

She blinked her eyes clear of sweat and grit. She couldn't see the Death Stalker. Her finger trembled on the trigger. She closed her weapon up into a handbag; it was going to have to be hand-to-hand combat.

She fought to control her breathing. Then something flickered in her peripheral vision. She jumped and whirled, bringing her bag around. A claw came at her from the darkness and she froze. At the last second she swung her bag up, whacking the claw out of the way. She spun away from it, losing track of the Death Stalker's location again. She had to calm down and listen.

"Coco, we're here," Fox sent. *"Don't shoot us."*

"Are you okay?" Yatsuhashi asked. *"We heard the gunfire."*

The rest of the team had arrived. And they had brought light. Coco flinched as a flashlight illuminated the space—

No, not a flashlight, but Velvet and a hard-light weapon, a copy of Yatsuhashi's sword. That was better.

The cavern was wider than it had seemed, but there wasn't a lot of room to maneuver. Fox hacked at the Death Stalker's legs with his weapons, doing little more than distracting it. Yatsuhashi pulled the stinger out of Linus's leg, and the man crawled away with his wife's help. Velvet slashed at the Death Stalker's tail with her glowing sword. It scraped against the Grimm's hard exoskeleton, again doing little damage, but getting it to turn toward her.

Fox and Velvet traded off blows, keeping the Death Stalker moving back and forth between them.

"When I fire, run!" Coco said.

"Hold on—" Yatsuhashi said.

She fired, drowning out whatever he was going to say. This time she didn't hold back, and the Death Stalker crumbled under her explosive rounds.

Unfortunately, so did the tunnel.

"Run!" she said again, unable to hear her own voice over the falling stone and the ringing in her ears.

They ran.

"Careful, it's slippery up ahead," Fox said.

Coco ran and slipped up a muddy slope, the stone of the cave giving way to soft earth, bathed in moonlight. She came out on the bank of a stream, just above the rushing water. Velvet was just ahead of her, knee-deep in the middle of the stream with Linus and his family. They were surrounded by Ursai.

Velvet was now brandishing a pair of hard-light daggers.

"Why'd you pick those, Velvet?" Coco muttered. She needed to get better at sizing up her enemies and choosing the best weapon and fighting style to take them down.

An Ursai snapped at Velvet and she smacked it in the side of the head with one dagger, knocking it back. It shook its head, lunged for her again, and she threw the second dagger into its open mouth. The glowing blade protruded from the back of its head. The red faded from its eyes and it went down.

Velvet turned and tilted her head at Coco, eyebrows raised.

Another Ursa attacked. Velvet parried its blows with her remaining dagger. Fox sped ahead of Yatsuhashi and Coco and took down an Ursa with a series of jabs and slashes from his arm blades. Yatsuhashi skewered the one beside it and tossed it away from its pack.

The refugees ran through the opening in the ring of Grimm toward Coco.

"What are you doing?" she hollered. She laid down covering fire as three Ursai pursued the family. Linus fell, and Rhea and Leander went back for him. She yelled something at the children and they ran on.

Coco picked one of the Grimm off, then another. But then her gun clicked. She needed to reload.

"No!" she shouted as the third Ursa grabbed Linus in its teeth. The man howled, and then he went silent. Rhea collapsed to her knees, screaming.

The Ursa turned on her, but a glowing hard-light dagger caught it in the back. It spun and faced Velvet as the blade vanished. She fiddled with her camera for a moment before summoning another weapon: a re-creation of Sky Lark's halberd. She lowered the axe-head and fired rounds at the Ursa, giving Rhea time to run away.

The kids passed Coco as she reloaded and joined Velvet in firing on the Ursa. They huddled behind her, silent and wide-eyed, until their mother joined them.

"Get away from here," Coco shouted. More Grimm were descending into the valley, boxing in CFVY and the family they were trying to protect.

"We can handle them," Coco said. Because they had to. Then the ground rumbled behind her.

Coco turned. She looked up. And up. And up. For the first time, she thought she was about to die.

On the other side of the stream, Velvet froze.

"That sounds bad," Fox said.

"It's very bad. A Goliath," Yatsuhashi said.

The shadowy Goliath lumbered up the bank of the river, looming over Coco and the family, who looked tiny in comparison. Its bone-white faceplate was streaked with red, and it had one massive, curved tusk—the other had been broken halfway, but the splintered end was just as sharp and deadly looking.

Now they knew what must have destroyed Lower Cairn. And it was here to finish the job.

The Gray children shouted. Velvet snapped out of it and watched as the family scrambled back into the cave.

"No!" Coco shouted.

The Goliath advanced toward the stream. Coco fired her gun at it, but it didn't seem fazed at all. It slid down the slope, crushing the cave entrance and the people inside.

Velvet dropped to her knees. "Oh no. No," she said. The halberd fell to the ground and faded away.

Yatsuhashi ran toward the Goliath, sword raised.

"Hold on," Fox sent. He looked up.

A Bullhead descended toward them, firing heavy artillery at the Goliath, pushing it back. Professor Port crouched in the open door of the transport, firing his blunderbuss at the Grimm around Velvet and Fox.

"Get in!" he shouted.

"Coco, Yatsuhashi, we have to go," Fox sent.

Velvet shook her head, climbing to her feet.

"No, we have to fight." She flipped through her camera, searching for the right weapon that could solve everything.

"We have to leave," Fox sent. He pulled on her arm. *"We have to* live.*"*

She shoved him away. "No! We can still save them. We—"

"They're gone," Fox said. *"I can't—I can't sense them anymore."*

Velvet choked back a sob and followed him.

"I don't retreat," Coco said. *"I'll hold them off."*

"Don't be stupid," Fox said.

Yatsuhashi winced. He looked at Coco.

"Save it. There's no convincing her," Yatsuhashi said.

"Thank you." Coco started to head back toward the fight. Then she felt herself swept up in Yatsuhashi's arms.

"Yatsuhashi! Put me down!"

Yatsuhashi winced as Coco's blows landed hard on his

shoulders—she was too strong for him to hold on to for long. He ran toward the Bullhead, which laid down covering fire that cut through the scattering Ursai. The Goliath had turned and was walking away slowly, as if they weren't even worth paying attention to anymore.

Yatsuhashi hurled Coco into the airship and jumped in after her. As it flew up and banked toward home, they looked down at the ruins of Lower Cairn.

"We failed," Velvet said.

CHAPTER TWELVE

From inside the wagon racing across the desert, Velvet watched as the blue sky turned a sickly orange-gray. The sun was a dull bright orb overhead. The van shuddered as the wind rocked it. The sand outside was undulating. It drifted across the peaks of dunes around them, rising and whirling in flurries around their group. It was magical. It was terrifying.

"We aren't going to make it," Slate said.

"We will," Coco said.

Slate tapped the dashboard. "We're almost out of fuel. We don't have enough to get to the canyon. We'll have to lash the vehicles together and shelter inside them." She squinted. "But this looks like a really bad one."

They trundled along while they considered all their options, which seemed fairly limited.

"What if we could get above the sand?" Velvet asked.

"You have an airbus on call we don't know about?" Coco asked.

Velvet pointed. "I was thinking about climbing that plateau."

"I know this desert, kid, and there are no plateaus in these parts," Slate said.

"Then what is that?"

Yatsu looked in the direction Velvet was gazing. It was hazy out there, visibility dropping as the air filled with sand. He shaded his eyes and waited for a clearer view.

"She's right, there's something out there. It's huge, with a flat top, and four, no—five outcroppings," Yatsu said. He blinked. "But . . . I think it's moving."

Slate pulled a pair of binoculars from a compartment near her seat. Velvet noticed a pistol tucked in the back before she closed the door.

"Where?" Slate asked.

Velvet pointed.

Slate's mouth fell open.

"Well, I'll be. That's no plateau! That's a flatback slider!"

"A what?" Coco asked. "You mean it's alive?"

"Alive, and very rare in these parts. I've only seen it once in my life, when I was a little girl. From a distance. It could even be the same one."

"But what is it?" Velvet asked.

"A sand turtle," Slate said. "One big enough to ride on."

"You mean a tortoise?" Yatsuhashi asked.

Slate gave him a look. "If I'd meant a tortoise, I would have said tortoise, young man. That there is a turtle. It's not walking on the sand, it's swimming in it. And it looks like it's trying to get away from the sandstorm, same as us. It'll travel for a bit and then retract its head and wait it out. It's so big, it will hardly notice it, but the sand has shaped it, too, over time, just like the rocks and canyons."

The sandstorm was coming from the other side of the turtle, driving it northeast, along the same path they were taking.

"You said it's big enough to ride on?" Velvet asked.

Yatsu stared at her. "You're bonkers," he said.

"We're desperate," Coco corrected him. "And I happen to think this is a terrific idea."

"Me too," Slate said. "The sandstorms typically reach around fifty to sixty feet—we could ride above the storm easily."

"And how high up is the back of that turtle?"

"Probably one hundred feet." Slate fell silent, considering. Then she yanked the wheel, angling the van to the right. "We might have enough fuel to intercept it, and I've always wanted to see one up close."

The other vans adjusted course to follow them, a long line stretching behind them, sending up a sand cloud of their own. Velvet had to admire Slate—her people were following her without question. Velvet glanced at Coco. Coco smiled.

"Are we doing this?" Velvet asked.

"Oh. We are doing this!" Coco said.

They gradually caught up to the turtle. When they were running on fumes, they passed in front and clambered out of the vehicle to wait for it. The rest of the caravan joined them, gaping at the humongous creature as they crawled from the vans.

It was slow-moving, maybe going ten miles an hour. It was hard work swimming through sand, even with a storm at your back.

Carmine approached with Gus; they'd been traveling in the van behind Slate's.

"What are we doing? And what fresh headache is that?" Carmine gazed at the turtle drifting toward them with a mixture of awe and terror.

Slate caught her up on their plan.

Gus's eyes went wide. "You're climbing it?"

"*We're* climbing it," Coco said.

"Crazy enough to work. Who's going up first?" Carmine asked. "Any of us could make it up that thing without much trouble, but what about them?" She swept a hand out to include the townspeople clustering and muttering. The sand was swirling around their ankles now, already piled up around the wheels of the wagons. They wouldn't be moving them anytime soon, even if they had enough fuel.

"Good point. We'll have to send someone up to secure some lines to get everyone else to the top," Coco said. "Are these turtles dangerous?"

"*Now* you ask. I don't think so. I hear they're only dangerous if they see you," Slate said. "Fortunately they have terrible vision, and they usually ignore tiny, short-lived things like us. She may be as old as the Great War."

"So this will work," Coco said.

"I've heard of some people who camp on them for days or weeks. There's no better way to travel through the desert, if you're lucky enough to find one. Just seeing one is considered a good omen."

"We can use a good omen right now," Coco said.

"I'll go first," Velvet cut in.

Coco considered her. Velvet braced herself for the protest, the insistence that she go instead.

But Coco grinned. "Go."

Velvet loaded her belt with tough but light ropes that had been intended for tying the vans together for shelter. If all went well, they would be much safer above the storm.

She bounced on her heels, getting ready to climb as the front of the turtle slowly slid past them. Slate was right, it never even looked down or took notice of them. They were basically as insignificant as bugs.

"You sure about this, V?" Yatsu asked.

She nodded. "Give me a boost?"

"You got it."

Yatsu stepped back from the turtle a bit and drew his sword. He held it in both hands and slung the broad, flat side of the blade over his shoulder like a baseball bat.

"Good luck," Coco said.

"It's supposed to be good luck to see one, isn't it?" Velvet said. "So climbing it must be really lucky."

"I hope so."

Gus smiled up at Velvet. "I'm worried, but I think you can do it."

"Thanks." She ruffled Gus's curly hair, and he ducked his head.

Then she jumped up onto Yatsu's shoulder and walked along his greatsword. She crouched on the flat blade close to the tip.

"Ready!" Velvet called.

Yatsu swung, low and then high—and fast. As his arms fully extended with the sword pointing straight out, Velvet launched herself, using the momentum to carry herself twenty-five feet up. She landed on one of the turtle's massive flippers.

Already a quarter of the way up, Velvet thought. *Thanks, Yatsu.*

She could barely tell that she and the turtle were moving but when she looked down, she saw her friends following along beside it at a brisk pace. They wouldn't be able to keep that going forever, and wind was still picking up. Velvet's face itched as sand brushed against it.

The giant flipper she stood on was firm. She knelt and pressed her hand against it. It was definitely warm and alive, but the creases in the tough skin, which had the texture of a rubber tire, were filled with sand and rocks. The sand turtle was the color of the desert it swam in, rich oranges and yellows and reds. She felt the powerful strength of the animal as its muscles worked to propel it through the shifting earth below.

As Velvet raced up the flipper, she thought that racing up a gargantuan turtle swimming in the desert had to be the most exciting thing she had ever done. Her speed carried her to the lip of the turtle's shell. She grabbed it, turned herself around, and then flipped her legs up and over so she was standing on the edge.

The obsidian shell was worn down here, almost glasslike. She was maybe forty feet up now, still on the edge of where sandstorms would have blasted it smooth. The dim sun glinted off it, and Velvet saw her image reflected in the surface, warped like in a fun house mirror, so she appeared shorter and wider—a cartoonish version of herself.

It was slippery, so she had to jump to catch a handhold; higher up, the shell was pockmarked and pitted, the black-and-gray coloration around faded by exposure to the sun. Then there were natural ridges and joints that made it straightforward but arduous work to climb.

Slow and steady now, she thought. Falling would not only likely injure her but also delay her progress, and they were nearly out of time.

She was above the storm line now, and the air felt lighter and fresher than it did below. The full heat of the sun returned, and the sky was once again blue. She glanced down as she moved upward and couldn't see the ground through the thick soup of hot wind and sand swirling below her.

And then she crested the shell and sprawled on her back for a moment, catching her breath. She sat up and looked out at the desert. On one side, the thick, cauliflower clouds of sand were almost upon them. Below her, the ground was still obscured in a dismal layer of sand and dust. She hoped her friends and the townspeople were okay.

And farther out, the desert looked as it usually did, untouched and unbothered by anything happening here and now. The desert was old and it would outlast all of them, all of the people Velvet knew or would ever know. It wasn't uncaring; it was indifferent. Everything that they held dear and struggled for, the battles with Grimm, with other kingdoms, with Cinder Fall and the White Fang and their mysterious allies—none of that mattered to Vacuo, the desert or the creatures who roamed it.

Velvet found the thought sobering. It gave her some perspective on what had happened at Beacon and ever since. No matter what she did, whether she lived or died, the desert would always abide.

But it all mattered to her, and the people below who were counting on her. She wandered the sun-bleached surface of the shell, as flat and stable as any plateau, and blissfully free of sand. Astonishingly, there were abandoned tents here, evidence of campfires, and even trash. Something must have happened to the people who left this stuff up here, as Vacuans were typically more respectful and less wasteful than anyone else.

She poked her head into one of the tents and grimaced. She had found the last people to scale this monstrous beast: a couple lying on worn pallets, reduced to skeletons by birds or insects, still wearing the threadbare clothing they had died in.

Velvet closed the flap and backed away. She tripped over something.

"Clumsy," she said. But what had she tripped over?

The center of the shell had a number of pitons driven into it. *Perfect!* she thought.

She hoped it hadn't hurt the turtle whenever that was done, and she hoped it wouldn't hurt if she used them to secure her ropes.

She tied off the ends of two long lines and then returned to the edge. She threw them over the side and watched as they arced out and tumbled through the rising layer of blowing sand. She felt like she was fishing.

One line went taut, then the other. They had hold of them.

Velvet continued to explore the shell. It was about an acre in size, plenty of room for all the settlers and then some. She worked her way to the front and watched the back of the turtle's head as it slowly bobbed backward and forward with its motion. Watching it made her feel slightly queasy, so she looked past it.

The sand on the horizon was moving in concentric circles, almost too slowly to detect, like the gradual motion of a clock's hands. The wild country was dotted with clusters of wagons and tents, but nothing as large as Feldspar had been. She saw an oasis far to the east, perhaps the one that Carmine and Bertilak had talked about. She saw the canyons to the west, their original destination. There were patches of green scrub dotting the landscape, belying the desert as a lifeless place. Birds winged in the distance.

Vacuo could look beautiful, it turned out, when looked at from above.

And there, in the distance, a four-level pyramidal structure rose up above the desert: Shade Academy.

She didn't feel the same way looking at it as when she thought of Beacon Tower, but she had been living there for more than a year, and the familiarity was reassuring. She even missed it, she supposed.

Velvet's Scroll buzzed on her belt. She grabbed it and saw Coco's picture. She answered.

"Hey," Velvet said. "I guess we're close enough to Shade's CCT tower to get a signal."

"It's . . . weak down here, but hopefully . . . enough." Coco's voice was breaking up.

Velvet hurried back to the lines she had tossed over. A woman's head appeared over the edge of the shell. Velvet reached down and helped her climb up.

"I've got it." The woman pushed away Velvet's hand as soon as she was standing on the shell and walked away from her.

"You're welcome," Velvet said. *I only climbed up here and tossed you a rope to save your life and everything.*

Uh-oh, Velvet thought.

She looked over and saw more people emerging from the dust below, ascending by holding on to the rope and walking up the side slowly. They were arguing and complaining, not acting at all like people who were in the midst of a miraculous rescue.

"Are you just going to stand there?" A red-haired woman stretched a hand out. Amaranth again, and her son, in a sling wrapped to her back.

Velvet took her hand and pulled her up.

"You okay?" Velvet asked.

"Pffpt," Amaranth said. She unwrapped Ash from her back. "Wasn't it enough that I carried you inside me for nine months? I wish you'd hurry and carry your own weight."

Velvet's eyebrows shot up.

"Uh, Coco? Everything okay down there?"

Coco cursed at her. "What do you think?" she asked.

"I guess Fox came back with Edward," Velvet said.

"What . . . you say that?" Coco asked.

"He's not?"

"Haven't seen them yet."

"The folks up here are kind of moody," Velvet said.

"They're outright fighting down here," Coco said.

"If Edward isn't back, what's making everyone act up like this again?"

"It could just be the stress of facing a deadly sandstorm and the prospect of climbing to the top of a mythic beast," Coco said. "I mean, that's kind of putting me on edge."

Velvet looked out onto the horizon again. There was another dust cloud out there, coming from the south, back the way they'd come.

"I think we have a situation developing," Velvet said.

"Another one? What else?"

Velvet snapped a photo with her Scroll and sent it to Coco.

"Another sandstorm?" she asked.

A moment passed. Then Slate came on the phone with Coco.

"Storms don't move like that," Slate said. "Looks like a Blind Worm to me."

The fear in Slate's voice was unlike anything Velvet had yet heard from the leader.

Something leaped out of the small cloud—a long, black, spiky worm thing, with a fiery red eye in the center of its head, which also featured a circular maw with razor-sharp teeth.

So, not blind, then. But it was the largest Grimm she had ever seen, easily as wide as a Nevermore from wing to wing and the length of six Goliaths.

The Blind Worm landed back in the sand, causing another cloud to ripple out. It then continued to burrow toward them— toward the largest source of negative emotions for miles around.

"Get up here!" Velvet said. "Get everyone up here now!"

"We're working on it," Coco said. "Although maybe we should stay on the ground after all if we're about to be attacked."

"Everyone else will be safer up here," Velvet said. "If we can't defend our position, we'll engage the Grimm and draw it away from the turtle and the group. But the most important thing is getting the others out of harm's way."

"Good call," Coco said. "But are you really suggesting we fight a giant worm on the back of a giant turtle?"

Velvet steeled herself for Coco to shoot it down as another silly notion.

"That's the idea," Velvet said.

Coco smiled. "Sounds like fun."

CHAPTER THIRTEEN

Fox was down.

He lay with his face in the sand, his head throbbing. His right eye was swollen shut. He couldn't breathe.

Something heavy—*someone* heavy—had gotten the jump on him. And now they were gloating.

"Get up," the voice said. "So I can finish you off fair and square."

It was Bertilak Celadon.

Sand and wind roared around them. The sand was already piling up on Fox; if he waited much longer, he would be buried.

Fox pushed himself up on his hands and shook his head. The earbud fell out of his left ear. He scooped it up, but he could tell it was broken. His right earbud was fritzing, fading in and out as Ada tried to feed him information on the man who was trying to kill him.

"Opponent: Six feet six inches tall. Two hundred and seventy-five pounds. Very fit. Weapons: Ball mace. Update: Spiked ball mace. Update: Spiked ball mace with chain. Likely projectile capability." A bang, and then the sand exploded in front of Fox.

"You think?" Fox muttered.

Fox's Semblance was fading in and out, too, which explained why he hadn't been able to detect Bertilak's mind before he could attack.

Fox's mouth was full of sand. He got up. He spat and wiped his mouth with the back of his hand.

"You call ambushing me 'fair and square'?" Fox said.

"Over here." Fox turned to follow the sound of Bertilak's voice. The man was circling him in the sand.

His Scroll's proximity alert was going haywire because of the sand blowing around them, decreasing visibility and messing with the motion sensors.

There was an old saying in Vacuo: "Listen to the desert." It was meant on a philosophical level, that those who became one with the desert could survive in it. It also highlighted the fact that if you truly paid attention, you could hear—and see—that the desert wasn't as lifeless as it appeared to be.

Fox tore the earbuds out of his ears and stuffed them in his pocket. He listened to the desert.

When he concentrated, he thought he could hear Bertilak moving. He even might be able to judge the Huntsman's position from the sound of sand flying into him. Strangely, it reminded Fox of raindrops hitting the windowpane in his room at Beacon.

"What are you planning for Edward, Bertilak?" Fox asked.

Bertilak laughed. "Trying to keep me talking so you can keep track of me?"

Fox oriented on him again and confirmed that listening to the sand around them was effective as a crude sensor.

Bertilak rushed toward him. Fox backed up in time and brought his arm blades down in time to deflect a blow from Bertilak's mace. He grabbed for where he thought the chain was, connected with it, and pulled, but it slipped out of his hands. Something sharp dug into Fox's left forearm.

Bertilak's mace dragged in the sand, splitting Fox's attention and making it harder to pinpoint where Bertilak and his weapon were.

"Why would you kidnap a defenseless old man?"

"Defenseless?" Edward protested.

Fox turned slowly in the sand, following Bertilak's motion, so the Huntsman would know he could follow him whether he was talking or not. Meanwhile, he kept trying to send a message to Edward: "*Stop blocking our Semblances. I need to be able to see him. I need to be able to talk with you, mind to mind.*"

"My boss is interested in people with powerful Semblances," Bertilak said. "Like someone who can create mood bombs and trigger Grimm attacks. But it looks like I got the wrong guy. I thought something was up with those two. Well played, old man."

"You work for me!" Edward said.

Bertilak laughed. "We only convinced you to hire us so you would trust us and we could stay close until it was time to deliver you."

"You were taking him west. But you wanted to go to the city this whole time?" Fox said.

"Unfortunately, we got saddled with protecting every damn settlement we ended up at. We've been trying to get the Caspians away from the main group, but Edward is pretty stubborn."

"Hey, who's your boss, anyway?"

"You don't know them, but judging by your team's abilities, they probably have a nice fat file on you," Bertilak said.

"That's creepy," Fox said.

"I don't care about Edward," Bertilak said. "But I can't have you trying to stop me."

"You're going after Gus next," Fox realized.

"Believe it or not, he'll be safer with us, and all of you will be safer without him around. Don't worry, we won't even *charge you*!"

Bertilak lunged forward and punched Fox in his left side before he could react. Fox bent over and covered his side. He staggered away, spinning around to make sure he was facing Bertilak again. Where he had last heard Bertilak, anyway.

The problem was, he didn't know the range of Bertilak's weapon. He couldn't dodge bullets, either. Right now, Bertilak was playing with him.

Fox's legs were swept out from under him and he fell hard on his back. He rolled away, coughing on sand. Frustrated, he zipped toward Bertilak and slashed out with his arm blades. His left blade glanced off metal, but the right made contact, and Bertilak bellowed with pain and rage. Bertilak grabbed Fox's ankle and flung him away.

"Have to save Gus. Have to save Gus. Have to save Gus." It took Fox a moment to realize that he was picking up on Edward's thoughts. The channel was open, which meant he could now communicate with the older man. Which meant—

Fox focused and fixed on Bertilak's position, his consciousness a presence in Fox's mind, easy to pick out in the barren wasteland. The only other person close by was Edward, his thoughts sputtering and sparking but holding together. Beyond, Fox picked up on other, smaller, slighter minds, a sort of background hum of the desert creatures sheltering from the storm under the sand, in hidden crevices and natural hollows in the rock. Farther out, Fox felt the faint suggestion of other people, that tiny, phantom connection with Coco, Yatsuhashi, and Velvet was enough to urge him on.

"Edward! Listen, it's Fox," he sent.

"Fox?"

"I need your help. If I can't see what Bertilak is doing, I can't fight him."

"The storm is pretty bad now. I can't see more than two feet in front of me."

That was good to know. If Bertilak couldn't see Fox, either, they were more or less on even ground.

"Hold on, I just spotted him," Edward sent.

"What's the range on his weapon?" Fox sent. He climbed back to his feet and headed toward Bertilak. The man had stopped moving. What was he waiting for?

"He can send the spiked ball on his mace out about seven feet," Edward said. *"Careful, though—it also fires bullets. But he can only load one at a time, and he's low on ammo."*

"Good. Anything else?"

"Yeah, he's a real bastard."

"Even I can see that," Fox sent.

As Fox approached Bertilak, it seemed to be getting hotter and hotter. The sandstorm was still raging around them, though, the sun all but obscured in the sky, so what was causing this heat? It was radiating in waves—from where Bertilak stood. The closer Fox got to him, the hotter it was.

So that's his Semblance, Fox thought. He thought back to moments when the temperature inside had been more unbearable than outside, and Bertilak had always been close by. Apparently he could turn up the heat, especially when he was angry.

Fox gritted his teeth and pushed onward.

"So I'll have to beat him quickly," Fox said. "Before this heat knocks me out."

"Good luck," Bertilak said. Fox felt him approaching—as much from the ambient heat shield as from his mental presence and the sand blowing around them.

Fox and Bertilak circled each other. "You're a disgraceful excuse for a Huntsman," Fox said.

"It's easy for you to say, with all those lofty ideas Ozpin and Theodore drilled into your heads. 'Being a Huntsman is a calling and a privilege, not to be taken lightly.'"

Fox had heard his professors at Beacon and Shade give exactly that speech.

Bertilak spat. It was so hot, Fox heard the liquid sizzle and evaporate as it hit the sand.

"They're just words. You think your headmasters and professors are model Huntsmen? They're worse than all the rest of us. You want to know why I barely graduated? I was tired of being used as a tool."

It was so hot, Fox was feeling feverish, weak, muddled. He couldn't keep this up much longer before succumbing to heatstroke.

"You're still a tool," Fox said.

It got even hotter. Oops.

"On your left!" Edward said.

Fox dodged to the right, felt a wave of heat pass on his left side. He struck upward with his left blade and Bertilak bellowed.

"You got him again," Edward said. *"Duck!"*

Fox ducked. Then he turned it into a forward roll, a handspring, and his feet connected with Bertilak's face. Fox followed through as Bertilak fell backward.

He heard Bertilak hit the sand. The temperature dipped slightly, for just a moment, but even those two degrees of relief felt amazing.

"Come on, boy. I've seen you fight Grimm. This is no different," Edward said.

Edward was right. If Bertilak had been a Grimm, Fox would have been done with him by now—sandstorm and heat notwithstanding. But there was one huge difference: He wasn't trying to kill Bertilak. In fact, he was specifically trying *not* to kill Bertilak. He had to finish this differently. Had to draw him closer and lull him into a false sense of security.

"He's behind you," Edward said.

Fox turned his head left and right, as though he were trying to listen hard. He fired a shot from his weapon out into the desert, away from Bertilak and Edward.

"Can you hear me? Fox? He's practically on top of you," Edward sent. *"Dammit."*

Fox felt Bertilak close by. He heard him swing the chain of his mace, and just as he expected, he felt the chain slip over his head. He brought his arm blades up just in time to prevent the chain closing around his throat. Bertilak squeezed. Fox pushed hard—and his tonfas helped him slip out of its embrace, slicing into Bertilak in the process.

Bertilak bellowed and shoved Fox forward, making him stumble headfirst into the sand.

"You're going to pay for that," Bertilak snarled.

Fox spat sand out of his mouth as he rolled and leaped back onto his feet. Then he did a handspring toward Bertilak, his boots colliding with Bertilak's face. Bertilak groaned and fell backward with the motion until Fox was sitting on his chest, knees pressing the man's arms down. Fox began punching.

Fox's Aura depleted with the force of each blow, but so did Bertilak's. And just before Fox reached a critical low, he felt Bertilak's Aura shatter, followed a moment later by his nose shattering with a satisfying crunch.

Bertilak screamed and heaved Fox off him. He scrambled to his feet. Even without Aura, the Huntsman was still somehow on his feet, fight left in him.

Fox tried to recover as he braced for a blow from Bertilak's weapon. One more hit and his own Aura would shatter.

Bertilak roared and then Fox heard metal clash against metal.

"Really, old man?" Bertilak said through his broken nose. "That's a cool toy, but you're no match for me."

Fox heard the two of them fight. He lay in the sand, willing himself to get up, but every time he did, he got dizzy. He tried to vomit, but all he coughed up was gritty sand he had inadvertently swallowed. His head pounded and he kept forgetting where and when he was, reliving childhood memories of living in Vacuo.

A rainstorm was a special treat, not only because it provided much-needed water for the nomads and desert plants and animals, but it gave them enough water to make mud bricks for building. But they had to work quickly, shaping and setting the bricks before they dried in the heat and became too brittle.

"I want to help," Fox said. "I can do it."

"Darling, I know you can, but we don't have time to explain how to make them right now," Fox's father said.

"It'll be faster if we do it ourselves," his mother agreed. "Why don't you go play on your own for a while?"

Only the littlest kids played in the mud, making sand castles instead of doing useful work. Fox was insulted. So he went off to prove his parents wrong. He would make the mud bricks and make a whole house of his own. He would show them.

As he worked, the other kids came to watch and make fun of his mis-shapen bricks, the lopsided structure he was building. Fox's face burned with embarrassment and anger, but he kept working. He would show them all what he was capable of.

While Fox worked, something terrible was happening nearby. The first sign he had that something was wrong was when the outer walls of his castle fell, and he felt the vibration in the earth. A quake? He knew whatever had caused it was big, and happening in the center of his settlement. He ran to warn everyone, but he was too late.

Later, when Uncle Copper found him hiding in the remains of his mud house more of a tomb-shaped mound, he learned that a giant sinkhole had formed in the sand, caused by the sudden, heavy rains. It had swallowed half of the settlement—including Fox's parents and their home—before the sand finally settled.

Oddly, it wasn't the fact that the desert had killed his family and friends that bothered Fox the most; that was what the desert did, and you couldn't blame it for being what it was. Fox's own father had told him that after los-ing his own parents in a sandstorm when Fox was four years old. Every Vacuan, from the youngest to the oldest, knew and accepted the risks and dangers and had felt loss—death was simply their way of life.

No, what bothered Fox most was that their deaths had been random, impersonal. Meaningless. And they had been powerless to do anything about it.

After grieving—a brief process in Vacuo, where you had to literally pick up and move on—Fox had vowed to leave Vacuo one day and live someplace where he could protect people who couldn't protect themselves. Where you had a fighting chance to survive. And he swore that his death one day would have some purpose behind it.

A knocking sound woke Fox. A banging.

He rolled over and took a breath. He could breathe again. The temperature had cooled back to the desert's normal range, perhaps a bit cooler because of the particles in the air blocking the sun. The wind had died down, so he was no longer taking in mouthfuls of sand.

Fox sat up. The banging sound that had woken him was metal on metal, accompanied by guttural sounds of pain.

"Edward?" Fox sent.

"Rise and shine," Edward sent back. *"Looks like I've still got it, but I wouldn't expect it to last much longer,"* Edward cried out. *"Mostly because I wouldn't expect* me *to last much longer."*

Fox climbed to his feet. He swayed, but his head was clearer and he didn't feel like he was going to be sick again.

He staggered toward the sound of combat.

"How . . . strong is . . . this shield?" Bertilak yelled in between blows from his mace.

"My arm will break before it does," Edward said.

"Works for me!" Bertilak picked up the pace.

Fox softly crept up behind Bertilak.

"Watch out behind you," Edward said.

"Like I'm falling for that," Bertilak said.

Fox wrapped his right arm in a choke hold around Bertilak's throat, pulling him off Edward. His arm blade prevented Bertilak from reaching up to grab at him. He struggled for a bit, then jabbed backward with the handle of his mace, knocking Fox backward. Bertilak coughed.

"Good one, kid." From the sound of his voice, he had turned to face Fox. Fox heard the chain extend and went into his fighting stance. Arms up, blades out.

In the suddenly quiet desert, still recovering from the storm that had passed through, sounds took on a new quality. The creak of leather in Bertilak's clothing, the sand shifting as he moved, the whirring of the spiked ball on its chain.

Fox listened to the desert.

When the whirring sound changed, Fox got ready. Instead of dodging the incoming weapon, he went toward Bertilak. He brought both of his blades up over his head and slammed them down with all his strength, cutting through the chain. The ball went flying off into the desert and Bertilak sprawled from the sudden shift in weight. Fox caught him and pushed him down as he brought his knee up, connecting with Bertilak's chest and then knocking him back.

Bertilak came for him again, attacking with the handle of his broken weapon. Fox easily parried the blows and got a couple of punches in.

He heard Edward bashing Bertilak with his shield from behind. Then Bertilak was retreating while Fox and Edward traded blows with him, side by side.

"Two on one? What would Theodore say?" Bertilak said.

"He'd say it's payback for ambushing a blind guy and an old man in the desert," Fox said.

"Yeah, but you can fight," Bertilak said.

"Flattery will get you—" Fox turned and delivered a round-house kick that made solid contact with Bertilak's thick head. "Flattened."

Bertilak did not get up.

"Finally," Edward said. "Now I can sit down."

Fox bound Bertilak's hands and feet with rope from his own pack and then grabbed his Scroll. He wanted to find out who Bertilak was working for.

He collapsed next to Edward. The old man clapped a hand on his back. Fox winced—everything hurt—but it also felt good. He suddenly missed his uncle Copper. Fox hadn't even tried to find his old settlement and his people, Kenyte, since moving back to Vacuo. He decided he would when they were done with this mission; he wanted to introduce his two families to each other.

"You did it, my boy," Edward said.

"*We* did it. Are you all right?"

"My buckler's seen better days, and I think my wrist is fractured. But I haven't felt this good in a long time. My head feels clearer somehow from the fighting. I suddenly remember things I'd forgotten."

"Like what?"

"I knew something was up with Bertilak and Carmine. I knew they weren't behaving like real Huntsmen." Edward slapped his knee. "I remember when I called for help. I brought you here."

"*You* did?" Fox asked. He didn't know whether the man was being delusional again, but he seemed lucid—and *someone* had called Shade Academy for assistance. Maybe they hadn't come forward because they hadn't remembered doing so. The mind could be a funny thing, especially out in the desert.

"Bertilak and Carmine . . . they knew that we were causing those emotion bombs." The old man kicked a light dusting of sand in Bertilak's direction. "I hired these fools to take us to safety, but over time, I realized they weren't taking us west at all, at least not directly. By the time I figured that out, though, we were already in the desert and the Grimm were following us— we needed the Huntsmen to survive. So I figured I'd try the distress call, see if it brought anyone in."

"Your plan worked." Fox handed Bertilak's Scroll to Edward. "Can you find anything useful in this? Ideally, the name and address of Bertilak's boss."

"Never cared for these things myself," Edward said. "Lucky! No password."

"Why would a big, strong Huntsman need a password? He probably thought he was all the security he'd ever need," Fox said.

"Or Carmine got tired of him asking her what his password was. He isn't exactly the brains of the operation."

Carmine! She was Bertilak's partner, he wouldn't have been keeping his intentions toward Edward and Gus to himself. He wouldn't have been able to—she was way too smart.

"Crap. Check the call log. Has Bertilak been communicating with Carmine since he brought you out here?"

He heard Edward tap at the screen.

"He sent her a message about twenty minutes ago." Edward clicked on it.

> They tricked us. E is useless. I'll ditch him, you get G
> to the boss. I'll catch up.

Edward groaned and got up, his bones cracking and popping. "We have to get back to the others."

Standing was the last thing Fox wanted to do right now, but he got up anyway. There was no telling what Carmine would do, especially if the rest of Fox's team put up a fight to protect Gus.

"Help me with Bertilak," Fox said.

"Help you what? Bury him?" Edward asked.

"No. *Carry* him."

"Let's just leave him here."

"He'll die on his own like this."

"He deserves worse. He'll slow us down."

Fox shook his head. "We don't leave people behind. Even people like him."

Edward sighed.

"Is that what they're teaching Huntsmen these days at the academies?"

"It's just something a true Huntsman knows already. Right?" Fox asked.

Edward was quiet for a moment. "But what if they're really heavy?"

CHAPTER FOURTEEN

Fox, Coco, Velvet, and Yatsuhashi stepped out of the Bullhead. All hopes of avoiding attention and getting back to their room quickly and quietly were immediately dashed—it seemed like the entire school was at the cliffside docks.

"Damn," Coco said. "That's today?"

It was the day the Vytal Festival assignments were being given out to students. It was a bigger deal for the First-years, who had yet to go on a real away mission with their new teams, but for most of the classes it was the first big outing. It was also a great PR move for Beacon Academy, a show of both strength and goodwill, a reminder to citizens in Vale and beyond that Huntsmen and Huntresses were watching their backs.

Or they were supposed to be. If Coco hadn't volunteered her team for that mission in Lower Cairn, they would be here now, getting some routine job patrolling an obscure region. On the other hand, they might have had to work with Professor Port again; for some reason he got assigned to mentor Team CFVY an inordinate amount of the time.

Coco had thought that Team CFVY was above all this, but their recent failure had her rethinking that. It had her rethinking everything.

She sighed. "Well, here we go. Let's put on a good face."

"Maybe no one will notice us because there's too much going on," Yatsuhashi said.

Fox started counting, wearily: *"Three, two, one—"*

"Hey, Team CFVY is back!" a student called out.

Velvet's shoulders slumped.

All eyes turned to them and several students rushed over to see them up close.

"It's showtime," Fox said.

He led the way as the team crossed the courtyard, heads held high but trying to convey that they really didn't want anyone to talk to them right now. It all fed into their persona as rock stars at Beacon, though they certainly didn't feel like they deserved a hero's welcome.

Coco kept pace with Fox, but Velvet fell behind. Yatsuhashi slowed down so he could keep an eye on her. They had all been preoccupied on the way home, lost in thought, replaying and analyzing everything they had done over the last week. But Velvet seemed to be taking it the hardest. She was the soul of the team, so much so that she almost literally wore her heart on her sleeve. Coco, Fox, and Yatsuhashi all kept big parts of themselves protected and hidden away, but Velvet put it all on display.

Team RWBY watched CFVY from the sidelines with the same admiration as the rest of the school, but slightly less awe.

The two teams saw a bit of themselves in each other, as two of the teams that stood out at Beacon—that Professor Ozpin had chosen to draw attention to.

There seemed to be one special team every year, whether to motivate the rest or to push that team harder to be models for the rest, to be as exceptional as everyone expected them to be. The big surprise was that RWBY was outshining Pyrrha Nikos's team, though everyone in CFVY agreed that Team JNPR was still impressive, considering.

Yatsuhashi was relieved when he saw Team RWBY hurry up to Velvet. She could probably use someone else to talk to. Given everything that happened, CFVY hadn't had much to say to one another since they had been rescued. Coco was angry at Yatsuhashi for pulling her away from certain death by a Goliath and swarms of other Grimm. Yatsuhashi was angry at Coco for falling apart under pressure. And they were all sifting through their actions, wondering what they should have done differently to save that family.

"Velvet! Are you okay?" Blake asked.

Velvet lifted her head and turned around. She appreciated the concern from her friends, but the last thing she wanted to do right now was talk about what had happened.

She was *still* trying to figure out what had happened. And a part of her wanted to forget all of it.

"I'm fine," Velvet lied. "I had Yatsuhashi to look out for me." Velvet gestured at him as he passed by and flashed him a quick smile.

She hoped that things were still okay between her and Yatsu. She hoped Team CFVY could come out of this one. They'd had defeats before, but this was the first time they'd lost the people they were trying to protect. It felt wrong that they had been rescued at the last moment and that poor family . . .

"Your mission was supposed to end a week ago," Weiss said. "What happened?"

"N-nothing happened. It was just . . . There were just so many." Velvet looked down. She could still see the swarms of Grimm moving in, the Goliath marching toward them. The cave entrance collapsing with the Gray family inside.

Yang, Ruby, Weiss, and Blake looked at one another nervously.

Velvet couldn't do anything about her and her team's failure, but she could at least make sure that her friends succeeded on their first real mission. She wanted to tell them that no matter what they did, they still could be beaten. That the stakes out there were real, and not only could they die, but other people might die. And they really, really needed to be able to trust one another and work together.

But there would hopefully be time for all that later, and maybe they would need to learn those hard lessons for themselves. Right now, all they needed was reassurance, and that was all Velvet had to offer.

"Oh, but don't worry. You First-years are just shadowing Huntsmen, so you should be fine." Velvet gave them a shaky smile that she hoped was convincing.

Yang squinted. "Riiight."

Velvet was worried that if she stayed there any longer, she would break down in tears.

"I should go." Velvet backed away and raised her hands. "Be safe, okay?"

As if those empty words could make sure they came back in one piece.

Velvet hurried away. Her team hadn't waited for her. She started after them, but then she decided she could use some time alone. She turned to head for the gardens, where she often went to think—and almost ran into Professor Goodwitch.

"Oh! Pardon me, Professor." Velvet avoided making eye contact and tried to get around the older woman. But Professor Goodwitch held up a hand, palm out, to stop her.

"Ms. Scarlatina. Welcome back. Are you all right?"

Velvet held her breath. She blinked back tears. She nodded.

"We're all relieved that you made it back safely to Beacon. I know you could use some time to recover, but Professor Ozpin would like to see you in his office."

Velvet froze. "Me? What for?" she blurted out. Her face flushed. "I mean, of course. What time?"

"Now."

"Now?" Velvet swallowed. She looked for her team but they were long gone. Maybe they had already been summoned and she would find them there.

"Right. Lead the way, then."

Velvet followed Professor Goodwitch toward Beacon Tower.

She had never been one to get into trouble at school, and students didn't get called to the headmaster's office often.

"Hey, Velvet!" Sun Wukong hurried to catch up to her, followed by his teammate, Neptune Vasilias.

Velvet had only met them a couple of times, when they were hanging out with Team RWBY. She didn't know much about the Haven students, who composed half of Team SSSN (Sun). But she appreciated that Sun was always kind to her, and it felt good to know another Faunus, even if he was only around during the Vytal Festival. She had learned a lot more from him about Vacuo, where he had grown up, than she had from Fox, who rarely talked about his childhood there. Nothing she had heard made her remotely interested in visiting Vacuo, even if it was one of the most welcoming places for Faunus-kind.

"How'd your mission go?" Sun asked.

Velvet shook her head.

"Hi, Professor Goodwitch," Neptune said, turning on his charm.

Professor Goodwitch gave him a withering look over her glasses. "Don't you have somewhere to be?" she asked.

"Not until tomorrow," Sun said. "Crime scene investigation in Vale."

"So we're around tonight, if you want to do anything." He seemed to be speaking to Velvet, but he was looking at Professor Goodwitch.

She rolled her eyes. "We have official business for Professor

Ozpin, so please excuse us." She marched ahead. Velvet shrugged her shoulders unhappily and followed.

"There's nothing to be worried about," Professor Goodwitch said as they rode the elevator up to Professor Ozpin's office at the top of the tower. "We just need you to tell us everything that happened."

The doors opened.

"Absolutely everything," Professor Ozpin said. He had been waiting at the elevator to greet her. "Welcome, Ms. Scarlatina. We're very glad to have you back with us."

"Th-thank you, Headmaster." Velvet looked around. "Where's everyone else?"

"I assume you mean your teammates," Ozpin said. "We prefer to speak with you each individually so we can get a more complete picture of events." He walked her over to his desk and gestured to a chair. Velvet couldn't help but look around at his office. They were inside the clock at the top of the tower; the window behind the headmaster's desk formed the clockface, and numerous cogs and gears moved on the walls and in the rafters above.

"I apologize for not giving you a chance to rest after your ordeal." Professor Ozpin sat behind his desk and steepled his fingers. The desk was so large, he looked like a kid playacting at his father's desk. The comparison seemed even more appropriate when Professor Goodwitch took up position behind him to his right, standing with her arms clasped behind her back.

Velvet hoped Professor Ozpin's Semblance wasn't reading minds.

No one knew much about him. He was a mysterious figure, often seen at Beacon events and walking around campus, quietly observing. He seemed to have a genuine interest in his students and an almost carefree attitude about life, which was a stark contrast to Professor Goodwitch's no-nonsense bearing. He somehow appeared to be both younger than his physical age and much older. He didn't teach any classes at Beacon himself, and no one had ever seen him fight—but rumor had it that he was a formidable Huntsman in his own right.

"Anything I can do to help," Velvet said.

"Thank you. The reason I wanted to speak with you first is because of your uncanny observational skills and attention to detail. No one is blaming your team for what happened in Lower Cairn—as your teacher and headmaster, Professor Port and I take full responsibility for the mission. But people will have questions . . . *We* have questions. And it is our responsibility to understand what exactly went wrong."

Velvet nodded.

"But first, would you like anything? Water? Hot chocolate? Cookies? I know students concentrate better when they are fed."

"No, I'm fine," Velvet said.

"Very well. Let us begin. At the beginning, if you please."

Velvet folded her hands in her lap. Unfolded them. A tear dropped to her sleeve.

"When we got to the village, it was already lost," she said.

"The Grimm had taken over, and there was no sign of survivors . . ."

Yatsuhashi had been looking forward to eating at Curry Up, one of the many pop-up restaurants in Vale for the Vytal Festival, but he didn't have much of an appetite for once. In fact, only Fox was eating the rice curry he'd ordered, and he didn't even seem to be enjoying it. They were all starving after their mission, but they were also preoccupied by what had gone down in Lower Cairn.

"We could have made it," Coco muttered.

"Are you kidding?" Yatsuhashi said. "We're lucky we got out of there alive." He stopped himself before adding, "Not everyone did." They were all aware of how badly they had screwed up.

Coco lowered her head. She wasn't even worried about the failing grade on their mission; she was haunted by the things she'd seen, by the people she'd failed. Not to mention being rescued by Professor Port at the last minute had been a tremendous blow. After he had picked them up in the airship, he had looked at each of them solemnly, making sure they weren't hurt—and then he had sat down in the front without saying a word for the entire trip home. She didn't know if he was just giving them space to reflect, or if he couldn't deal with his disappointment in them.

"Professor Port seemed a little surprised at that Goliath, too," Fox sent.

"You think so? He looked like he wanted to jump down there and take it on single-handedly," Yatsuhashi said.

Maybe that accounted for his disappointment, then.

Coco poked at a curry-soaked potato with her chopsticks. "We didn't have enough information about what we were getting into. They couldn't have expected us to handle it without—"

Yatsuhashi pounded his fist on the table. Their plates and glasses jumped. "Which is it, Coco? Could we handle it or not? Or do you mean you think *you* could have handled the situation, on your own?"

Coco's mouth fell open. "No! Yatsuhashi, that's not what I—" She sighed. She slipped her glasses off and rubbed her eyes. "I don't know what I mean. Of course I couldn't have handled it alone. If anything, it's all on me. I'm the leader. I . . ." She shook her head. "I should have gotten us out of there sooner. Called for reinforcements. I was just too proud, too eager to prove ourselves. Myself. And then my fear, in the cave . . ."

Fox shook his head. *"It's on all of us. We have to take responsibility for what happened. We aren't always going to have enough intel, or correct intel, about a situation. We have to be able to handle anything that comes our way, at any moment. Even if 'handling it' means a strategic retreat."*

Coco nodded. "You're right."

"You need to tell Velvet that," Yatsuhashi said. "She's shouldering a lot of the blame herself."

"Wait, where is Velvet?" Fox looked around.

"I assumed she just went off by herself, like she does," Coco said. "With Ruby and the others."

Yatsuhashi didn't correct her. Coco thought Velvet went away to hang out with other friends, but he knew that Velvet took things very personally. She disliked feeling useless, or like she'd failed her team. Having to hide her Semblance from their potential rivals didn't help—Velvet wasn't the kind of person to hide something that was much a part of her, one of the things that made her special. Of course, Coco never picked up on any of that.

"She probably isn't with Team RWBY now. All the First-years are heading out on missions," Yatsuhashi said.

He tried to call her on her Scroll, but it went straight to voice mail.

Then he saw Team JNPR—Jaune, Nora, Pyrrha, and Ren—walk into the food stand with Sun and Neptune from Team SSSN. So not all the First-years had left Beacon yet.

"Have you seen Velvet?" Yatsuhashi called.

Sun and Neptune glanced at each other. "Yeah, we saw her a little while ago, with Goodwitch."

"What?" Coco said. "Where were they going?"

"They said they were on some business for Ozpin."

Yatsuhashi and Coco stood up. Fox slid Coco's plate over and started shoveling food into his mouth.

"Is something going on?" Jaune asked. "Is she in some kind of trouble?"

"I cannot imagine Velvet ever doing anything wrong," Pyrrha said.

"She didn't," Coco said. "We did."

"And we should all be there," Yatsuhashi said.

Fox finished eating and slapped his fork down. "So let's go."

Coco led the way to Professor Ozpin's office, having been called there once or twice in her time at Beacon.

The elevator doors opened and Yatsuhashi stormed out, closely followed by Coco. Fox lingered in the doorway. He was bothered that Velvet had been singled out for their failure in the village, too, but he didn't think storming the headmaster's office was going to make the situation better for any of them.

"What's going on in here?" Yatsuhashi stomped toward Professor Ozpin's desk. Velvet turned.

"Yatsuhashi?" she said. Her eyes were red and her face was wet with tears.

"Are you all right?" Yatsuhashi asked.

Professor Goodwitch moved swiftly to stand in front of Ozpin, smoothly drawing her crop and pointing it at Yatsuhashi. He levitated off his feet.

"Whoa." He flailed his arms.

Professor Goodwitch flicked her crop upward and Yatsuhashi zipped all the way up to the high ceiling.

"It wasn't Velvet's fault," Coco said.

Fox slowly strode into the room and stood next to Coco. If this was happening, it was going to happen to the whole team.

Professor Ozpin rose. "We were just having a conversation." Then his voice lowered and became ominous. "To which you were not invited."

"You need to have some respect for this office," Professor Goodwitch said.

"Guys, just stop," Velvet said.

"They shouldn't have brought you here by yourself," Yatsuhashi called down from above.

Coco folded her arms. "As team leader, I take full responsibility for everything that happened in Lower Cairn."

"*We* take full responsibility," Fox said.

"As you should." Professor Ozpin rose. "Let him go, Glynda."

She glanced at Yatsuhashi and then pointed her crop at the floor.

Yatsuhashi thudded to the floor. Professor Goodwitch stepped back.

"I deserved that." Yatsuhashi winced as he got back on his feet.

"You okay, Velvet?" Coco asked.

"I'm fine." Velvet was a little shocked, and a little embarrassed at her team's overreaction, but she was also happy that they had come to her defense.

Professor Ozpin walked around his desk and down the line, looking at Coco, Yatsuhashi, and Fox. Velvet stood and joined her team.

"The first thing I want to say to all of you is . . ." Professor Ozpin sighed. "I'm sorry."

Velvet sniffled.

"I know it's a hard thing to lose anyone, people who need

you. But it happened. It, in all likelihood, will happen again. But that doesn't make the loss any less painful. Take the time you need to grieve." He looked at each of them. "Now is a time to come together and lean on each other like you never have before."

His voice regained its former steel. "From what Velvet told us, I know each of you played a role in how events turned out at Lower Cairn. The outcome was regrettable, but it also seems to me that you did everything you could." He turned and crossed his arms, looking out the window. "Which is all we ask of you as students. I am proud of you for stepping up and taking responsibility for the lives lost yesterday, but I am also here to take responsibility myself. If you fail, as Huntsmen and Huntresses, or as good people out there in the world, it is in part because we have not prepared you well enough."

Coco started to say something, but Fox nudged her.

"Let him talk," Fox sent.

"But I must also trust that you take your education seriously. Since you became a team, you have performed admirably. But until you truly learn to work together, trust each other, rely on each other—you will be Team CFVY in name only." He faced them again and spread his hands. "For all of your successes, it is only now, in your worst moment of defeat—when you came to the defense of one of your own, with no regard for your well-being—that you have truly shown yourselves to be a team."

Professor Ozpin walked back to his desk, as if every step weighed him down, and sat heavily. "I have made many mistakes in my life, and I am still learning from them and growing. I'm still trying to make up for some of my larger failures. But I can't do it alone."

He glanced at Professor Goodwitch.

"Life will test each of you, but if you face your challenges together, you can overcome almost anything."

Thoughts, unbidden, came flooding back to Coco, to the moments before they'd found the Gray family in the underground cavern. Standing alone, pointing fingers, assigning blame. If she'd been a better leader, if she'd been able to refocus and rally her team, would that have made a difference? Could that have saved lives? The numbness she'd felt from the battlefield up to now suddenly shattered, and she felt untold anger at herself for letting this happen, for making her team go through this.

Professor Ozpin leaned forward. "Though it might be hard to tell around here lately, we do have rules. And rules are crucial to keeping everything moving like . . ." He looked around. "Well, like clockwork."

Professor Goodwitch stepped forward. "Each of you is to turn in a written statement of everything that happened in Lower Cairn to Professor Port by the end of the week. You will also have faculty supervision on all escort and rescue missions from now until we deem you ready to operate on your own again. Understood?"

Coco let out a breath. She had been waiting for the other shoe to drop, and there it was. She nodded. "Understood." A moment later she added, "Thank you."

"One more thing," Professor Goodwitch said. "I believe you all are behind on your classes. If you don't make up any exams and assignments you've missed by Monday, I'm afraid you'll have to sit out the Vytal Tournament. You are dismissed."

CFVY piled into the elevator. Without consulting one another, they waited until they were outside and walking back to the dorms before they spoke.

"Thanks for coming for me, guys," Velvet said. "I was so nervous, worried I would say the wrong thing."

"If you told them the truth, you can't say the wrong thing," Yatsuhashi said. "I'm sorry we let them bring you in alone."

"All of our heads have been somewhere else," Fox said. "I'm sorry I got us lost back there. It was all my fault."

"No, I should have fought better," Velvet said.

"I kind of overdid it a bit, when I caused that cave-in," Yatsuhashi said.

Coco was quiet for a long time. "I let this happen. I have to be a better leader." She shrugged. "I'm sorry I failed you."

"You didn't fail us," Velvet said. "Like Professor Ozpin said. We all succeed together, and we all fail together. In the forest . . . we were exhausted and in over our heads . . . we fell apart."

Coco tried to smile from behind her sunglasses, but fooled no one.

"I have to say, as scary as it was to be interrogated like that, it felt kind of good to talk about it." Velvet looked at her teammates as they walked toward the dorms. "I needed to talk to someone."

"You can always talk to me, V," Coco said. "It's something I need to work on. I have to listen to all of you more."

"We should be able to talk to each other about anything," Yatsuhashi said. "If we can't trust each other, we're not going to survive out there."

"Group hug?" Fox sent.

The team huddled up—it was a bit awkward with Yatsu's height, but everyone felt better for it.

"Before, I couldn't wait to graduate from Beacon and get out there in the real world," Coco said. "But it's a lot different than I thought."

"I'm glad we have another couple of years to go," Fox said.

"And I'm glad we're doing it together," Velvet said.

CHAPTER FIFTEEN

People's emotions were frayed and arguments were breaking out. They didn't have time for this—they needed to get everyone up on top of the turtle. Yatsuhashi walked around helping Slate restore order.

Of course, they had slightly different approaches. Slate gently insinuated herself between people and talked them down to defuse the situation and get them thinking clearly again. Yatsuhashi got a little more physical.

"Stop that," he said to two men at the start of a pushing contest. He put his hands between them and knocked them apart from each other.

"Hey!" one of the men shouted. "Who asked you?"

Yatsuhashi didn't mind diverting their anger away from each other toward himself. Once he had their attention, he pointed them—or picked them up and faced them—in the direction of Coco, who was near the base of the turtle, directing nomads up the dangling ropes.

"Get up there, quick," Yatsuhashi said. "If you don't want to die."

Sometimes just the sight of Yatsuhashi coming toward a fighting group was enough distraction to snap them out of it. Telling them a giant Grimm worm was approaching usually was enough to get them moving, no matter how reluctant they were.

They just didn't have the luxury of talking out their feelings right now. If they were lucky, there would be plenty of time for all that later. Yatsuhashi couldn't understand how Edward's mood bomb Semblance could still be affecting them so strongly with him out in the desert somewhere, but maybe that meant Fox was on his way back with the old man.

Yatsuhashi himself also wasn't immune to the effects, and the nonstop adrenaline rush of preparing for a big battle wasn't helping. He was impatient and irritable. He needed to sit somewhere quiet to clear his mind, but that wasn't going to happen anytime soon. He looked forward to taking out his anger on the approaching Grimm.

"That's nearly everyone," Yatsuhashi said after dropping off a brother and sister he had caught pulling each other's hair.

Slate joined him and Coco. "Thank you for helping to get everyone to safety."

"Don't thank us yet," Coco said. "We may just have moved them from one mess into a different sort of trouble."

The three of them jogged alongside the turtle, easily keeping pace with it. Was the creature aware of them down there, or the dozens of people now hitching a ride on her back? If she suddenly noticed them, what would she do?

"I still appreciate the effort. We all do, even if everyone is too preoccupied to realize it right now," Slate said.

"Slate, why doesn't Edward's Semblance affect you?" Yatsuhashi asked.

"Who says it doesn't?" she said.

"You've been completely relaxed this whole time. And you seem to be able to make other people relax, too," Yatsuhashi said.

Slate smiled. "Most people try to hide their feelings. They're ashamed of them, or they worry about how they will make other people feel. That's never been me. I always say what I'm thinking, and I don't lie to myself about what I'm feeling." She shrugged. "I don't know if that's the answer, but I guess I'm just more aware of my emotions than most people. I can tell when they aren't coming from inside me."

"You also genuinely care about people," Coco said. "Edward's Semblance doesn't only boost negative emotions, it seems to enhance all emotions—even the positive ones. When it's affecting us, maybe you're just caring even more than you already do—and that outweighs everything else you're feeling."

Slate raised her eyebrows. "I hadn't considered that."

"So the solution is to be more positive," Yatsu said.

"I don't think that's much of a solution, since it's easier said than done," Slate said.

"But wouldn't that be nice, if we all just could turn our bad feelings into something more compassionate?" Coco looked off into the distance.

Slate patted her on the arm. "It's the hardest thing for any leader to accomplish." She glanced up the rope. "Looks like it's my turn."

"See you up there," Yatsuhashi said.

Coco and Yatsuhashi waited until the last of the nomads were on their way up before they took to the ropes themselves. Velvet met them at the top. She looked concerned.

"Is Gus with you?" Velvet asked.

"No," Yatsuhashi said. "There's no one else down there. I assumed he was already up there."

"I haven't seen him, either," Coco said. "I should have realized, since I was sending everyone up . . ."

A call came in on their Scrolls. "It's Fox!" Velvet said.

Coco patched him into their call. Edward's face appeared on the screen.

"Edward?" Coco said.

"Is Fox okay?" Yatsuhashi asked.

"He's fine," the old Huntsman said. "He's got his hands full."

The image tilted as Edward turned the camera to show Fox trudging through the sand with Bertilak slung over his shoulders. The Huntsman's face was covered in blood.

"Oh," Velvet said.

Fox smiled weakly and waved, then panicked as Bertilak started to slide off his shoulders. He caught him in time and sighed.

"What happened?" Coco asked.

"It's a long story, but you need to get Gus away from Carmine right now."

Coco looked around. "Has anyone seen Carmine?"

Yatsuhashi and Velvet shook their heads.

"Like I said, she isn't up here," Velvet said.

"She must be with Gus. You have to find them," Edward said.

"Turns out Carmine and Bertilak were bringing Edward to someone who's collecting people with powerful Semblances," Fox said.

"Only . . . it's really Gus they're after," Edward said. "We lied to you—my Semblance is to block other Semblances. Gus—"

"Creates the mood bombs," Yatsuhashi finished.

"That explains a lot." Coco sighed.

"When the Grimm kept coming after Bertilak took Edward away, Carmine must have figured it out and made off with Gus," Edward said.

"We should have, too," Coco said.

"We'll watch out for Gus," Velvet said. "Don't worry."

Edward's breath hitched, and Yatsuhashi didn't think it had anything to do with the exertion of hiking across the desert.

"As soon as we find him. We need to get eyes on Carmine and Gus." Coco headed toward the edge of the turtle shell.

"Edward, where are you and Fox?" Yatsuhashi asked.

"Maybe an hour away. Fox is tracking your location, but we'll have to hurry up if we're going to catch up to you. He says you're moving pretty fast."

"Look for the large flatback slider, and/or a Blind Worm," Yatsuhashi said.

"Look, over there." Velvet pointed.

"Yatsuhashi, I think we have a bead on Carmine and Gus. What do you make of this?" Coco said. She pointed to a funnel-shaped cloud of whirling sand moving ahead of the turtle, toward the Vacuo capital city on the horizon.

"Another storm?" Yatsuhashi said.

"Look closer," Coco said, pointing to the heart of the cloud. Two dark spots were at the bottom of the dust devil.

"Is that them?" Yatsuhashi asked.

"Somehow Carmine can control the sand or create localized weather patterns," Coco said.

"Bertilak can affect the temperature of the environment around him," Fox said. "Maybe it's something similar."

"I'm going after her and the kid," Yatsuhashi said.

"Took the words out of my mouth," Coco said. "Do it. Bring Gus back."

"I'll help," Fox said. "Think we can pick up the pace, old man?"

"No way, Fox. You don't even have enough energy to use your Semblance right now, let alone fight. You get here as quickly as you can, but you're sitting this fight out. You've already done plenty," Coco said.

Fox scowled. "You're right, and it's annoying."

"Coco, Velvet, you'll be okay here?" Yatsuhashi asked.

"Of course," Velvet said. "You know I can handle myself." Yatsuhashi nodded.

"It's an even bet which way the Blind Worm will go, now

that Gus is out there with Carmine," Coco said. "He's got to be feeling pretty stressed right now. Hopefully, it will come for us, but it might head for them instead. Either way, we'll be ready."

"Don't worry, Yatsu," Velvet said. "Go save Gus. We've got this!"

Yatsuhashi grabbed on to a rope and slid back down the side of the turtle.

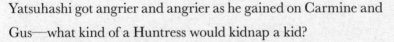

Yatsuhashi got angrier and angrier as he gained on Carmine and Gus—what kind of a Huntress would kidnap a kid?

He had the woman in his sights. The dust storm was swirling around her and Gus; however she was doing that, it was preventing Gus from getting away, and also giving them cover in the desert and hiding their tracks, unless you looked closely at the sand funnel and realized it wasn't a natural phenomenon.

"Hey, Yatsuhashi," Fox sent.

"Fox! You must be close. I can see Carmine just ahead of me." Yatsuhashi was glad he didn't have to speak aloud. He was already breathing hard from running.

"I can see you, too. Turn around," Fox sent.

Yatsu skidded to a halt and turned. Fox was approaching, moving much faster than Yatsuhashi could, and it was even more impressive because he had a heavy Huntsman on his shoulders. Edward wasn't far behind him. His mind might be going, but he was still in peak physical form, even at his age.

When Fox reached Yatsuhashi, he tossed Bertilak at his feet. *"I hate to ask, but this guy was a bastard to fight. Think you can take care of him?"*

Edward stumbled over, panting. "What? After all this, you're going to let *him* kill Bertilak?"

"Not kill."

"I don't know," Yatsuhashi said.

"It's not gonna hurt anything, Yatsuhashi. We can't keep carrying him, and we can't worry about him while we're taking on Carmine."

"While *I'm* taking on Carmine. *You're* going to keep resting and get your strength back up," Yatsuhashi said.

Yatsuhashi knelt by Bertilak, who was snoring loudly and coughing whenever he breathed in sand. Fox was right: He would probably wake up soon.

He touched his fingers to Bertilak's temples. His hands trembled and he forced them to steady. He didn't need to be in physical contact when using his Semblance, as he'd discovered all too often, and disastrously, as a kid. But it helped him focus, would make sure he didn't accidentally wipe Fox's and Edward's memories, too.

He hated using his Semblance. His parents had seemed to forgive him for misusing it, but he had never forgiven himself. And unlike them, he remembered each and every incident. At Beacon Academy he had learned to control it, but even then he used it sparingly, and only in direct combat. In those rare instances, Yatsuhashi usually only erased a second or two of short-term memories to disorient his opponent and get the element of surprise.

Yatsuhashi looked at Fox. "How far back should I take him?"

Fox tipped his head back thoughtfully.

"How about a little before he dragged me into the desert?" Edward said.

"So, about a day," Fox sent.

Yatsuhashi closed his eyes. "Forget," he whispered. He pictured a black hole, a spinning mass of darkness, and nudged Bertilak's mind *just so* to temporarily block his memories from the last day. The effect took the same amount of time he was taking away to wear off, so in a day those masked memories would come flooding back to Bertilak. No doubt, he would be pissed, but hopefully he would also be in police custody.

"Okay." Yatsuhashi stood and brushed sand off his hands.

"I saw what you did," Fox sent him privately. *"It was like his consciousness dimmed for a second. And its shape is different. I don't know how to describe it. It's like how Edward's mind seems brighter right now."*

"Edward, keep an eye on Fox," Yatsuhashi said. "I'm going after Carmine."

"I can help," Edward said.

"Don't you start, too," Yatsuhashi said.

"No, really. He can," Fox said. *"That's the other reason we came to you. Edward, think you can block Carmine's Semblance to stop that storm so Yatsuhashi can grab Gus?"*

"I think so." Edward licked his dry lips. "Just tell me when."

"I'll keep the channel open," Fox said.

"Good plan. I'm going in." Yatsuhashi took off.

When he drew closer to Carmine and Gus, Yatsuhashi slowed to creep up on them. Sneaking around wasn't his specialty, and he was convinced she would turn at any moment and see him.

"Maybe you should tell Gus what we're doing so he'll be ready," Yatsuhashi sent.

"I don't want to startle him. It might get her attention," Fox said.

"Good point." Yatsuhashi drew Fulcrum and prepared for the fight ahead. He didn't have time to meditate, but he briefly closed his eyes and pictured his mother. She had taught him exercises to practice mental discipline and control, not only for his ability, but also for his emotions. It was how Yatsuhashi had worked on overcoming his fear of unintentionally hurting others, mentally or physically. Imagining her soft voice saying, "Breathe easy, Yatsu, clear your mind," was enough to center him.

When Yatsuhashi was just thirty feet away from the dust devil, he sent a message to Edward: *"Block her Semblance now."*

"Go!" Edward sent.

Yatsuhashi started running toward Carmine. The dust devil dispersed, raining sand around them. Carmine looked around, confused.

Yatsuhashi brought his sword back and swung it down toward Carmine. She spun around, bringing up her dual-sai—and caught his sword on one of the prongs. She twisted and his sword turned over, but he held on and spun with it, yanking his blade free.

"Gus! Run!" Yatsuhashi yelled to the boy, who turned and

ran. "Your grandfather is back there." He pointed in the direction he'd come from with his sword, then brought it around toward Carmine. She parried it easily with her own weapon.

They continued trading blows with their blades as Yatsuhashi circled her, but Carmine held her ground.

She was fast. She couldn't get in close to Yatsuhashi with her own short sword, but she wasn't letting any of his attacks make contact, either. Perhaps he could tire her out eventually, if they were able to keep this up for a while.

And then one of her punches landed on him, and he went flying backward.

He shook his head and scrambled onto his feet. Bellowing, Yatsuhashi brought his greatsword back and put all his might behind it. The massive blade hit her sword and knocked it out of her hands.

Carmine ducked under his weapon as he regained his balance, grabbed the blade between the palms of her hands, and pushed it backward. The pommel of his sword hit Yatsuhashi in the breast bone and he went down with an "Oof!"

His chest felt like a giant bruise. He kept his balance, but now he was unarmed. Carmine was still holding on to his sword. She flipped it up by the blade and caught the handle. She tested the weight, tossing it from hand to hand.

"Not bad. I think I'll keep this," she said.

"*—when you hear me let me know when you hear me let me know when you hear me,*" Fox sent.

"*I hear you,*" Yatsuhashi replied. He'd forgotten that in order to block Carmine's Semblance, Edward had to block all Semblances. That explained why he hadn't heard from Fox in a while.

"Damn," Fox said. *"That means Edward's not blocking—"*

Sand swirled around Carmine and her red hair rose and spread out behind her. She grinned.

"—her Semblance," Fox said.

"Give up now, boy," she said. "And maybe I'll go easy on you."

"I think I can take you."

"You don't even have a weapon," Carmine said. She tilted her head. "Here, you can have mine."

Something knocked into Yatsuhashi's left shoulder from behind. He grunted and dropped to his knees. He looked down and saw Carmine's dual-sai hovering over him. The blade levitated in front of his face, and twirled dangerously with the tip pointed at his eyes.

So that was her Semblance. Telekinesis.

He lunged for the sword, but it darted out of the way and thwacked the top of his head.

"We've sparred with Telekinetics before. And I'm willing to bet you're not as good as Goodwitch."

Yatsuhashi moved fast, knocking her sai aside with his arm. It darted back toward him. He parried it again, thinking how odd it was to be having a fistfight with a flying sword. Then it zipped back to Carmine and she caught it. Now she had two weapons, and he had none.

Sand started swirling around her again, drifting slowly like a ring around a planet. Then she waved her hand, and the ring expanded quickly. Sand blasted into Yatsuhashi, pushing him backward, stinging his face, getting into his eyes, his mouth, his armor. He brought his hands up to shield himself from the worst of it, but he was itching and blinded for a moment.

"Look out! Above you!" Gus called.

Yatsuhashi rubbed sand out of his watering eyes and looked up to see sand gathering over his head, a growing ball of grit.

He tried to dodge to the side, but the ball dropped and he was buried under a ton of sand, just like that.

Yatsuhashi roared and burst out of the pile, and another large mass of sand punched him in the side. He went tumbling away.

I can't do this on my own, Yatsuhashi thought.

Yatsuhashi dug himself out of a second sand pile and zeroed in on Carmine. She spun her sword rapidly, gathering sand toward it in a spiral column, and then she pushed her hand forward and fired the sand at Yatsuhashi. He ran toward it and vaulted over it, but the sand blast redirected upward and propelled him high into the air. More sand gathered, like she was turning up the force on a water hose. Pushing him higher and higher. Then the sand fell away and Yatsuhashi dropped after it. He landed hard on his back in the sand and the wind was knocked out of him.

"Hey! You started the party without me."

"Bertilak!" Carmine shouted.

Yatsuhashi looked over and saw Bertilak Celadon standing ten feet away from him, holding his broken weapon—and Gus. Why had the kid come back to help Yatsuhashi?

"Well, I'm screwed," Yatsuhashi sent.

CHAPTER SIXTEEN

"Don't worry, Yatsu. Go save Gus. We've got this!" Velvet watched Yatsu drop down the side of the turtle, wishing she felt as confident as she had sounded. She didn't want Yatsuhashi worrying about her when he had his own dangerous task ahead. But the Blind Worm heading toward them was more than a little disconcerting.

The turtle seemed to agree. It suddenly shifted its course to the left, turning away from the Blind Worm. Velvet almost lost her balance. A few people standing too close to the edge of the wide, flat shell tumbled, but Coco and Slate caught them and pulled them back up.

"Grab those ropes," Slate said. "We need to secure everyone."

The turtle was now racing away from the Blind Worm, but the Grimm was gaining on it. It just couldn't swim very fast in the sand, while the worm was built for speed.

Several of the nomads had pulled the ropes up and were using them to lash everyone together, securing them with the hooks and pitons embedded in the turtle's shell. Velvet had the horrible image of the turtle rolling over, crushing everyone, or burrowing into the sand, dragging them down with it. It didn't look like the turtle was prepared to fight, and unless it could shoot laser beams from its mouth or do something equally useful, it was going to be up to her and Coco to defend it and everyone on board.

"It's almost on us!" Coco unfolded her bag into its gun form. She looked at Velvet. "Get ready."

Velvet nodded. She would need some powerful weapons for this fight, and this wasn't the time to hold back.

The first weapon she called up was a pair of armored gloves loaded with circular saws. When the hard-light weapons formed, Coco said, "Oh."

There would be no replacing these. Roy Stallion was presumed killed during the Battle of Beacon—he'd last been seen in the clutches of a Nevermore. No one knew where the rest of Team BRNZ (Bronze) was, either, missing or dead.

"Good-bye, Roy," Velvet whispered. She raised her arms. "Ready?"

Coco nodded.

The Grimm worm bore down on them, and it looked even more horrific and eldritch up close. They could see its teeth rotating around its circular maw and feel its hot breath wafting over them. Coco fired her gun into its mouth, while Velvet fired the spinning saws at its eye. The worm closed its mouth and abruptly burrowed down into the sand.

Velvet and Coco glanced at each other. "It couldn't have been that easy," Coco said.

It wasn't.

The worm burst out of the sand and shot over the turtle. Coco fired off another round of bullets, joined by gunfire and a hail of arrows from the nomads. Nothing seemed to be able to penetrate its thick hide.

It landed and turned around, surprisingly fast. Velvet got off another shot with Roy's saw. Her aim was true, just as his would have been, and the razor-sharp discs struck between two of the worm's armored segments. Something hot and green spewed from the wound; Velvet raised her shield and kept most of the splatters off her and Coco. But where it touched her uniform, the fabric burned away and her skin sizzled and blistered.

"Ow!" Velvet said. "What is that stuff?"

"Acid," Slate said. "Blind Worms are nasty things. Maybe the nastiest in a desert of nasty things."

The worm shuddered and rolled over, spreading its green ick over the sand. The turtle shifted direction again to head in the opposite direction. This time Velvet fell over and bumped into Coco, knocking her down.

"Sorry," Velvet said.

"You okay?" Coco asked.

Velvet nodded. Her shield armored gloves disappeared and were replaced by Neptune Vasilias's rail gun.

Coco raised her eyebrows.

"They're no good to us if we're dead," Velvet said. She knew Coco thought she should be holding on to these pictures for emergencies, but if this didn't qualify, then what did? She couldn't afford to be sentimental about the irreplaceable photographs of their friends, either. Last she'd heard, Team SSSN was still out there, anyway, though no one knew where Sun Wukong had headed off to. He'd always been nice to Velvet, and she hoped he wasn't getting into too much trouble, wherever he was.

The worm recovered and barreled toward them again. They both fired on it. Velvet concentrated the energy blasts from Neptune's gun on the worm's eye, which began to burn and scar and bubble under the assault.

But that didn't stop it from advancing toward them. It rammed into the side of the turtle. The world tipped over, but the turtle frantically worked to right itself. And the blind worm disappeared.

The turtle withdrew, pulling its flippers and head into its shell. It had clearly had enough. Its sturdy shell might protect it from the Blind Worm's attacks, but everyone on the shell was exposed—and they weren't moving anymore.

"Should we jump off?" Velvet asked.

"Not yet," Coco said. "We're still a tougher target up here. Down there in the sand, that thing could swallow us up in seconds."

They waited, but all seemed still.

Velvet and Coco stood back-to-back. Velvet was ready to call up her next weapon when a target presented itself.

"I never wanted to come here," Velvet said quietly.

"What?" Coco said.

"I didn't want to come to Vacuo. I wanted to stay in Vale," Velvet said. "We never should have left Beacon."

"It was a lost cause," Coco said. "It was unsafe."

"I thought we don't believe in lost causes."

"You should have said something."

"I tried. But your mind was already made up. And the boys were on your side."

Coco pursed her lips. "I'm sorry. I didn't want to leave Vale, either, but I thought this was the best thing for us. I think we . . . *I* needed to get away for a while. It was hard to stay there, without our friends, with the place destroyed like that. All those Grimm."

"But, like, Vacuo?" Velvet said. "This desert? You really thought this would be better? At least we had a home there."

"I needed to protect you . . . and Yatsu and Fox. After we lost that family in Lower Cairn—after we lost Roy and Penny and Pyrrha and Ozpin—I couldn't lose you, too. I couldn't bear it," Coco said, closing her eyes against the desert wind. She breathed in slowly. "We'll get back there one day, I promise. And when we do, we'll be ready to win it back. That's the reason we're here. To become better Huntresses. To save our home."

The sand rumbled and Velvet looked down in time to see the Blind Worm launching straight up the side of the turtle shell toward her and Coco. The shell shuddered and she felt herself pitch forward. Then someone grabbed her from behind and she was spun around to safety. She glanced back as she flew toward the center of the shell and saw Coco tumble backward over the side. The worm rose up past the side, hung in the air for a moment, and then fell back down.

Velvet rushed to the edge to look for Coco, but she was gone. The worm had swallowed her.

CHAPTER SEVENTEEN

A typical school day for a second-year student at Beacon Academy:

7:30 a.m.—Breakfast

8:00 a.m.—Plant Science, Professor Thumbelina Peach

9:45 a.m.—Military Strategy, Professor Peter Port

11:15 a.m.—Weapon Crafting and Upkeep, Professor Harold Mulberry

12:30 p.m.—Lunch

1:30 p.m.—Stealth and Security, Professor Ann Greene

2:15 p.m.—Legends of Remnant, Professor Dr. Bartholomew Oobleck

4:00 p.m.—Combat Training, Professor Glynda Goodwitch

5:00 p.m.—Sparring, Self-Directed

6:00 p.m.—Dinner

A typical school day after the Fall of Beacon:

5:00 a.m.—Breakfast

5:15 a.m.—Fight Grimm, Dr. Bartholomew Oobleck

12:00 p.m.—Lunch

1:00 p.m.—Fight Grimm, Professor Peter Port

6:00 p.m.—Rebuilding, Professor Glynda Goodwitch

7:30 p.m.—Infirmary

8:00 p.m.—Night patrol, Self-Directed

The best thing about Beacon Academy, what made it stand out above the other major Huntsmen training academies, was its emphasis on practical education. They sent more students on supervised missions than Atlas, Haven, and even Shade, and they gave them more one-on-one time with their teams and trained Huntsmen. Add in the fact that Vale was beautiful year-round and a cultural center with a diverse population, and it was no wonder that it was the first choice for students from all over Remnant.

That was before it was destroyed and taken over by Grimm. After that terrible night of fire and devastation and so much loss, life at Beacon became one never-ending training mission—only, training was over, and lives were at stake.

"We aren't making a dent here," Coco said wearily. She and Velvet, Yatsuhashi, and Fox were eating ration packs in a classroom building on the perimeter of Beacon's campus—as close as they'd been able to get to the Academy, and one of the few areas they had been able to secure from Grimm . . . for the moment. It was looking more and more like they would have to fall back farther from school grounds.

"They just keep coming." Yatsuhashi lifted his head from his hands. He didn't have much of an appetite these days. He didn't like to take even this short break from clearing out the city. The last few weeks had been grueling for them, a constant cycle of sleeping, eating, fighting. They were among only a dozen students who had remained there—the rest being Third- and Fourth-years—and the endless battle was taking its toll on them.

They hadn't been able to say good-bye to most of their friends before they had scattered in the chaos or gone home or retreated to the temporary shelters in Vale, waiting to see whether there was any hope for Beacon.

Then there were the friends they would never see again. They had all watched Penny die in the Vytal Tournament, but they had only heard about others who were gone, like Pyrrha and Roy and Professor Ozpin, with no idea what fate had befallen them.

"It's that thing," Fox said, too drained to even use his Semblance to speak telepathically. He nodded out the window toward what was left of Beacon Tower, with the giant winged Grimm frozen at the top. "It's attracting them. Until we figure out how to kill it or get rid of it, this will never stop."

No one knew what had frozen the beast there, or if they did, they weren't talking about it. The only thing *everyone* knew was there had been a bright flash of light, and it had been stuck up there since. There were rumors that Ruby Rose had been at the Tower at the time, and it wouldn't have surprised anyone if the precocious First-year had been involved somehow.

"Goodwitch is working on that," Velvet said. "Port, Oobleck, they all are. We just have to stick it out, do what we can until they figure it out, and everything can go back to normal."

Yatsuhashi shook his head. "Things will never be normal again. And we can't wait for someone else to save us."

"There are too many Grimm," Coco said. "They're seemingly coming from nowhere. On a good day we kill as many as are coming in, but on a bad day . . ." They were having more bad days than good. "It's only a matter of time before they overwhelm us. The school is already a ghost town."

"Don't say that! We just need more Huntsmen to join the fight," Velvet said.

"But they're leaving. Everyone is leaving tomorrow," Yatsuhashi said. "We have to decide—do *we* stay or go?"

"And if we leave, where do we go?" Fox sent.

Vale had scraped together enough resources to send the last remaining refugees home, but only to their own kingdoms.

"I want to finish what I came here for," Coco said. "I want my Huntress license."

"The combat schools are taking in displaced Beacon students," Velvet said. "We could still stay in Vale and help out here."

Coco laughed. "Been there, done that. We've learned everything they can teach us. That would be a huge step back."

"Atlas? Haven? Shade?" Yatsuhashi said.

"Atlas was partly to blame for what happened here," Fox said. "I don't think they can be trusted."

"And they don't tend to take in transfer students, even in the best of times," Yatsuhashi said.

"I bet General Ironwood would make an exception for *us*," Coco said.

"What about Mistral?" Yatsuhashi asked.

"I'm not going to Mistral," Velvet said sullenly.

"Mistral wouldn't be good for . . . us," Fox said.

"Looks like it's Shade, then." Coco adjusted her sunglasses. "Knew these would come in handy."

Velvet opened her mouth to protest, but Fox spoke up first.

"Shade is rough," he said. "But nothing we can't handle."

Velvet looked at Yatsuhashi, but he was staring out the

window. "It would be good to have something to look forward to, something we can work toward."

"I'm tired of being surrounded by . . ." Coco gestured at the rows of empty desks that might never be occupied again. "Failure and misery. I want to live in hope again."

Velvet waited for someone to ask her what she thought, what she wanted, but no one did.

"When we're trained, we can come back," Coco said. "We can find our friends. We can save our home."

Velvet shook her head. She tried to form the words, but it was clear what Coco, Yatsuhashi, and Fox wanted was different from what she wanted. What if they left her just as easily as they had decided to abandon their school and their home?

When they told Professor Goodwitch that they would be leaving, she seemed relieved. She had set up her office in the city library, and there were stacks of books piled up around her desk and littering the floor.

"I understand, and I support your decision," Professor Goodwitch said. "I have appreciated your help these past few weeks, and your commitment to Beacon and Vale, but this is no place for students right now."

She pulled a thick folder from a drawer, then wrote something on a sheet of Beacon Academy letterhead and signed it. She slid everything into an envelope and sealed it. Then she stood slowly, like the weight of the world was on her shoulders. Coco wondered if the professor had been sleeping at all since taking over as temporary headmistress—an empty title, for an empty school.

Professor Goodwitch rounded the desk and handed Coco the envelope. "Give this to Headmaster Theodore. If the CCT were working I would just call him, but sometimes a personal touch is nice. And please, give him my best."

"What is it?" Coco examined the envelope.

"Your transcripts, and a letter of recommendation." She tipped her head and smiled. "And a warning. He's never seen a team like yours before."

Coco tucked the envelope away. "Thank you."

"As much as we've been worried about your safety while you've been here, you've shown that those concerns are unnecessary. I'm proud that you will be going out into the world to complete your training, and I have no doubt you will be exemplary Huntsmen and Huntresses—because you already are." Professor Goodwitch spread her hands and looked at each of them. "You won't have the privilege of hearing Professor Ozpin deliver his graduation speech, but there's one thing he tells every class that I want to share with you."

She clasped her hands behind her back and thought for a moment. "'Beacon Academy is not a place. It is an idea, which has taken root in each and every one of you. *You* are Beacon, and you must now go forth and serve as a hopeful light for others. It is your privilege and your burden as Huntsmen and Huntresses to protect not only those who cannot defend themselves, but to watch out for each other, always.'"

Professor Goodwitch closed her eyes and lowered her head. "'Now get out of here.'"

Velvet's throat was choked up, and Fox was pretending that he had something in his eyes. Yatsuhashi had listened with his eyes closed the whole time, imagining that Professor Ozpin had been there delivering those words himself. Coco was feeling excited about living those words and honoring the headmaster's legacy. He had brought Team CFVY together, and she wouldn't have been the person she was without him, or her friends.

Professor Goodwitch looked up. "That last bit was part of his speech, too. He always kicked the students out after that. He hated long good-byes, and so do I."

They left the next morning, while Professor Port and Dr. Oobleck were on patrol. Fox could have gotten a ride to Vacuo, but he chose to travel with his team instead.

"Anyway, you'd never find your way to Shade in the desert without me," he said. But really he just didn't want to be separated from them.

It would take them about three months to make the journey, but Coco hoped they could cross over into Vacuo before winter and then reach Shade in time for the second semester. She had no doubts that they would accept the team as transfers and that they would be able to face whatever came at them—as long as they were together.

They were a team, and they would watch one another's backs. Always.

"Let's go." Coco pushed her glasses up and looked ahead— to their bright future.

CHAPTER EIGHTEEN

It was pitch-black inside the Blind Worm.

Coco took her glasses off, but that didn't help at all. Maybe that's why they called it a Blind Worm, because if it swallowed you, you couldn't see inside its stomach, or whatever this was.

Or maybe it was called a Blind Worm because you never saw it coming. Only she *had* seen it coming, and she'd ended up inside the damn thing, anyway. She had pulled Velvet out of the way, only to take her friend's place. Coco figured sacrificing your life for your teammate was one way to be remembered as a good leader, but maybe that was just cheating.

The air was warm and wet and foul smelling. And the darkness was even more disorienting because the worm was moving—fast. She was inside a living, runaway train with no idea how to get out.

"The only way out is through," Coco muttered, her voice muffled and lost, like she wasn't even there. She held back a scream.

She turned her Scroll on, but the light almost made it worse. Now she could see just how tight the space was, how it glistened and pulsated.

Coco screwed her eyes shut. She was back in that cave in Lower Cairn, scared of the dark. Scared of failure. Scared of dying.

Her hands trembled. She was losing it. She opened her eyes. "Get yourself together, Coco," she said aloud. The heavy darkness swallowed the sound.

She wasn't going to let the nomads end up like the Gray family back at Lower Cairn. Coco clenched her hands into fists and held to the strap of her purse. She wanted to move, she wanted to fight, but still she was rooted to the spot.

"*Fight*, Coco," she said. She unfolded her Gatling gun and tried to identify a weak point, but it all looked the same, a seemingly endless expanse of mottled gray flesh. She planted her feet, aimed at the wall opposite her, and fired.

The world turned upside down as the worm lurched and rolled. Coco tumbled around it, cushioned by the spongy lining on the walls. She watched her gun slide deeper into the beast and saw a bright light bouncing around—her Scroll, which soon went dark. There went her only communication with the outside and the only source of light in this oppressive blackness.

"Great," she said.

The inside of the Grimm trembled, and it continued to whip her back and forth, more a roller coaster than a train ride now. She started crawling, hoping she could recover her weapon, but she wasn't even sure which way she was going. She stopped and curled up in the center of the creature, arms wrapped around her knees.

Guys? I need some help, she thought.

But what could they do for her out there? Fox was spent. Yatsuhashi was busy fighting Carmine and Bertilak, and if they were very unlucky, they would be joining her soon inside the Blind Worm. The way it had picked up speed suggested it was moving toward a new target rather than engaging the turtle and going after the refugees.

She hoped when the time came that Yatsuhashi, Fox, and Velvet wouldn't hesitate to kill the Grimm without worrying about her.

Light appeared. She blinked at it and realized she was looking out of the Blind Worm's wide mouth. Its teeth raced around the circular opening. It was bearing down on Fox, and he didn't notice it coming.

"Fox, look out!" Coco yelled.

She scrambled and tried to run for the opening, but it reared up, knocking her back again. She fell head over heels and slipped farther back.

The worm shuddered—something was attacking its armored hide from outside, and it was getting angry.

The light disappeared and a flood of sand sprayed over Coco, pushing her farther down.

She flew up and slammed into what she thought of as the ceiling. The worm was diving, trying to get away, or launch a fresh surprise attack. Then it abruptly stopped, sending Coco pitching forward.

Enough already, she thought.

"*Coco, are you okay?*" Fox sent.

"*Define 'okay,'*" Coco said.

"*Alive?*"

"*Barely. What's going on out there?*"

"*Velvet is rescuing you,*" Fox said.

"*What? How?*"

"*You have to get out before the worm burrows back into the ground. The skin is tough, but it's thinnest in the back. Can you get to the last segment?*"

"*I'll try,*" she said.

"*Go,*" Fox said. "*Hurry.*"

It was an uphill climb, as the worm was wriggling and trying to escape. Grimm didn't usually turn away from a fight, but big ones like this and the Goliaths—very old ones—had a stronger survival instinct. And they demonstrated a better understanding of people, choosing their battles and acting strategically.

Coco stretched her arms out. She could just touch the curving sides of the worm with the tips of her fingers. She hurried and soon she was pressing against them with her hands.

"*Almost there, I think,*" Coco said.

She kept going and tripped over something. She reached down, groped around in the darkness, and then found something very familiar in a shallow pool of viscous, burning liquid—Gianduja!

"Come to Momma." She picked her gun up and reduced it back into her handbag, then slung it over her shoulder. The top of her head brushed the ceiling. She reached up and felt the ick in her hair; she had lost her beret somewhere along the way. She sighed.

"I'm as far back as I can get," she sent, hoping they were still listening.

All was quiet.

"Fox?" Coco said. *"Hello?"*

"Stand back, Coco!" Velvet sent.

"Velvet?"

Then the worm flooded with a bluish light as a glowing line sliced through the worm, only two inches away from Coco's face. As it passed, she realized it was a replica of Brawnz Ni's claw weapons.

She stumbled backward as the weapon faded. A beam of sunlight appeared on the ceiling and spread quickly down the curved walls and along the floor, widening as the tough skin and flesh and sinew separated—as Velvet pulled them apart. She had hacked and slashed all around the creature and then let it pull itself apart as it tried to dive under the ground. The front portion of the worm disappeared into the sand in front of Coco, spewing ichor that turned the sand black.

Coco leaped out of the remains of the worm, falling right into Velvet's arms.

"Coco!" Velvet called. "Are you all right?"

"Do I look all right?" Coco asked.

Velvet wrinkled her nose, holding her friend at a distance. "Um."

Coco reached into her belt and retrieved her sunglasses. She slid them on.

"That's better." Velvet smiled.

"Thank you," Coco said. "I always thought Brawnz's weapons sucked."

"The right tools for the right job, I always say." Velvet winked. "I'm glad you made it out of there. And thank *you* for saving *me* first."

"Who's keeping count?" Coco asked.

Fox came over and slapped her on the back. *I am,* he sent.

Coco looked at Velvet. "That was a really good plan. Better than anything I could have come up with."

Velvet blushed happily.

Yatsuhashi joined them. "Looks like I missed all the action." He turned as the tail end of the Grimm twitched and then wriggled into the sand and vanished. He stepped back, horrified.

"Ew," Velvet said.

"There goes my Scroll and hat," Coco said.

"Will that piece grow into another Blind Worm?" Yatsuhashi asked.

Fox nodded.

"I take it back. That was a *terrible* plan," Coco said.

Velvet pouted.

"Speaking of terrible plans . . ." Yatsuhashi pointed behind Coco. A short distance away, Carmine was fending off attacks from both Bertilak, firing bullets from the shaft of his mace, and

Edward, who fought her at closer quarters with a bladed disc in his hand.

"Bertilak! What are you doing, you idiot?" Carmine screamed.

"You always think you're smarter than me! Well, who's laughing now?" Bertilak said.

"That doesn't even make sense, moron." Carmine punched toward Bertilak and sand hit him in the face.

"What . . . is happening?" Coco said.

"Bertilak thinks that Carmine tried to double-cross him and take Gus on her own," Fox said.

"How'd you convince him of that?" Coco asked.

"He doesn't remember trying to get away with Edward, and Fox fighting him." Yatsuhashi rubbed the back of his neck.

"And Gus seems to be revving their emotions up. He must be getting more of a handle on his Semblance," Fox said.

"Nice," Coco said.

As Team CFVY raced toward the fight, they watched Carmine blast Bertilak and Edward with a wave of sand. Bertilak protected himself with a wall of heat that fused the wave into glass, but Edward was knocked back and buried.

"Grandpa!" shouted Gus.

Coco glanced up, where three Ravager Grimm were winging overhead. The Blind Worm might be gone, but now other Grimm were closing in. This battle was going to get out of hand pretty quickly.

"Flank her," Coco said. She opened up her Gatling gun and laid down covering fire, shooting at Carmine. The first round of bullets hovered in front of the Huntress, but she strained as they built up. Some of them broke through, clipping her in the arm.

Carmine sent the wall of bullets flying toward Velvet, who batted them away with a hard-light version of Dr. Oobleck's telescoping thermos and then fired several blasts at her. Carmine somersaulted away from the attack, and ended up right in front of Fox, who unleashed a flurry of blows.

Carmine broke her sai into two halves and struck out with both blades, flipping them over and driving them into each of Fox's thighs. He cried out as his Aura flashed, flickered—and shattered. There was a crack and a sizzle and he jolted from a burst of electricity from the pronged weapons. He collapsed in the sand, wisps of smoke rising.

"Fox!" Coco said. Her gun clicked. Out of ammo. She transformed her weapon back into a handbag and ran toward Carmine. The Huntress was breathing heavily, covered in sand and sweat and blood.

"That's all you've got?" Carmine asked.

Coco smashed the purse into Carmine's face. The woman went down.

"I can't believe I thought you were cute." Coco spat.

Carmine got back up. She prodded the left side of her face gingerly.

"I thought you were supposed to be some kind of hotshot students, but none of you can take me down."

Coco swung her bag around in a circle.

"*None* of us is right," Coco said. "But together . . ."

On her left, Yatsuhashi slashed the wall of glass that Bertilak's heat had created while Velvet launched herself at it, sending it toppling over onto Carmine. She looked up and screamed as it fell on her. Sand flowed around her and upward, but the fountain of sand couldn't support the heavy glass.

"See? Glynda could have lifted that," Yatsuhashi said.

Coco stepped gingerly on the slab and looked down, expecting to see a flattened Huntress through the murky glass. Instead, she saw a hole in the ground, which was quickly filling with sand.

"Uh-oh," Coco said.

"Huh," Bertilak said. "I didn't know she could do that."

She scanned the terrain around them. Then she realized what Carmine's move was. "Gus!" Coco said.

They turned as one toward the boy. He stared at them in alarm for a moment, then a hand reached from the ground and grabbed his ankle. He screamed.

Velvet was closest. She raced toward him as he began sinking into the sand. She reached him and grabbed his hands when he was waist deep.

"I've got him!" Velvet said, straining to keep his head aboveground. But Carmine had her, too. Velvet began slipping into the sand, while Gus held on to her desperately.

Coco was out of bullets, but she had another idea. "Yatsuhashi!" she shouted as she ran toward Edward.

She need not have bothered. He was already on his way to

help Velvet. He drew his sword and plunged it into the ground at Carmine's position.

Coco heard a muffled shriek. Carmine let go of Gus.

"She's on the move!" Fox sent.

Yatsuhashi studied the area around him and brought his blade down, sending a geyser of sand up. He picked up the blade and brought it down again a few feet to the right. He spun around and struck again. It reminded him of a game of Whack-a-Grimm at the Vytal Festival fairgrounds.

Suddenly a Ravager dove at him, raking his back with its claws. Yatsuhashi spun his blade around and sliced it in half. A second Grimm swooped down and pecked at the sand. The spot swelled, knocking the black bird back.

Bertilak was fighting a third Ravager, backing away and firing bullets from his broken weapon as it advanced on him.

Sinkholes began forming around the desert. Yatsuhashi got to his feet and pulled Gus and Velvet out of the sandpit. He lifted Gus to his shoulders.

Coco leaped over a hole as it appeared in front of her, eyes on Edward.

The old man was lying in the sand, disoriented. He mumbled incoherently.

"Edward," Coco said. "We can't do this without you. You have to concentrate, block Carmine's Semblance. Block everyone's, whatever. Just do it now."

"I . . . can't . . ." Edward closed his eyes and his hands trembled.

The sand opened up beneath them, and they began slipping beneath the desert.

Coco squeezed his hands reassuringly. "You have to," she said. "Be that legendary Huntsman one more time. For your grandson."

Edward's breathing calmed. His forehead crinkled in concentration. And then he smiled.

They stopped sinking.

The holes around the desert filled in, and the sand stilled. The dead Ravager near Bertilak smoked and faded away like the other defeated Grimm. Everyone looked at one another, wondering, was it really over?

Bertilak scrambled over to a mound of sand and started digging. Yatsuhashi spotted the hand sticking out of it and joined him. They worked quickly, but the sand fell back into the hole as soon as they could scoop it away.

"We're losing her," Yatsuhashi said.

"Keep digging!" Bertilak grunted.

Velvet fiddled with her camera, walking toward Bertilak and Yatsuhashi.

"Stand back," she said.

"Velvet?" Yatsuhashi looked up as a hard-light hologram formed in Velvet's hand. A glowing blue trumpet. It flickered and dimmed in the sunlight. Velvet was nearly out of Light Dust.

"What good is that?" Bertilak asked.

Yatsuhashi's eyes widened. He grabbed Bertilak by the back of his armor and hauled him away.

Velvet put the trumpet to her lips, leaned back, and blew a clear note. Sound waves blasted out of the trumpet and blew sand away in sheets. Carmine was uncovered in a second, just as the trumpet disappeared, the note slowly fading away.

Bertilak hopped into the canyon and picked Carmine up.

"Good going, Velvet," Coco said. She looked around. "I think we won."

It was slow going as the group dispatched the remaining Grimm and followed the path of the turtle toward the Coquina settlement, which was the closest settlement to the city of Vacuo. Then the path of the turtle veered off, and there were signs of a big struggle.

"The Blind Worm," Yatsuhashi said.

"No . . . that can't be, after everything we did?" Coco looked around, wondering what had happened, kicked at the sand in anger.

"I think I see something." Velvet squinted and pointed. "A group of people ahead."

Coco picked up the pace, which was challenging because they had Bertilak and Carmine tied up securely so they couldn't cause any more trouble, and Fox was still recovering from his injuries. They were all tired from their fight, and the sun was relentless. She missed her beret.

They finally caught up to the refugees, a long line of them winding through the desert toward their new home. Slate was in the rear. She called a halt to the march when she spotted Team CFVY and their group. The message passed up the line, stopping people as they received it.

"I'm glad to see you lot," Slate said. "Looks like you've had an adventure."

"You too," Coco said. "We saw you had another run-in with the Blind Worm."

Slate nodded. "We did as you said and ran for Coquina, but we didn't get far before the Blind Worm came up on us. We thought we were goners, but then four Huntsmen came to our aid."

"Four Huntsmen?" Fox turned to Coco.

"Hey, it's Team CFVY!" someone called out.

Coco looked up. She blinked. It had to be a mirage, but—

"Sun!" Velvet cried. She ran ahead to greet Sun Wukong excitedly.

"Well, how about that," Fox said. "Team SSSN is here?"

"Never thought I'd see those guys again," Yatsuhashi said.

The two teams came together.

"Where have you been?" Coco and Neptune Vasilias said simultaneously.

The groups laughed. "It's a long story," Sun said.

"Same," Velvet said.

"We have a lot to catch up on," Coco said. She had so many questions.

"You guys look terrible," Neptune said.

Coco lowered her sunglasses and glared at him. He held his hands up.

"But you're still a sight for sore eyes." Neptune rubbed the back of his head nervously.

"We were on our way to Shade Academy, when we ran into Slate and her people," Sun said. "Didn't realize we were cleaning up your mess. Man, you guys used to be the best."

"We're still the best." Coco folded her arms. "Better than you, anyway. It's just been so long, you're probably overdue for a reminder."

"You're heading for Shade? We've been studying there," Velvet said.

"Maybe we'll get a chance to settle this in class," Yatsuhashi said.

"Looking forward to it," Sun said.

Coco nodded. "But first let's get these people to their new home."

Velvet smiled. "And then *we* can go home."

EPILOGUE

Teams CFVY and SSSN spent a couple of days at Coquina, recovering from the fight, and learning all about what Sun had been doing with teams RWBY and JNR at Haven Academy, of all places.

"Sounds like we missed out on the action," Coco had said. "Maybe we picked the wrong school after all."

"There's plenty going on at Shade, don't you think?" Velvet said. "And it's kind of nice not to have to defend our school from a major threat every year."

Coco and Velvet exchanged a knowing glance.

But they had only scratched the surface of everything that had been happening in the wider world; no one did isolation better than Vacuo, especially with CCT communications down. They would have a lot to talk about on the way to Shade, and both teams CFVY and SSSN were raring to go. Sun Wukong seemed to have a problem staying in one place for very long; Velvet wondered if he'd be able to stick it out at Shade Academy for the long haul.

When it was time to go, CFVY gathered up their things. They hadn't brought much, but the villagers had loaded them down with whatever they could offer as a thank-you. Coco tried to reject all their gifts, but Fox couldn't resist hauling in at least a few pounds of extra mole crab meat. And Edward wouldn't hear of letting them go without at least a bit of money for their trouble.

"I wish you could stay a little longer," Gus said to Velvet. "I'll miss you."

"I'll write, and I'll come visit you at Oscuro," Velvet said. She mimed boxing. "Show you and your new friends a few things."

"I don't know if I'll ever be a fighter like you guys and my grandfather. I just want to learn to control my Semblance so I don't hurt any more people. Maybe figure out how it can help people one day."

"You don't have to be a Huntsman to protect others," Velvet said. "You've been doing a great job with your grandfather." She followed his gaze to where Yatsuhashi and Edward were meditating together under a stand of palm trees.

Gus smiled and Velvet felt a surge of hopefulness and happiness. But she couldn't attribute her feelings to his ability this time—these emotions were her own.

Velvet hoped things would work out for both Gus and Edward. It was better than Edward's other plan: to go after Bertilak and Carmine's secret employer. They were relieved that Headmaster Theodore had sent the authorities in Vacuo City to Coquina to collect the Huntsman and Huntress. CFVY was getting tired of looking over their shoulder every five minutes.

"Hey, everyone! Look at this!" Fox sent.

Yatsuhashi's eyes snapped open and he scowled. "Fox!" he roared. "Not while I'm meditating!"

"Shouldn't you be more peaceful or something?" Fox asked. He was under the shade of another tree, where he had been building a sand castle with Sun and Neptune for the last hour: a very impressive sculpture of Beacon Tower. Velvet wandered over to take a photo.

"I'll show you peaceful." Yatsuhashi got up and promptly fell over. He smacked the ground in frustration. The sand rumbled and rippled away from him.

"You meditated your legs asleep again." Fox laughed. "Very peaceful."

"Hey, this is really good, Fox," Velvet said.

Fox beamed.

"Roar!" Coco rose slowly from behind the sand sculpture, arms raised threateningly. "I am Grimmzilla!"

"Coco, no!" Velvet shouted.

Coco swatted the tower down, then stomped through the sand. "Grrrr!"

"Guys? What happened?" Fox asked. "Is my castle okay?"

"Yeesssss . . .?" Sun said.

"Looking good, man," Neptune said.

Coco hefted her bag and the backpack full of crabmeat, handing the latter off to Fox.

"It's time to go," Coco said.

Velvet shook her head. "One second."

She ran back over to Gus and his grandfather. "Can I take your picture?" she asked.

Edward nodded. He put an arm around Gus and they both smiled.

"Oh, come on—take out your weapon! Show us your battle face!" Velvet cried.

"Oh, like this?" He lifted the disc from his belt and separated the sharp outer ring from the curved shield, which had been reforged in town.

"I like it," Velvet said as she snapped a photo.

Yatsuhashi came over to say good-bye to the pair, too. They all exchanged hugs.

"Thanks again," Gus said. "For everything."

"Take care of yourself," Velvet said.

Yatsuhashi knelt and put a hand on Gus's shoulder. "You were great out there. I noticed you coming back to help me, when you could have run. And you helped us defeat Bertilak and Carmine by distracting them with their own emotions." He smiled. "I know how scary a powerful Semblance can be, but don't be afraid of it. Learn to control it, and use it for the right reasons."

Gus nodded, his eyes a little misty.

Finally, the two teams of students set out for Shade. Coco seemed strangely quiet.

"What's up?" Velvet asked.

"I've been thinking a lot about who hired Bertilak and Carmine."

"Who cares? They're in custody now."

"If someone out there is kidnapping people with powerful Semblances, I don't think they have good intentions. Do you?"

"Coco, we won."

"We won the battle, but not the war," Coco said. "Mission's not over."

Velvet covered her eyes. "You're not going to let this go, are you?"

"Don't you know me by now?"

"You're not going to let this go."

Coco tilted her head back. "And I know my team well enough to know you're going to help."

Velvet groaned. "Do we have a choice?"

"Of course. But I'm right about this one." Coco nodded ahead. "There's Shade."

Velvet looked up at the pyramidal castle rising on the horizon. She smiled.

There was no place like home, and somewhere along the way Velvet had realized home was wherever Yatsu, Coco, and Fox were. For now, that was Shade Academy, but she didn't know where life would take them beyond that or even what tomorrow would bring. They never could have imagined themselves in Vacuo, for instance.

It didn't matter as long as they were doing what they were meant to do, protecting others as Huntsmen and Huntresses—together.

About the Author

E. C. MYERS was assembled in the U.S. from Korean and German parts and raised by a single mother and the public library in Yonkers, New York. He is the author of numerous short stories and four young adult books: the Andre Norton Award–winning *Fair Coin*, *Quantum Coin*, *The Silence of Six*, and *Against All Silence*. E. C. currently lives with his wife, son, and three doofy pets in Pennsylvania. You can find traces of him all over the Internet, but especially at ecmyers.net and on Twitter @ecmyers.